BY DELILAH S. DAWSON

Minecraft: Mob Squad
Minecraft: Never Say Nether
Minecraft: Don't Fear the Creeper
Mine
Camp Scare
Servants of the Storm
Hit
Strike
The Violence

STAR WARS
Phasma
Galaxy's Edge: Black Spire
The Skywalker Saga

BLUD
Wicked as They Come
Wicked as She Wants
Wicked After Midnight
Wicked Ever After

THE TALES OF PELL (with Kevin Hearne)
Kill the Farm Boy
No Country for Old Gnomes
The Princess Beard

THE SHADOW (as Lila Bowen)
Wake of Vultures
Conspiracy of Ravens
Malice of Crows
Treason of Hawks

MINECRAFT™
MOB SQUAD

DON'T FEAR THE CREEPER

MINECRAFT™
MOB SQUAD

DON'T FEAR THE CREEPER

DELILAH S.
DAWSON

DEL
REY

NEW YORK

Copyright © 2022 by Mojang AB. All rights reserved.
Minecraft, the MINECRAFT logo, and the MOJANG STUDIOS
logo are trademarks of the Microsoft group of companies.

Published in the United States by Del Rey,
an imprint of Random House, a division of
Penguin Random House LLC, New York.

DEL REY and the CIRCLE colophon are registered
trademarks of Penguin Random House LLC.

Published in the United Kingdom by Century,
an imprint of Random House UK, London.

Hardback ISBN 978-0-593-35581-7
International ISBN 978-0-593-59771-2
Ebook ISBN 978-0-593-35582-4

Endpaper illustration: M. S. Corley

Printed in the United States of America on acid-free paper

randomhousebooks.com

2 4 6 8 9 7 5 3 1

First US Edition

Book design by Elizabeth A. D. Eno

To you.
Yes, you.
There's a great big world out there,
and you have the heart of an adventurer.
Never settle for potatoes.

MINECRAFT™
MOB SQUAD

DON'T FEAR THE CREEPER

1.

ELDER STU

 So here's what you need to know: My name is Stu, I'm the Eldest Elder and the second oldest person in the town of Cornucopia, and YOU NEED TO STAY INSIDE THE TOWN WALL.

D'you hear me, kid? DON'T EVER GO OUT INTO THE OVERWORLD.

The town Founders built Cornucopia for a reason. It's scary out there. Real dangerous. There are terrifying monsters and bloodthirsty animals and strangers who do not have your best interests at heart.

Sure, there might be good scenery and interesting people and untold riches beyond the wall. Forests and seas and emeralds and axolotls, whatever they are. And yes, some people might tell you that the fine folks of Cornucopia are all descended from grand adventurers and that we all hold the potential for bravery, valor, discovery, and creativity, blah blah blah.

Poppycock, if you ask me.

Utter nonsense.

Stay within the wall, child. We have everything you need.

Don't go out there.

You never know what you'll find.

It might be your own doom.

Now get out of my shop. Out you go. Children are noisy and annoying. That's why I never had any of my own. I like my life like I like my town: quiet, calm, and boring.

Before you leave, would you like to buy a hoe? Potato farming—that's the way to go. Just rows of potatoes as far as the eye can see. Potatoes for dinner every night. A nice, solid potato never did anyone any harm.

You don't need a sword or armor. You don't need one of those newfangled horses.

You just need to settle down inside the wall with your potatoes and wait for old age to claim you.

Mark my words—the Overworld is the last place you want to be.

The wall is your friend.

2.

LENNA

 So here's what you should know: My name is Lenna, I'm the apprentice of the oldest and weird-est person in town, and you shouldn't listen to a single thing Elder Stu says. He doesn't know what he's talking about. He's never once been outside the wall around Cornucopia, even though there's currently a great big opening in it so that our people can come and go freely.

Or—well, kind of freely.

They still don't like it when me and my friends go out into the Overworld.

Even though we were the first people in our town to venture beyond the wall in four generations, and even though we've saved the town—twice!—Stu and the other Elders still think we're up to no good.

Of course, we're used to people in the town treating us differ-ently. They used to call us the Bad Apples, and some people still do. We're not as normal as they'd like us to be.

Like I said, I'm apprenticed to the oldest, weirdest person in town, my friend Mal's great-great-great-grandmother Nan. She keeps the lore, and we're creating a library for everyone to use, so they can learn about our history and the world beyond the wall — the biomes and flora and fauna that we don't have around here. Nan also taught me how to shoot my bow and arrows, how to craft a few things, and how to bake her famous cookies. Maybe more important, she taught me that there's nothing wrong with being different. My family made fun of me all the time for getting lost in daydreams and being, as they said, a bit loony, but Nan tells me it's a gift. I'm starting to believe her.

My pockets are stuffed with cookies as I head through downtown and past the Hub, which is the very center of Cornucopia. Most of the Elders and more traditional families live here, where the old houses are tall and skinny and jumbled together, but my friends and I have all chosen to settle down a bit farther out. I live in a little cottage by Nan's house in the forest farthest from the middle of town, right up against the wall. Nan's great-great-great-granddaughter Mal lives with her parents on a cow farm out where the houses have some space to breathe and room to farm. Chug and his brother Tok now live behind their store in New Cornucopia, which is a recent settlement just outside the wall. And Jarro, who used to be our bully but has become our buddy, set up shop right beside them to raise horses and llamas and rent them out to travelers.

I'm on my way to have breakfast with my friends. Actually, it's halfway between breakfast and lunch, which Chug has decided to call lunfast. He loves naming things, but he's not particularly good at it, which is why his pet pig is named Thingy. My own pet, a tamed wolf named Poppy, jogs beside me, tongue out and tail wagging. She loves lunfast, too, because she can play with Thingy and also Tok's cats, Candor and Clarity.

I used to fear the Hub, because Jarro and his minions Edd and Remy would always pop up to bully me, but now Jarro is on my side and Edd and Remy have been deemed old enough to go to work. They both found jobs in my family's mine, and they're welcome to each other. I always knew they were dumb as rocks, and now they can spend all day with their kind. It's a relief, walking through town with only a few dirty looks and no rotten beetroots slamming into my back.

Mal is waiting for me in front of her house, sitting on the fence and scratching her favorite cow, Connor, behind the ears. He moos happily, and I present him with a sheaf of wheat I plucked from an overgrown pasture along the way.

"You brought more than wheat, right?" Mal asks, jumping off the fence and joining me on the road.

"I've got a pocket, got a pocket full of cookies," I sing. She fistbumps me, which is nice. My friends know I don't generally like being touched. This is our compromise.

It's not too far from Mal's farm to the wall, and she tells me about all the ores and gemstones she's discovered in the small mine she's digging out behind the cow pasture. It's funny how I was born to a mining family but hate it, and she discovered mining out in the Overworld and realized she loved it. Maybe things would've been different if I was an only child working with cows all day instead of the youngest of ten very serious kids raised by very serious parents in a very serious mine, but I guess we'll never know. I'm just glad I found Nan and she saw my potential. I'm happy now, and so is Mal, and when the boys see how many cookies I brought them, they'll be happy, too.

The door in the wall comes into view, and my spirits sink as I recognize the people blocking us from leaving town.

"Oh no," I mutter.

Mal looks ahead and sighs.

My oldest brother, Lars, steps into our path.

"Names, please," he says. He puts away his sword and pulls out a book.

Mal and I look at each other.

"Names?" she asks, because she's a lot braver than I am, especially in front of my family. I'd rather face a hundred zombies than my older sister Letti, and Lars is only a year younger than her and not a bit more understanding.

Lars puffs up his chest. "Names. The Elders have decreed that we must keep track of who enters and leaves the town at all times. So give us your names."

He's in full iron armor—which my friend Tok made—with his sword hanging at his side. Whoever gave Lars a weapon clearly wasn't thinking straight.

"You know who we are," Mal says. "You two are siblings. And we're third cousins."

The other guard swings around and glares at us. It's Jami, one of the town's main sheep farmers. I don't know him super well, as he's an adult and usually sticks to his farm, but he has definitely called us Bad Apples in the past. He, too, has a sword.

"The Elders don't want your family tree, kids. They want names. This is a new process, and you're expected to comply. So just state your names, and we can all go back to our very busy days."

I look around. There is no one else on the road to or from the wall, not a single living creature visible in the Overworld as far as the eye can see.

"What are you busy doing?" I ask.

"Explaining the rules to rude children," Jami says through clenched teeth.

Mal and I look at each other, confused, and she shrugs. "I'm Mal. That's Lenna. Can we go now?"

Lars writes our names in the book, his tongue poking out between his teeth. He was never that great at writing. "Mal and Loony Lenna." I wince at this old family nickname that he just won't let me forget. "Okay, then my initials and the date. Destination?"

"Destination?" Mal echoes.

Lars sighs dramatically. "Where are you going? We're keeping track of comings and goings, so you have to tell us where you're going."

"We're going to have lunfast with Chug, Tok, and Jarro in New Cornucopia. You know, the other part of our town that's outside of the wall?" Mal says, her face swiftly growing as red as her hair.

Lars writes that down, too. "There, was that so hard? If you would just follow directions, we would've been done already."

"Are we free to go?" Mal asks.

Jami and Lars step back like they've been training to move in unison. It's creepy.

"Be careful out there, citizens," Jami warns, trying to sound authoritative. "The Overworld is a dangerous place."

I blink at him. "Have you ever been outside the wall, Jami?"

"That's neither here nor there!" Jami barks. "I'm a guard entrusted with guarding the wall, and so guard the wall I will."

"You'd better get out of here before you make him mad," Lars says with a sneer. "Guards now report to the Elders on a daily basis, and you wouldn't want to get a demerit."

"What's a demerit?"

His sneer twists, and he snickers. "You'll see."

Mal and I hurry away toward New Cornucopia, and I can't stop wrinkling my nose like I smelled something bad.

"What was all that about?" I say. "I can't believe anyone would willingly give Lars something sharp. He used to drop pickaxes on his toes all the time. That's why they moved him to the sorting yard outside the mine."

Mal tugs on her braid as she thinks. "I bet it's Elder Stu and Elder Gabe. They don't like the door in the wall, so they're making it harder to use, maybe." She shakes her head and glances back. "It used to be one guard in regular clothes, just whoever was available and mainly to welcome visitors, and now it's two guards in full iron armor with weapons giving orders. We were last out here, what, two days ago? And it wasn't like this. I wonder what happened to make them change the rule? We need to tell Nan after lunfast."

"Do you think we should call it brunch instead?"

She rolls her eyes. "Yes, but I'm not telling Chug that. It would break his heart. You know how proud he is of lunfast."

A mouthwatering feast is waiting for us at a table outside the shop where the brothers sell everything Tok makes with his crafting table and brewing stand. Chug has prepared delicious pies and steaks and potatoes and bread, and Mal has brought a bucket of fresh milk. Jarro walks over, followed by his cat Meowy and an adorably spotted baby horse. I can hear Tok hammering away at his crafting table as usual, but as soon as we sit down Chug shouts, "Tok! Hurry up! It's lunfast time!"

Tok looks great—all his hair and his eyebrows have grown back after he learned to make proper potions on our last expedition. He's smiling, his cats and their latest kittens cavorting around his feet.

"So I came up with the perfect name for that baby horse," Chug says.

"Foal," Jarro corrects.

"No, that's a terrible name. I was thinking—are you ready for this? Sir Horsely."

Jarro is momentarily lost for words, and it's hard to believe he used to bully all of us around; he's really kind, now that he's away from his mom and ex-friends. "No, I mean, a baby horse is called a foal. And his name is Al."

Chug deflates a little and mutters, "Okay, but the next one is gonna be Sir Horsely, right? Because that's a great name. I would also accept Lord Wuffles."

Jarro chokes on his stew, and Chug helpfully thumps him on the back, completely unaware that he's the cause of Jarro's current breathing crisis.

"Hey, Lenna," Tok calls, pulling my attention away from the scene. "Do you know if Nan has any books on redstone?"

"What's redstone?" I ask, because I grew up in a mine and I've never heard of it.

"Sometimes I find these red blocks," Mal explains. "And they make this weird red dust . . ."

"And I've been experimenting with it." Tok leans forward, excited, his eyes alight. "It's kind of like back when I was inventing things but they never worked. There's some secret to redstone, and I feel so close, but—"

"But at least he's not still blowing things up," Chug finishes for him.

I shake my head. "I've never seen anything like that in a book, but Nan's collection is mostly about plants and mobs and biomes, not mining. My folks back at the mine might know more."

"Gross," Chug mutters under his breath, and I smile because it feels good to know my friends have my back.

"Yeah, not worth asking them." Mal looks toward the wall as she chews and frowns. "I can't believe Lars signed up to guard the wall."

I sigh. "I can. Some people will do anything to feel important."

"Hey, remember that time Lars fell face-first in a cow patty?" Chug asks.

"Yeah, because you pushed him." Tok grins.

"Whoa, that was you? I was always jealous of that. Nice!" Jarro holds out his hand, and he and Chug do an elaborate handshake that ends with a fart sound.

We all laugh, remembering that day, and I never dreamed I could ever be so happy. We eat until we're all groaning and rubbing our bellies, and Poppy falls asleep in the grass covered in kittens and one mud-splattered pig. When it's time for Mal to go back home and do her chores, we help clean up the dishes and say our goodbyes and head back toward the wall.

This time, when Lars asks for our names, we just say them and hurry past, eager to be away from his arrogant grin. I'd love to remind him of his time in a cow patty, but I know he would just find some way to punish me—especially now that he thinks he's tough. As Mal milks the cows, I enjoy the pasture, watching bees and sketching birds for the book I'm writing about flora and fauna. The cows love Mal, but they get fussy when I try to help, because my mind tends to wander and they don't really like being squeezed that hard by someone who's not paying attention.

Once the milk is all lined up in pails, Mal and I hurry down the road and through the Hub, carefully carrying a bucket of fresh milk for Nan. Elder Stu glares at us from his store, and I wonder why he is the way he is, why he's so scared of everything that isn't exactly his way. Not all the old people are like that—and Nan is definitely not like that.

I smile as we near her cottage, with the bright flowers we planted together in the window boxes and the sleepy bees humming around their hive. Nan is usually sitting outside at this time of day, reading a book in her rocking chair as she enjoys the afternoon sun—and waits for her milk. The door, oddly, is open. And when we push inside, we see why.

"Oh no!" Mal cries. "Nan!"

3

MAL

 So here's what you need to know: My name is Mal, and I can't think about anything else right now because my great-great-great-grandmother is clearly in trouble.

Nan is on the floor, stretched out on her belly like she fell. She's the oldest person in town, over a hundred, but she's always seemed so strong and spry. I kneel and gently turn her over with Lenna's help, and Nan blinks and shakes her head as she coughs. Her skin is grayish and slack, her eyes unfocused.

"Nan," I say softly. "What happened?"

"Mara, is that you?" she mumbles, and I flinch, because that's not me—it's my mom.

"Nan, it's Mal."

"And Lenna."

"Yes, and Lenna, too. Did you fall? Are you hurt?"

Nan shakes her head harder and licks her dry lips as she struggles to sit up on her own. "Nothing happened. I'm just old, that's all. Needed a little nap. Help me into bed, will you, Mara? This floor leaves a good bit to be desired."

We carefully pull Nan up and help her stagger to her bed. Once we've got her under the covers, she settles back against her pillow with a weary sigh and closes her eyes.

"She was fine this morning, I swear," Lenna says, exasperated and worried. "She woke up before me. She scolded me for not weeding the window boxes!"

"Nan, tell me what you're feeling," I ask, holding her hand.

She blinks, her eyes searching for me.

I've never seen her like this before, and it's terrifying.

"Mara, change your shirt," she mumbles. "Always covered in cow hair, that girl."

"No, Nan. It's me. Mal. Mara's daughter. When did you start feeling bad?"

She coughs, and her eyes find mine. "I was outside reading, and my heart started fluttering. I came inside to get a drink, and everything began swaying around like I was on a boat. I fell down, and I was just too tired to get up. It's the strangest thing. Now let a body rest, would you? Humph. Children. Pesky things."

Her eyes flutter shut, and I look to Lenna. "Have you ever heard of an illness like this? Maybe in one of your books?"

Lenna shakes her head. "I can look, but I don't think so."

I gaze out the open door, back toward town. "Will you stay with her? I'm going to the Hub to get Tini and Elder Gabe. Maybe they'll know more."

Lenna tucks in Nan's feet and goes to a bookshelf, already pulling down an old book. "Go on. I'll keep an eye on her."

I nod and take off, running for the Hub like I'm being chased by a thousand skeleton horsemen. Luckily, we're not too far away, and I skid into Tini's shop, gasping for breath. She looks up from her counter, frowning. Then again, our town healer is mostly frowning when my friends and I are in view. I guess when you sell rare potions stored in glass bottles, a bunch of rowdy kids are your worst nightmare.

"Help," I manage to mutter. "It's Nan."

Tini stands, straightening her robes and smoothing back her gray hair. "What's wrong? Did she fall?"

I shake my head. "She's . . . sick. So she fell, but because of something else. She's in bed now. Doesn't seem like she broke any bones, thank goodness."

Tini's brow wrinkles down. "Then what do you want me to do?"

"I don't know!" I shout. "Fix her! That's your job—to fix people!"

Hands on her hips and nose in the air, she says, "That is my job, yes, and your job is to respect your elders. Have you conferred with Elder Gabe?"

"I came to you first."

At that, she preens a little—Tini is in the running to be our next town Elder, when whoever is oldest finally dies. As the healer, I guess she has extra insight into that sort of thing, but it's always seemed a bit morbid to me, actively waiting for someone to kick the bucket.

"Then let's go get Elder Gabe and we'll go together. It's good that you came to me first."

"We need to hurry!"

She flaps a hand at me. "Emergencies are rarely a matter of time, child."

I goggle at her. "Yes, they are! That's why they're emergencies and not—not—tea parties!"

Tini harrumphs. "Potions will fix things or they won't. Five minutes won't change anything."

I dance from foot to foot as she takes her time, closing her ledger and locking her potions closet before walking to the door so slowly I wish Chug were here to pick her up and carry her. She motions for me to go outside and carefully locks that door, too. I take off running for Elder Gabe's store, but Tini's walk is stately and calm, as if she needs everyone to see her performing her duty.

As I nearly jog in place beside her on our way to our town's oldest and grumpiest potions expert, I have to ask, "Tini, why don't you have an apprentice yet?"

She side-eyes me with a frown. "Oh, that time will come when I'm a bit further along. I'll choose one of my daughters and teach her my secrets. I think Livi might be a good choice."

"But if you taught her now, she could keep the shop open for you. What if there's another emergency while you're out seeing Nan?"

Another hand flap. "It'll take care of itself. You know our town's ways. We typically take on apprentices when we become Elders or are in our decline, not when we're still capable of working."

Now it's my turn to frown, because I understand what she's actually saying. If she trained anyone else, if she shared the secrets of her craft with them, then she might lose business to them. That's why tools were so expensive before Tok learned how to craft—Elder Stu was the only person in town who knew how to work a crafting table, and he guarded that information so jealously that no one else even knew it could be done. Our Elders don't pass down their knowledge until they have no choice . . . which is why there are so many frustrated young people. Maybe that's why my friends and I got into a ton of trouble before we started going on adventures beyond the wall—we didn't have anything useful to do because no one would teach us how to be useful.

Even at Tini's slow-as-dripping-honey pace, we soon arrive at Elder Gabe's storefront. She pats her hair and settles her robe into place before entering, and he hears the door chime and emerges from the curtain that hides his wares with a theatrical flair.

He instantly deflates when he sees who it is.

"Ah, young Tini," he says, even though Tini is old enough to be my grandmother. "What brings you to my fine establishment? Need some more potions?" He waggles his tufty white eyebrows.

Because, again, Elder Gabe won't teach Tini how to make potions. She has to buy them from him and then use them to heal people. When Tok learned how to craft tools and brew potions, it really shook up the town economy, which is probably the only reason they let him move outside the wall—so Elder Gabe wouldn't lose as much business.

"No, Elder Gabe," I break in, because I honestly don't have time to listen to Tini explain it. "We have a big problem—"

"Who is it? What did you see?" he barks, looking around frantically and brandishing his walking stick like it's a weapon.

I don't know why he's so jumpy, so I just tell him, "Nan is really sick. I'm not sure what's wrong with her, but she needs help."

He exhales in relief and nods sympathetically, his hat slipping off his bald head. "Yes, well, little Mal, that's called getting older, and it happens to us all."

I shake my head, my braid flying. "No. That's not it. She was fine this morning, and then she suddenly got very, very not fine."

Elder Gabe and Tini share a look of surprise.

"Well, you see," Elder Gabe says with a pitying look, "that's impossible."

"Then come to her cottage and see. Because I assure you, it's very possible."

"Children have such big imaginations," Tini says with a shrug.

I glare. "So you think that I'm imagining my great-great-great-grandmother being deathly ill?"

They share another look, and Elder Gabe sighs heavily. "Very well, then. I will have to charge you for the visit either way, you understand."

"We both will," Tini hurries to add. "Lost time, lost revenue . . ."

"Fine! Charge the oldest person in town. I'm sure she'd prefer that to dying," I bark. "Now come on!"

I march toward Nan's cottage, and Elder Gabe and Tini trail behind me. At first, they both try to go slowly, each looking more aristocratic and stuck-up than the other, with Elder Gabe's walking stick clacking on the cobblestone. But then, once we're out of the Hub, they pick up the pace, probably realizing that the faster they get back to their shops, the faster they'll get back to selling their wares. I bust through Nan's door and find very little changed. Nan is in bed, asleep and breathing shallowly, and Lenna sits on a chair beside her, a stack of books by her side and a big blue book in her lap.

"Wee Gabe," Nan says, blinking annoyedly. "You'd best not bother my cow again, you scalawag. It spoils the milk."

Elder Gabe clears his throat. "Hello, Nan. How are we feeling?"

Tini elbows her way in front. "We're feeling how, there, Nan?"

Nan sits up, frowning. "I feel like a steak left out in the rain.

Weak, achy." She sighs and deflates a little. "I would say I'm getting old, but I've been doing that for twenty years with no ill effects."

Tini and Elder Gabe take turns inspecting Nan from her eyeballs to her ears and nose, right down to her feet. They mumble to themselves and mutter at each other, but neither of them really seems to know what's wrong. Lenna pages furiously through her books, muttering to herself and tossing each book on the ground as it fails her.

Finally, Tini sighs and brushes down her robes. "This is not a known illness. It would appear that age has simply caught up with you."

"Balderdash!" Nan roars, and I grin to see a bit of her old fire. "I've got thirty years left in me! At least!"

"There's nothing we can do," Elder Gabe concurs, head hanging. "We can only keep you safe in bed and feed you a steady diet of beetroot soup."

"I'd rather die!" Nan barks.

"Well, it would appear you're going to do that either way. I'm so sorry, Nan." Elder Gabe tries to take her hand, and she flails at him, almost like she's trying to punch him in the nose.

"I'm not dying!" she cries, but it ends in a fit of dry, hacking coughs. "Get out of here, you bumbling old fool!"

"We must discuss consultation fees—"

"So bill me! And if I die, I'm not paying!"

Elder Gabe and Tini hurry out of the cottage, and Nan settles back down. I grab her hand, and she sighs deeply and looks to me with wet eyes.

"They can't help me," she says. "With their potions. This is beyond potions, whatever it is."

"Then what can we do?" I ask, my eyes tearing up, too. "Maybe Tok can craft something new. Maybe—maybe we can go to the Nether and find something. Whatever it takes, Nan, we'll do it. We can't lose you."

Nan's eyes go far away. "There is one thing . . ." She trails off, her eyes fluttering closed.

I shake her gently. "Nan! Nan! What? What is it? Whatever it is, we'll get it for you."

Her eyes pop open, wide and dreamy, like she's looking at a far-off sunset.

"The enchanted golden apple," she murmurs before falling unconscious.

4.

TOK

Here's what you need to know:

No. Wait.

Here's what I need to know: What is an enchanted golden apple, and how can I get one for Nan?

And, I guess, how can I keep Chug from eating it first?

Don't get me wrong—my brother loves Nan as much as I do, but he definitely isn't known for his self-control.

As soon as Elder Gabe and Tini said they couldn't help Nan, Mal ran all the way through Cornucopia and back to our place. I've never seen her so scared and anxious, and I've seen her half dead from poison. She filled us in on what had happened and asked me if maybe there was a potion in one of my books that could help. Chug and Jarro and I stuffed a bunch of my books and potions into our pockets and ran to Nan's house as fast as we could. Well, as fast as Lars and Jami would let us, thanks to that ridiculous new protocol at the door.

My potions book didn't have anything useful in it, so now Lenna and I are going through all of Nan's many old books, back from the time of our town Founders, scanning each page for anything related to an enchanted golden apple. It's hard not to get distracted, because these are Nan's special books that she never, ever lends out, and they're full of things we've never even heard of before. As Lenna and I pick up books, page through, and toss them on the ground in heaps, Chug paces and Mal holds Nan's withered old hand.

"Nan, please," she murmurs. "Please wake up. You have to tell us how to get that apple."

"Or any apple," Chug says, rubbing his stomach as he paces. "Lunfast was so long ago."

"You know," Jarro says from the corner where he's been sitting, slowly deconstructing a flower. "They said potions wouldn't fix her, and Tok's book wasn't very useful, but maybe potions would help enough to get Nan talking? I bet Elder Gabe and Tini didn't want to use any potions because they don't want to fail—or be responsible if she takes a turn for the worse. If people heard that our town's specialists treated Nan but couldn't save her, everyone might start to doubt them."

I look up. It's a good point. "That makes sense. They're just not willing to take the risk and fail. But I am. I'll make as many potions as Nan needs." I look to Mal. "If that's what you want?"

Mal's face is red and tear-streaked. "I don't see how it could get any worse."

"I do," Chug breaks in. "What if one of the potions turns her into a strider? Her shirts wouldn't fit because she wouldn't have arms. Or—or a slime? Although I guess then we could subdivide her to make more, smaller Nans . . ."

"Just try healing potions, maybe," Mal says. "But yeah, please don't turn my great-great-great-grandmother into a slime."

I line up all the potions from my pockets, and Lenna pulls all of Nan's potions out of the secret compartment in her armoire. I know what each of my potions does because I made them, but Chug just grabbed things randomly, which isn't going to help us much. I start with a Potion of Healing, dripping the bright red liquid into Nan's mouth. She splutters and then sips, her eyes blinking open.

"Nan!" Mal cries.

Nan shakes her head and turns her face away. "Stop that yelling. I'm old, not deaf."

"Do you feel any better?" Lenna asks.

Nan sighs and slumps down, almost like she's becoming a liquid. "No. I don't think I'll ever feel better. Just like you woke me up from a nice dream. Now let an old lady sleep." She closes her eyes, and I tip a little more potion into her mouth. She swallows it and eyes me suspiciously. "You're up to something."

"We just need to know how to find the enchanted golden apple," I say.

"Or we can just keep feeding her Potions of Healing for every moment of the rest of her life?" Chug says hopefully.

Nan's nose wrinkles up. "That would be like waking you up every two minutes that you were asleep for the rest of your life. I won't have it. Now listen up, because I'm only going to say this once."

We all surround her bed, and she sits up a little and gives each of us a stern look. "Nobody start crying, you hear me?"

"No promises," Mal says with a sniffle.

"As you all know, our town had eight Founders," Nan begins.

"Your ancestors. When they began building Cornucopia, I was just a little girl, even younger than you. But here's a secret, children . . ."

We lean close.

"There were originally ten Founders."

We all exchange looks.

"How have we never heard this?" Mal asks.

"Because the people who stick around write the histories," Nan says. "Efram and Cleo were written out of the narrative. As the Founders journeyed here, they had to cross a great ocean. Cleo was lost to a drowned, and Efram went mad with grief. He no longer wanted to found a great city. He wanted to stay by the sea where he'd last seen his wife. He told us he was going to build a home out in the middle of the ocean, where no one could ever bother him again. He was angry that out of everyone, only his love had been taken. It hurt too much, he said, the thought of seeing everyone else happy and thriving while he suffered. They tried to talk him into coming along, or at least going back to their original city and starting anew. But Efram would have none of it. He dove into the sea and was never seen again."

We all exchange bewildered glances.

"Great story, Nan," Chug says in the most Chuggish of ways. "Now tell us the one about the enchanted golden apple."

Nan coughs and harrumphs. "This *is* the story of the enchanted golden apple. You kids these days have no patience for theatricality." She settles herself down like a chicken sitting on eggs. "Now, the thing about Efram was that he loved hunting for treasure in odd places, and one time, he found a golden apple that shimmered with violet magic. He wouldn't use it for any reason. He was saving it, he told us, in case anything bad ever happened to Cleo. But then when tragedy struck and she was pulled down into the water, there was no way to give her the enchanted golden apple he'd saved to rescue her from death. The adults reckoned that irony broke his mind."

"Those old people were hard-core," Chug whispers to me and Jarro.

"So you're saying that this Efram guy might still have the enchanted golden apple?" Lenna asks, cutting to the chase as usual.

Nan nods sagely. "That's the only time I've ever seen one. Never even heard of one, before that or after that. Couldn't tell you how to find one. Efram never told us what he had to do to get it. He said it was too horrifying, got that faraway look in his eye. But I saw it once. He pulled it out to show it to Cleo, and it was the most beautiful thing I've ever seen."

"Okay, so how do we find Efram?" Mal asks. "Do we go to the ocean?"

Nan nods. "If he still lives, it's there. I don't doubt he's still alive, either, as he had all sorts of esoteric magical items. If I'm still kicking, he's still kicking, the crazy old coot. You find the ocean, you'll find him. In a house in the middle of the water."

"So we go to the village, get a map from the cartographer, find the ocean, and . . ."

Mal trails off, but Chug continues for her.

"And find a crazy old man living in his ocean hermit house and mourning his lost love, and we ask him for his prized possession that failed him during the greatest tragedy of his life. I'm sure he'll be real happy to see us."

Nan winks at Chug. "Sounds like a nice plan."

"We're going to need the horses." Mal looks to Jarro.

"I can have them ready immediately," he says, nodding. He's

still just glad to be one of us and would do pretty much anything for Mal.

"We already have a bunch of potions, but we're going to need armor and weapons," she goes on.

"Well, obviously," Chug says, chest puffed up.

"And I can bring my crafting table and brewing stand. I have a whole traveling workshop," I say.

Mal grins. "Bring all that and any ingredients you might need along the way."

"And we're going to need a lot of cookies. Like, a lot." Chug looks at Lenna.

She nods."I baked a fresh batch this morning." Mal wipes her eyes and straightens up, looking less like a lost little girl and more like our brave leader. "Then let's split up. Guys, head out to New Cornucopia and get the horses and supplies ready. Lenna and I will gather up food and meet you there."

Chug and Jarro run to the door, and Chug turns back and raises an eyebrow at me.

"I need to repack all these potions," I explain. "Just make sure you pack my crafting table, brewing stand, and furnace. Don't forget, okay?"

"Okay," he agrees.

I look past him at Jarro, who winks at me. Chug will forget, but Jarro won't. It's kind of neat how they complement each other when all they used to do was insult each other. They run off, and I focus on filling my pockets with potions and ingredients from Nan's secret stash. My fingers itch to bring along a few of Nan's books, but I know there's always the possibility of being robbed out on the road. It happened to us once before, when we were on our quest to stop Krog and his illagers from destroying Cornucopia, and we lost almost everything. Krog is in the town jail, and the bandits who robbed us are trapped in the Nether without a portal, but there are always more bad guys in the world . . . although probably not as many as Elder Stu would estimate.

Once Lenna's pockets are full of cookies and arrows and Mal's pockets are full of more boring foods, we head toward the wall and New Cornucopia. Without really talking about it, we choose a roundabout path that keeps us out of the Hub. We've left town twice before, both times against the wishes of our town Elders, who are pretty strict about children not being allowed to roam. We went out the first time to save the town, and my friends went out a second time to save me when I'd been kidnapped. We're willing to risk everything to save Nan, but our parents and the other adults won't share that view.

When we get to the door, Lars and Jami block our path.

"You know who we are, and we're in a hurry, so just let us through!" Mal starts.

But they don't move. They spread out to look . . . well, as menacing as Lenna's older brother and a sheep farmer can look while carrying weapons that they don't know how to use.

"Sorry, kids, but you can only pass through the door twice per day. In and out. That's it," Lars says with a sneer.

"Says who?" Lenna shoots back.

"The Elders! Do you think we make up rules on our own?"

Lenna shrugs. "Probably! You once told me girls weren't allowed to hold pickaxes!"

"Because you'd dropped a pickaxe on my foot!"

"No, you dropped a pickaxe on my foot!"

Jami puts an arm between the quibbling siblings. "We enforce the rules made by the town Elders for the safety of everyone in

Cornucopia," he says. "Now, this is a brand new rule, delivered just a few minutes ago, so it sounds like you kids must be up to no good again. Come back tomorrow, give us your names, and we'll be glad to let you through. Tok, in fact, can pass. He came in, so he can go out." He bows graciously as if making room for me, but I don't budge.

"Come on," I say to the girls. "Let's go downtown and have a talk with the Elders."

I watch Lars and Jami as we turn, and since their expressions don't falter, I'm pretty sure this new rule is a real thing and not just something they made up to mess with the kids who used to be called the Bad Apples. I lead the girls back up the road, and we turn in at Mal's farm.

"What are you doing?" she says. "We have to get outside!"

I keep walking, and they follow me. "And we're going to get outside. Just not that way."

When the wall is in view Lenna chuckles. "Oh, I see. Smart. Mal, do you have your pickaxe?"

Mal, too, barks a laugh. "Yeah, good point. How do they always forget this part?"

"Because the Elders want everyone to think the wall can't be touched, much less mined. Pretty silly, when you think about it," I say.

We've never had to do this before, but we're not going to let two snooty guards and a new rule stop us from saving Nan. If we had the time, we'd walk back to her cottage and hop out the secret window in back, the window that is actually in the wall. The first time Nan showed us that window and the Overworld beyond, everything changed. The Elders probably don't know about that window, but again, we don't have time to double back.

We have much easier ways of getting through a wall.

Lenna and I keep watch as Mal pulls her pickaxe out of her pocket and walks up to the wall. Every block is pretty much the same, with torches set every seven blocks. She picks a random place and mines two blocks, leaving a person-shaped hole. We slip through, and she replaces the blocks. It's impossible to tell that we even touched the stone, but now we're standing outside. It's kind of funny, actually, how many people have lived every moment of their lives in Cornucopia, never thinking about what else there might be in the world. And never thinking that a wall is just stone, and stone can't stop anyone who's made up their mind.

The wall was built to keep out hostile mobs and marauders, but over time it became a way to keep the people inside, where it's safe. We grew up never thinking there was anything beyond it. Then we learned better. We learned there was more. They gave us a door and the promise of freedom, but their increasingly constricting rules feel like a return to the way it used to be, before we knew about the Overworld.

One pickaxe, two blocks. That's all it takes to gain freedom.

We run around the outside of the wall and to New Cornucopia. Jarro has five horses lined up, and Chug is in a mishmash of diamond and netherite armor. My cats, Candor and Clarity, are sitting on my horse's saddle.

"You guys came from the wrong direction," Chug says.

"Lars and Jami wouldn't let us out of the gate," I explain. "They said there's a new rule—you can only go in and out, or out and in, once per day."

"That's stupid!" Chug says, his hands in fists.

Mal grins and holds up her pickaxe. "It's stupid, but it's even more stupid if you don't know how to mine a hole in a wall. Tok's idea, of course."

"The word is 'stupider,'" Chug says with a matching grin. "At least in regard to Lars and Jami. And of course it was Tok's idea, because my brother is a genius. Are we ready to go?"

I glow with pride as we mount up and follow the trail that now leads from our town to the nearest village, where a beacon was placed by the Founders long ago.

"Hey, you kids! How'd you get outside?" someone calls. "Get back here!"

It's Lars, running toward us, shaking his sword.

"Time to run!" Mal says. She kicks her horse, and we all take off at a gallop.

Doors can't stop us, and neither can guards.

We're back in the Overworld, and out here, we make the rules.

5.

CHUG

So here's what you need to know: My name is Chug, I'd forgotten how hard it is to ride a horse in full armor, and I'll do anything to help save Mal's Nan—and not just because she makes the best cookies in the world.

I mean, Lenna can make them now, too.

It's just—Nan is fun and feisty and funny, and she's the first adult I've ever met who wasn't a total stick-in-the-mud block. I definitely don't want to think about a world without her in it.

As we gallop away from the wall—and the protests of Lenna's second most annoying sibling—I'm grateful that horses exist, because I don't know what I would do if I had to fight Lars for the right to leave. The poor guy would have no chance. Luckily, even the slowest horse is faster than an out-of-shape guard who isn't used to running in armor.

Not that I like horses better than pigs, because I don't. I'd much rather ride my pet pig, Thingy. But he's slower, and I hate putting him in danger, and he's going to be a father soon. I couldn't bear to tear him away from Miss Pig and their cozy nursery sty. So here I am, clanking and clonking on my noble steed. This time I'm riding Mervin. Everybody says I'm not very good at naming things, but at least my names make sense. What the heck is a Mervin?

Soon we're far beyond Cornucopia and Lars's pathetic shouts. It's so weird when people shout, "Stop! Come back!" when you know full well that if you stop and come back, you're just going to get in trouble. They might as well be shouting, "Go! Hurry! Get as far away from me as possible!" Tok and I learned early on that if we hid in the barn for half a day, most things would just blow over. Something tells me that this new thing the Elders are doing with their guards and their rules and their books isn't going to blow over on its own, though. People who make rules like that don't just nicely withdraw them.

It's good to be out in the Overworld again. Sure, New Cornucopia is outside the wall, but it's still a calm little town, just like the one inside the wall. But out here, nowhere near any walls at all, anything could happen. That's how I found Thingy and how Lenna found her pet wolf, Poppy, who seems overjoyed to be back out in the world. She's darting into the grass, chasing rabbits, sniffing flowers, then gleefully bouncing back to Lenna's side. Lenna is smiling, and Mal seems lighter, almost like whenever we're at home, she's wearing invisible armor that weighs her down. Lenna is completely out of her parents' house and their mine, and Tok and I really only visit our folks' pumpkin farm for Sunday dinner these days, but Mal still lives at home on the cow farm and tries to be the perfect daughter. She never says so, but I think she feels torn. Once you've been to the Nether and fought a ghast, it's hard to accept being scolded for coming home five minutes late.

Jarro seems happy out here, too. His mother pretty much disowned him after he got kidnapped, along with all of her sweet berries. He started a new crop with the few berries we managed to salvage while following his trail, and he knows for sure that his mom sneaks over at night to pick his berries to restart her own farm. He lets her do it, but it makes him sad. Whenever he wakes up to find that the berries have been stripped off his bushes, I tell him it must've been birds. Really ugly birds. It makes him laugh. And then I make his favorite mushroom stew and get him laughing with some good fart jokes, and he seems okay.

So yeah. I think we're all happy to be back on an adventure. Maybe not Tok, though—he enjoys it the least of all of us. Whenever Mal, Lenna, and I go into the Nether for more potion ingredients, Tok just stays home with Jarro to guard the portal, and I know he worries about us. Considering he was kidnapped there and trapped by brigands while he sleeplessly made potions for them in an underground fortress, I can see why he wouldn't want to go back. He may not like adventuring, but he loves Nan, so I know he's going to do his best out here, even if he doesn't really excel with any weapons. I tried to train him, but he's kind of a menace. Considering every crafting table I make is wonky and wobbles, I guess it's lucky that we each have our specialty.

The first time we rode to the village, we had no idea what we were doing, really, and we bungled all sorts of things. We had to make our own trail there, but now there's a brown path cutting across the plains. Jarro's horses know the way, as he rents them out for town citizens who want to travel to the village to trade their goods. I don't really have to think much, which is good, because honestly, it's not my best trait. If something that needs to get destroyed shows up, I'll destroy it. Until then, I can daydream.

Okay, fine, daydreaming only works for about an hour until my stomach is growling. My armor amplifies the sound, and Lenna laughs and rides up beside me to give me a cookie. Everyone gets a cookie, and mine is gone in two bites. I'm already thinking about what I'm going to cook for supper, because to everyone's surprise, I'm the best cook in our group. Lenna must be thinking the same thing, as she pulls out her bow and arrows and goes after some rabbits and sheep.

"Do we need to stop soon?" Tok asks, nervously looking up at the sun, which is sorta kinda thinking about beginning to set.

"I'm not sure." Mal turns around to look at us. "I can dig pretty quickly, these days. We can go a little farther."

She's nervous for her Nan, just like I was nervous for Tok, the last time we were on this trail. The faster we go, the faster we get what we need, the faster we can come back.

"Actually, there's supposedly a permanent shelter," Jarro says. "I heard about it from when Inka last rented a horse to take her melons to the village. She said it was right on the road." He looks down at the packed brown dirt cutting through the tall grass. "Which I guess this is now. A road, I mean."

"Then we need to hurry if we're going to make it there by nightfall. We got a late start." Mal kicks her horse, and I groan as we settle into a trot. I hate this part, when it's all bouncy right before we gallop.

For a while, all I can think about is holding on to Mervin while I sound like a milk bucket full of rocks rolling down a hill. Jarro says galloping on a horse is the best feeling in the world, but I don't see the appeal. For our past two adventures, we've used a minecart track underground, but we're not headed to the woodland mansion this time. We're going to the ocean, whatever that is. Something about water? I don't pay much attention when they're talking about things I don't understand and can't eat. It saves time.

As the sun sets, we see an object rise on the horizon. Our horses slow down as we approach it, and even Lenna draws her bow and arrow, just in case. As promised, it's a sturdy little shelter made of wood. The door isn't as nice as the ones Tok makes, but it's a lot better than the dark, rough caves Mal usually hacks out of the ground for us. There's even a fenced paddock, big enough for all our horses. This is great, but it's also . . . well, maybe a little boring? Part of the fun of being on an adventure is not knowing where or when you're going to stop for the night, but now we know that anytime we want to go to the village, we can stop right here, in this place that will always be the same.

Inside, there are four bunks against the walls, but we always carry beds with us, thanks to the secret gigantic pocket trick Nan taught us. I start a fire outside and get to work on dinner while Lenna and Poppy quickly scan the area for meat or other food we might need later. Tok rearranges all his potions and ingredients, Jarro talks to his horses, and Mal stands by the shelter's door, hands on her hips, frowning.

"You okay?" I ask her. "You look like you're mad at the air."

She sighs and comes over to sit beside me at the fire. "I'm worried about Nan. And I'm worried about Cornucopia. It was bad enough when there wasn't a door in the wall, but now the Elders are making all these weird rules. After all this"—she gestures at the wilderness around us—"I find it hard to follow other people's rules."

"So move out to New Cornucopia, with us," I say. "Maybe start your own little cow farm. Or dig a new mine. Or both. If you live outside the wall, they can't make you stay inside."

"But then how do I visit my folks? Or Nan? Ugh!" She throws a rock into the grass, startling a rabbit. "I wish I could be an Elder and help make the rules. They need a young person's perspective. We're the town's future."

I chuckle. "Yes, exactly what old people want: the thoughts of young people."

She has to laugh at that, too. "Why can't they all be like Nan?"

I think for a second, and then it comes to me. "Because she's been outside the wall. Even if she was young, she lived a life of adventure. They haven't. I don't think a single Elder has set foot outside the wall, even with the door there."

We sit companionably as the sun sets, and we both feel a little nervous until Lenna appears with a single piece of sheep meat and a sad little carrot.

"Not a lot out here," she says with a shrug. "I guess the other travelers have been hunting, too."

My stew is ready, so we go inside the shelter and eat on our beds. I sit by Tok on his bunk, as I'll be putting my bed down in the middle of the shelter later. If anything should happen, I'm the best fighter and the person who can take the most damage. Not that we expect trouble. The door is sturdy, and with the local brigands trapped in the Nether and our old enemy, Krog, in jail back home, there's no real danger out here. Zombies, after all, can't turn doorknobs.

We sleep peacefully, eat breakfast, and get on the road again in the morning without incident. It's nice to travel with my friends like this, everyone doing their part and getting along. At one point, we pass an old shelter that we left behind, just a hole hacked in the ground, and it makes me feel a little weird to see the grass grown up around the rough door set in the dirt. This place kept us alive, but now it's just . . . abandoned? No one would stop here if they knew the bigger, nicer, newer shelter existed, but this rickety little pit saved our lives, once upon a time. The horses are well behaved, and we're soon speeding up as we approach the beacon the Founders left by the nearest village.

We know exactly where to go, and I notice there's a new iron golem patrolling along with Rusty and name him Mr. Clanksalot. Thanks to her new mine, Mal has plenty of emeralds, and she's able to buy exactly the map we need without too much trouble. Lenna trades some wheat she gathered for those pies we love so much, and Jarro sees his first nitwit, which is fun. Nothing particularly interesting happens, and I'm glad to get back in the saddle and back on the—

Well, not road.

Where we're going, there are no roads.

Because we're headed to the ocean. According to the map, it's a large, blue thing. I guess the blue is water. I hope it's not ice. I'm used to rivers that look like ribbons on the map, but I don't really know what to do with so much water that I can't hop across it using a log. Mal orients us using the map and leads us away into the plains.

"Hey, Chug."

Lenna always rides last, because she has her bow and arrow and can keep us all safe from a more reasonable distance than my sword. I stop my horse and wait for her to catch up, letting Jarro pass me by with a wave.

"What's up, Lenna?"

She looks all around, her brows scrunched down. "Does anything feel . . . weird to you?"

I also look all around, but I don't see anything unusual. "I mean, we're out in the middle of a new place, going to see our first ocean, where we're going to hopefully find a crazy old guy even older than Nan and convince him to give us his magic fruit, but other than that, no."

Lenna looks down at Poppy, and the wolf's fur is all standing up along her spine, her ears twitching nervously.

"Do you think it might be another pig?" I ask. I trust Lenna and Poppy, so I'm sure there's something weird going on, but the last time Lenna acted this twitchy, it was because Thingy was trailing behind us.

"No. I don't know what it is, and I don't know how I know, but . . ." Lenna looks behind us, to the swaying grasses, gray boulders, and scrub trees. "I'm pretty sure we're being followed . . . and not by a pig. It's definitely not something good." She meets my eyes for the barest second before looking away, her shoulders up around her ears. "I've got a bad feeling about this."

6.

JARRO

So here's what you need to know: My name is Jarro, I miss my cat Meowy, and I'm excited—if a little scared—okay, maybe a lot scared—to be part of this adventure. The last time I was out in the Overworld, it was because brigands kidnapped me, along with all my mom's sweet berry bushes. But this time, I was just accepted as part of the group. Nobody asked me if I wanted to go; they just assumed I was in and asked me if we could use my horses. It feels good, to belong.

But I'm also pretty sure none of them know I'm secretly worried.

When I first decided to start a horse farm, I had no idea if other people would even want to leave town, but business has been pretty much booming. I'm the only source for horses, llamas, and mushrooms in Cornucopia, and it feels good to have my own resources and find some respect among the rest of the town. Before our last adventure, I was . . . well, not so nice and definitely not respected, but now I'm an entrepreneur, even if I always smell like horse and have llama spit somewhere on my shirt.

Thankfully, my horses are behaving as we follow Mal's map out into a part of the Overworld even the Mob Squad has never seen. Up ahead, a strange new biome rises, almost like the mountains near the river but less triangular and more . . . cliffy. Sheer rock faces are topped with weird white stuff, and I can see bizarre animals jumping around from rock to rock. The horses have to work a little harder to carry us upward.

"Is this normal?" I ask. "These white mountains?"

Mal shrugs. "Everything is normal for the Overworld, even if it's unusual for us."

"They're just mountains," Lenna answers.

"But the mountains are white. And the llamas have short necks and cow horns," Chug says, mystified. "Mountains should be gray, and llamas do not need horns. They're dangerous enough as it is."

"The white stuff is snow, Chug."

"So why are all the horned llamas white, too? Is it to blend with the snow?"

Lenna exhales in annoyance; she's been on edge all day. "Snow is like if rain was frozen. It's cold. These animals aren't llamas—they're goats. They're like if a llama, a cow, and a rabbit had a shaggy baby, according to Nan's book on mobs. And, yeah, it probably helps them blend in with the snow."

She's got the book out in front of her on the saddle, and I'm glad she always carries a library in her pockets, because it looks like we're going to see new things on this trip. I like to see new things, but . . . well, I've taken damage before because I didn't already know what I was encountering.

Chug watches the goats hop around. "Can we ride them? Or are they like llamas, where they'll carry chests but not people? Or are they like cows and rabbits, and good for eating?"

"Can they hurt us?" I ask, a far more important question.

"I don't think so." Lenna flips the pages on the book. "The book says they're not hostile."

Chug stops his horse and jumps down. He pulls some wheat out of his pocket and walks toward a goat, calling, "Here, goaty goaty goat goat. How about a hug? I've got some nice wheat for you. Everybody likes wheat. I've got carrots, too. And a cookie, but you can't have it."

The goat sees him now and stops, staring intently at him. Chug stops, too, and returns the stare. The goat lowers its head, and I think it's going to walk over and take the wheat, but instead, it bounds toward him with frightening speed. I see the horns lower into position, and I see the horror on Chug's face, and then Chug is flying through the air like a bird. He's in the air so long that Lenna has time to say, "Whoa!"

Chug flops onto the ground, his armor clanking. Lenna already has her bow and arrow in hand and takes the goat out with a few shots. Her wolf runs over and snags the meat before Lenna can get out of the saddle. Tok and Mal dismount and hurry over to Chug.

"Chug, are you okay?" Mal asks, squatting down beside him.

"Talk to me!" Tok wails. "Are you alive?"

"Ow," Chug murmurs. He sits up, takes off his helmet, and rubs his head. "Looks like I found the only animal in the world as hardheaded as I am."

Lenna jogs over to them carrying something weird. She hands Chug a cookie and holds up . . .

"A goat horn," she says. "That might be the weirdest drop of all. What do we do with it?"

"Get another one and then attach them to my helmet," Chug says between bites of cookie. "So that I can strike fear into the hearts of my enemies."

Mal and Tok help Chug stand, even if he's a little wobbly.

"Yeah, that's gonna terrify the goats," Tok says. "Let's get you back in the saddle and past the goats before one rams you in the butt."

Chug shakes his head and wobbles back to his horse. "It was bad enough getting rammed in the head," he says. "It's not like I use it very much. But I use my butt a lot."

I've been in the saddle all this time, making sure the horses stay together—and making sure I don't get rammed by a goat. It's not that I'm a coward . . . okay, well, maybe I am. I just know that sometimes when we encounter a new animal, we get ridable horses, and sometimes we get nearly killed by a hoglin. Sometimes we discover striders, and sometimes I get partially exploded by a creeper. I'm always keeping an eye on Tok's cats, now that I know cats keep creepers away. I still have nightmares of that green, blocky monster skittering toward me and flashing, and I can't really relax out here because I know they can show up anytime, anywhere, day or night, rain or shine. I almost brought Meowy, too, but . . . well, I just can't risk him.

"Should we keep going?" I ask nervously.

Chug clambers up into his saddle. When he sees a goat nearby, he shouts, "I see you over there, Rambert! I'm not scared of you, now that I know you play dirty!"

We line up and continue, and poor Chug has to ask for another cookie, as his ears are still ringing. Or maybe he just wants another cookie. Both reasons are equally possible.

It's a little eerie how the mountains loom over us. They're so big it's hard to fathom, and it makes me think about how until recently, the wall was the biggest thing in my world. These mountains—I'm glad we don't have to go over them, that Mal is picking a path for us that zigs and zags between cliffs. The goats leap around, far overhead, but luckily none of them take a leaping dive for us.

"I sure would like to mine into these mountains," Mal says wistfully. "But we have to keep going."

"Maybe we'll still be in the mountains when it's time to stop?" Lenna offers.

"Maybe," Mal agrees, but I can tell that there's nothing in the world that would stop her from getting a few steps ahead on her quest to save her great-great-great-grandmother.

The day passes pleasantly enough. We eat in the saddle, gnawing on mutton and cookies and cold potatoes. We pass a pretty little river that glimmers in the sunlight. We see rabbits and birds and flowers. Nothing terrible happens—not that it stops Lenna from constantly turning in the saddle to look behind us, her bow and arrow at the ready. I would think she's just being paranoid, but the fur along Poppy's spine never really goes down, either. They sense something I don't, and that makes me feel uneasy.

Mal stops before the sun sets so we have enough time to make a shelter before it gets dark and the hostile mobs come out. The mountains are a bit smaller here, trailing down to hills, but Mal has halted us right by a promising sort of cliff face. No one really says anything; everyone just goes about their business with this nice, friendly feeling of cooperation. Chug starts a fire and gets a stew cooking before walking over to the river to fish. Tok pulls out his crafting table and starts making a door. Lenna slings her bow over her shoulder and heads off into the scrub, a grim frown on her face and her wolf at her side. And Mal takes out her diamond pickaxe and starts mining into the sheer cliff face.

All that's left is me, and I'm about to ask what I can do when I remember—I handle the horses. I have a job here. I contribute. And no one has to tell me to do it; they just expect me to get it done. It's a nice feeling. I knew this would happen, so I brought along enough fence pieces to build a paddock for all five horses. It's easy enough to set up the enclosure and get the horses inside, and I'm about to remove their saddles when I remember that when you're traveling in the Overworld, you make sure you can run the second there's trouble. I give the horses a few extra carrots to make up for their discomfort, and they don't seem to mind.

"Ha!" someone shouts, and I go on full alert, my enchanted golden axe appearing in my hand on instinct. But then I realize it was a happy shout. Mal walks out of the shelter she's digging holding a glimmering block of diamond.

"Time for a new chest plate!" she says, tossing it to Chug, who was also drawn by her shout.

Chug catches the diamond block and shoves it in his pocket. "Tok's gonna love that." He steps closer to the hole Mal's created in the mountain and looks around, hands on his hips. "So . . . you're making a pretty big shelter, eh bud?"

Mal blushes a little, her cheeks as red as her hair. "I know we're in a hurry to help Nan, but I, uh, may have gotten carried away. I've kind of exhausted my mine back home. Haven't seen a vein in days, you know? But this place—it's so different. It's exciting. Diamond!"

Chug pats her shoulder. "It's okay to have fun, you know. Like, yes, we're on a quest to stop your Nan from dying, but that doesn't mean you have to be miserable and worried every second of every day. You're allowed to feel joy. Just keep mining. There's more than enough room for our beds, and everything else is taken care of. I'll bring you a fish on a stick so you can eat while you hack."

Mal gives him a grateful smile. "I guess I never thought about it like that. It's just . . . I see something new, and I get so excited and full of energy and don't want to stop."

"Maybe that's the way it's supposed to be," Tok says, and Chug tosses him the diamond block like it's nothing. "Maybe that's how new things always get discovered."

Looking only a little guilty, Mal goes deeper into the shelter, and the moment her pickaxe is in her hand, it's like we don't even exist anymore. She's grinning fiercely, and I'm happy for her. I get that same feeling when I'm taming horses, when I'm so focused on what I'm doing that the world just falls away. It's a feeling I never experienced until I went on an adventure with the Mob Squad, a feeling I didn't even know existed. I see the same look in Chug's face when he's cooking stew and on Tok's face when he's making potions and on Lenna's face when she's writing and drawing in her books.

I have never seen that look on the face of my mom or Remy or Edd.

I wonder if it's something that only happens out beyond the wall.

And for just a moment, I feel sorry for the people back home who've never felt it.

Chug and Tok head out of the shelter, and I follow. Lenna has already disappeared, probably out hunting in the nearby forest with Poppy. I look around, but I don't think there's anything useful I can do—until I see a bee covered in pollen. My mom keeps a beehive near her sweet berry bushes, and I get excited as I think about something else I can contribute to the group.

Axe in hand because, after all, I'm walking into the woods alone, I follow the bee as it bumbles from flower to flower. When it picks up a steadier pace, I jog after it. There, finally, is the beehive, dangling from an old birch tree with a few honey drips on the ground beneath it. Perfect! I know exactly what to do and am chuffed that I have this skill. I can't wait to surprise my friends. Chug is gonna love it.

I build a fire under the hive, place an old carpet from my pocket over it, and pop the top off a glass bottle. It's so funny, to think I spent most of my life not knowing Nan's secret pocket trick, whereas now I can carry almost anything I could ever need, just in case. The smoke lulls the bees to sleep, and I collect two bottles of honey, shake out my carpet, and douse the fire.

As I walk back toward the shelter, I'm practically skipping. As much as I like being a horse/llama/mushroom farmer, it's nice to be doing something different—something that doesn't involve quite so much manure.

As I walk past a bush, a hand whips out and grabs me, and I try to scream, but something drags me down to the ground and covers my mouth. My entire body floods with panic—is it the brigands? Are they back to kidnap me again? Or punish me?

"Shh," Lenna says near my ear. "Don't say a word. I need to show you something."

I nod, and she releases me. She's a lot smaller than me, but she's strong. Poppy lies in the grass by her side and gently licks my hand as if in apology. As Lenna leads me through the bushes, we stay low to the ground, and I try not to make any noise, although I definitely am lacking Lenna's sneaking abilities, which I guess is how she was able to avoid me so much when I was the bully who made her life terrible.

She stops behind a tree and points down at the ground.

"Hoofprints?" I whisper.

She nods. "Not from your horses."

"There are always wild horses."

She raises her eyebrows, and I finish the thought. "But not in forests."

After a beat of heavy silence, she whispers, "I think we're being followed."

And it's an odd moment, because I spent a big part of my old life making fun of her for having her head in the clouds and saying weird things . . . but I've since learned that she's a really cool person, if very different. Lenna was the first one to see the vexes poisoning our town, and the Mob Squad were the only people who believed her. I'm one of them now, which means that even if it seems far-fetched, if I want to be her friend, I have to believe her, too.

"So what do we do?" I ask.

"We follow the hoofprints."

I nod, and when she takes off tiptoeing, I follow, doing my best to walk lightly. Poppy follows me, tongue lolling and fur ruffled up. We skirt behind bushes, keeping off the main path.

"Oh no," Lenna whispers. "Run!"

I look where she's pointing and see a creeper head staring at us from behind another bush. She doesn't have to tell me twice.

I run.

7.

LENNA

 Of all the things I was expecting, a creeper was not at the top of my list. I'm sure they leave footprints like anything else, but I really don't think they have hooves. There's no time to think about creeper biology right now, though. I shove Jarro ahead of me, and we run in the opposite direction, back to camp.

For a big guy, he moves pretty fast, and I keep glancing over my shoulder, bow and arrow at the ready and wolf bounding at my side. The creeper doesn't follow us, which is good, but . . . odd. That's kind of what they do. Maybe this one didn't see us, thanks to the bushes, and its empty black eyes were just aimed in our direction. I hope so. Poor Jarro is still traumatized from his last run-in with a creeper, and I know he's going to dash into the shelter and slam the door and grab a cat and not come out again until morning.

I can't blame him. He and Mal nearly died last time.

As we burst into camp, Chug stands from his place by the fire and immediately whips out his sword.

"What is it?" he barks. "What's wrong?"

"Creeper!" Jarro shouts. He does indeed dart into the shelter, but he doesn't close the door. My heart kind of crinkles, to think that he cares enough about the rest of us now to not flat-out doom us to being exploded out here.

I stand by Chug, arrow nocked and ready, as Poppy growls by my side but the creeper doesn't appear. After a few minutes, my arms are tired, and Chug's must be, too.

"Are you sure it was a creeper?" he says.

"We both saw it."

He shakes his head. "I didn't mean that I doubted you! I just meant that—well, okay, yeah, there aren't a lot of things in the world that look like green pig-spiders that skitter at you. If you saw it, you saw it, although it's weird that it didn't follow you." He perks up. "Hey, maybe that's why you think we're being followed. Maybe it's that creeper, but it can't get too close because of the cats."

"Maybe," I allow, but I don't buy it.

This feeling I have, that we're being followed—it's not just some mindless mob. I feel like we're being watched, like knowing eyes are crawling over the back of my neck.

Whatever's following us—it's thoughtful. And not in the good way.

"Let's go eat," Chug says, collecting all the bounty from around the fire. Normally we'd eat outside, especially on such a nice day, but we both know Jarro's not going to emerge before morning, not with a creeper in the area.

The shelter is big and roomy, with plenty of torches and two different wings for our beds, girls on one side and boys on the other. Tok places a table between the wings, and Chug lays out all the food. My mouth is already watering, and Poppy licks her lips. There's fresh salmon, mushroom stew, hot potatoes, and one pumpkin pie Chug must've saved from Sunday dinner with his parents. It's a feast, and Mal puts down her pickaxe to join us.

"I found this," Jarro says in a small voice, placing two bottles of honey on the table.

"What?" Chug splutters. "How? Bees?!"

"Yeah, I found some bees. My mom has a hive," Jarro explains, stepping closer. "But she made me do most of the work."

"You're like some kind of beastmaster." Chug nods, truly impressed. "Horses, llamas, bees. The last time I tried to steal—I mean *borrow*—some honey, I ended up—"

"Stung a million times and costing our family a lot of pumpkin pies," Tok finishes for him, shaking his head. "I still can't believe how much Tini overcharges for a simple healing potion."

We have a delicious feast in our beautiful shelter behind a sturdy door. We don't know precisely when night falls, but we grow sleepy and rub our bellies and yawn. I sleep well—as well as I sleep in my bed back home in Nan's cottage and a lot better than I used to sleep in the room I shared with my sisters, where I often chose to curl up under my bed just so they would leave me alone.

In the morning, Chug is the first one out the door, in full armor with his sword drawn, but there's no sign of a creeper or any other dangerous mobs. We pack up our beds and table and mount up, and Mal gives one last, longing look at the mine she's begun but must now abandon. When she looks at the cliffs, I know she sees endless possibilities and would happily mine here every day for the rest of her life, but Nan comes first.

After consulting the map again, Mal leads us toward the ocean.

We fall in line, and I take my place in back, bow over my shoulder. Like me, Poppy looks around, bristling, but whatever is following us is good at hiding. With Tok's cats on his shoulders, at least, no creepers dare approach us.

The morning passes with the sweet scent of flowers and grass. I take down the sheep and cows we pass to build up our food stores. We eat on the road and keep riding and as the evening sky starts to turn a pearly periwinkle, we stop to make a shelter in the middle of a hilly meadow. The mountains are long gone, and we should find the ocean tomorrow morning, judging by the distances on the map. There is no exciting new cliff face for Mal to mine, but she makes quick work of a shelter dug into the ground, happy at least to find a vein of lapis lazuli ore. We find no honey, no sweet berries, no interesting treats, but Chug does meet his first donkey and Jarro suggests we bring a breeding pair with us on the way back home.

"I'll be back for you, Little Heehaw!" Chug promises while I sketch a pair of gamboling baby donkeys in my book.

As the sun sets and clouds crowd in, everyone heads down into the shelter. Jarro hangs around outside longer than I thought he would, but he definitely keeps one of Tok's cats in his lap at all times. When everyone else is inside, I stand by the hole in the ground and scan the plains for something, anything that might be causing me this strange anxiety. It's not the donkeys. If it was a wolf or another predator, Poppy would let me know. She would bound out into the grass and fight it.

And yet she just stays by my side, bristling and softly growling.

I don't know what that means.

The first few drops of rain patter down, but my fist is tight on my bow. My family told me that my ideas were silly, that I saw things that weren't there. But my friends believed me, and Nan made me promise to always trust my gut. She said it was connected to my brain, and even if I wasn't sure about something, my stomach would tell me. Right now, my stomach is telling me that we're being followed by something dangerous.

I see a shape move, far away. I squint, but I can't see clearly through the rain, and I'm not about to run out into the tall grass by myself right as night is falling. Poppy spreads her front legs and bares her teeth and growls, and I put my hand in the raised hair along her neck, just letting her know that I'm with her and getting ready to grab her collar if she tries to run away and face whatever is out there alone.

"It'll keep till morning," I tell my wolf, and she whines softly.

We go down into the shelter and shut Tok's sturdy door. I move my bed so it's right by the door, my bow and arrow under my pillow. Poppy curls up beside me, but neither of us sleeps well that night. Maybe it's the rain pouring down on the wood, maybe it's the thunder shaking the stone around us, or maybe it's knowing that there's something mysterious out there in the tall, waving grass, something dogging our every step.

I'm bleary the next morning when Chug wakes me up with the promise of hot buttered bread with honey. I'm the first one outside, and the sky is a thick, dead gray, all the grasses heavy with raindrops. I scan the plains but don't see anything moving except the little gray donkeys. We mount up and trot toward the ocean, and Mal asks me if I'm okay, and I don't know how to answer.

"Something is wrong, but I don't know what," I tell her.

"We're all worried about Nan," she starts.

But I shake my head. "Something else. I feel like something bad is going to happen."

"I feel like that sometimes," Chug says, altogether too chipper. "But it's usually just gas."

"Ever since the creeper, I think I kind of always feel like something bad is going to happen." Jarro admits.

I can't explain it any more clearly because I don't really understand it myself, and there's nothing I can do about it, anyway. We have to get that enchanted golden apple before Nan—I don't even want to think about it. Before she gets worse. And that means that we press ahead, no matter what Loony Lenna thinks she feels.

The sun finally breaks through the clouds, and every raindrop on the prairie glistens. We top a small hill, and as we look down, we're nearly blinded by a blaze of golden light that shines like fire and twinkles like crystal.

"What is it?" Chug asks.

"That's the ocean," Mal replies, grinning. "Remember when we stood on the roof of the woodland mansion and saw a glimmering ribbon of light on the horizon? I think this must be it."

We all stop to gaze down at the ocean, a vast body of water that seems to go on forever. Where it meets the land, there's sand, and the water laps up in frothy white before roiling back into what I can now see is a deep cerulean blue.

"The ocean!" Chug cries. He kicks his horse and gallops down the hill toward it, and after a moment of thought, Mal follows him. Tok is hot on their trail because he's always on edge when his brother does dangerous things. Running directly for a huge body of water definitely falls into that category.

"Oh well," Jarro says before following, probably to stay close to the cats.

Now it's just me and Poppy. I turn my horse to face back the way we've come and scan the waving grass all around for anything suspicious, but I don't see a single thing. With no real options, I sigh and take off after my friends, and I'll admit that it's pretty fun, galloping down a hill toward something new. I end up shouting just like everyone else, and we're all lined up together, our horses racing, their necks parallel to the ground and their hooves pounding. Tok screams a different sort of scream, and I notice that both of his cats have their claws sunk into his shoulders for dear life; he did not think this part through.

As we near the sand, our horses fall off to a trot and then a walk. Chug leaps down and yanks off his boots, wading into the lapping water in his bare feet.

"It feels good!" he says. "Cool and—tuggy? Like it wants to play."

"Do not play with the ocean," Tok says, massaging his wounded shoulders. "If you slap it, it's definitely going to slap back."

"And we don't know what's in there," Jarro says nervously. "All sorts of new animals." He looks to me. "And hostile mobs, right? Didn't this Efram guy's wife get killed by something?"

"A drowned," I fill in, because I've been studying every book I can find on the ocean and what we might find there. Nan said this guy lives in the middle of the ocean, which means that's exactly where we have to go. "Basically, an underwater zombie."

"Sick!"

Tok rubs his eyes. "You hear the words 'underwater zombie,' and the first word that comes to mind is *sick*? Like, in a good way?"

"I've never fought one before," Chug explains. "And I always like hitting new things with a sword."

Mal is staring down into the ocean like she's just going to see

Efram down there waving back. "So I'm thinking we shouldn't all go," she begins.

"I'm going!" Chug squawks.

"Which means I'm going," Tok says with a heavy sigh.

"And I want to go so that I can record whatever I find down there," I add. But I look back the way we came, because that feeling that we're being followed has not lessened.

"Then I'll be the one to hang back," Jarro says, obviously relieved. "I'll feel better if the horses aren't left alone. And if Mal will leave me some of the stone from yesterday's mining and Tok will leave me a door and some torches, I'll build us a little shelter so we'll have somewhere to stay the night. If I'm in a sturdy shelter, none of the mobs can get in. And with the cats, that creeper that's been following us won't be able to get near me." He actually seems pretty relaxed—and maybe even excited—by the prospect.

This plan works for everyone, so Mal gives Jarro a bunch of stone and Tok gives him a door and some wood blocks. Chug hands over a pile of torches, and Jarro puts up the horse paddock and gets ready to start building. He's smiling, which is nice; he definitely worries a lot more than the rest of us, so I'm glad he's found a solution that works for everyone.

I'm about to ask how we're supposed to go underwater, but Tok, of course, is ready. He pulls four Potions of Water Breathing out of his pocket and hands one to each of us. I swirl the deep blue liquid around in its bottle before drinking it down. The funniest feeling comes over me—like I'm inside a bubble and as light as air.

"Hurry! It won't last forever!" Tok shouts, and then I rush into the water after my friends.

Right before I dive down, I turn back to Jarro. "Take care of Poppy, okay?"

"Of course," he says cheerfully, with two cats twining around his legs and Poppy sitting politely by his side. "We're all going to be just fine!"

I dive under the water, and everything changes.

8.

MAL

I am suspended in endless, wavy blue, weightless and floating. It's kind of like when we learned to swim in Inka's pond back home, but there's so much more water than I thought could possibly exist. I don't know how I'm breathing, but I am. Potions are just magic, I guess. The ocean is so much deeper than I ever imagined. And a lot more full of . . . stuff.

There are fish, plants, stones, squid. A playful gray creature glides by and stops to stare at me with intelligent eyes, and I long to ask Lenna what it is, but I'm not sure if I can talk.

"Dolphin," she says, her voice high-pitched and far away. "Harmless."

"I wanna—" Chug starts.

"Don't hug it," Tok finishes. "We're on a mission, and we don't need a redo of the goat-hugging incident."

"Ah, dolphins can't hurt me," Chug says. "They don't have horns."

"Let's spread out in a line and cover as much ground as we can," I call in my weird, squeaky, underwater voice. "We're looking for anything that looks handcrafted down here. A building, I'm guessing, probably of stone."

As if we were walking along a trail on land, we spread out in a line. Chug takes his place about twenty feet to my right, then Tok twenty feet to his right, then Lenna way on the other end. We swim like this, parallel and looking down. The deeper the water gets, the darker the blue. The ocean floor is like an upside-down mountain, not flat at all, and there are rocks and plants but nothing that looks like an eccentric old man's house.

"There he is!" Chug calls. "Efram! Hi! We're friends of—"

Something hurtles directly at Chug, glancing off his leg.

"Ouch!" he roars. "Efram, you're a real jerk!"

I see it now, the figure moving toward us, but it's not Efram. Unless Efram is a—

"Drowned!" Lenna shouts, realizing it at the exact same moment.

"Who did?" Chug asks, staring at us.

"No, that thing is not Efram, it's a drowned—an underwater zombie. Remember?"

Whoosh.

Another projectile whooshes past, a stick with three prongs on the end like a giant fork.

"Cut that out!" Chug bellows.

"You're going to have to fight it," Tok says quietly.

"How?" Chug asks.

The drowned is headed right for us, swimming swiftly, another giant fork ready to throw.

"Any way you want to, Chug, just go!" I shout.

He nods at me and turns, pulling his sword out of his pocket and fighting his way down through the water. It's tough going with only one arm, but Chug is determined. When the drowned throws its next weapon, Chug bats it away and goes in for a slice with his sword.

"I wish I could use my bow and arrow," Lenna says, appearing beside me. "But I don't know how the water will affect my aim, and I don't want to hurt Chug."

"He'll take care of it his own way," I say, watching him battle the weightless zombie. "He always does."

"I have a Potion of Healing ready," Tok says resignedly. At this point, I guess he's just all too accustomed to his brother running headfirst into battles.

"I don't like this guy!" Chug shouts as he stabs and grunts and parries. "It feels like he shouldn't exist."

"Maybe zombies like to swim," Lenna says in her Lenna-ish way. "Maybe the cool water is soothing."

"Let's see him swim when I chop off his arm!" Chug shouts. "Take that! And that!"

A long pause.

And then Chug screams.

I guess underwater zombies are harder to handle than land zombies.

I guess we know, now, what happened to Efram's wife.

I draw my own sword and kick down toward Chug, who's hurt and having trouble continuing the fight. Whatever the drowned's weapon is, it's brutal, and its teeth don't help the equation. Chug sees me coming and smiles his thanks, and then I land a solid hit across the drowned's back . . . which is great, except then it turns the full force of its rage and hunger upon me. The darkness of the water only makes its visage more terrifying, and I momentarily forget to hold up my sword. The bite burns my arm, and Chug lands a hit while I struggle to get enough space to use my sword.

Finally, finally, Chug takes it down, and it leaves behind its weapon, floating in the deep, dark blue. Chug pockets it and asks, "Are you okay?"

I hold up my arm, which looks pretty terrible, and Tok swims over, holding out potions for us. I'm not sure how we're able to drink underwater, but it works, and my arm heals before my eyes.

"That big fork it dropped is a trident," Lenna says. "I remember it from Nan's books. It's a really good weapon, actually."

"Not when it hits you directly in the chest," Chug says with a groan.

"Okay, but now imagine you're hitting the zombie directly in the chest," Tok begins, and Chug grins and pulls the trident out of his pocket, inspecting it with a critical eye.

I look down, scanning the ocean floor for more drowned or anything that could possibly be a hermit's home. "Still no sign of Efram."

"Well, that makes sense. If you want to stay away from people, you're not going to build your underwater lair right off the shore," Tok says. He snaps his fingers, but they don't make any sound, because we're underwater. "What if we head for that island over there and make a couple of boats. Then we could row around while we look for Efram. We'd be safer that way, we can see nearly as well, and it's a lot less work."

Chug raises an eyebrow. "It's a lot less work if you're not the one rowing."

Tok chuckles, caught out. "I'll give you my next cookie."

Chug's eyes light up as he shouts, "Deal!"

We can see a chain of islands far out, just a misty haze rising over the water with tall shapes that must be trees. Thanks to the healing potion, I have the energy to get there, and we again spread out in a line and carefully watch the ocean floor for enemies and any sign of Efram. We don't see any more drowned, but we do see a sea turtle, and there's no way I can stop Chug from trying to hug it. The sea turtle, at least, doesn't seem to mind.

As we crawl up onto the sandy shore of the first island, my body feels heavy but my head still feels weirdly light and airy— the Potion of Water Breathing hasn't worn off, so I guess my voice will just be high-pitched for a while. Chug starts chopping down trees for wood while Tok sets up his crafting table and brewing stand. Lenna surveys the island, and it's odd to see her walking around without Poppy by her side. They've been inseparable ever since the day she tamed the wolf, and Lenna seems a little jumpy without her companion. At least she has her bow and arrow out. After meeting the drowned, we're all on alert. In the Overworld, you never know what new creature you might meet.

"How can I help?" I ask Tok.

Without looking up, he says, "See if you can catch some puff-erfish. Just toss in your fishing line and wait. The fish we want will be orange with bulgy black eyes." He reaches into his pocket and drops a fishing rod onto the sand, and I take it and hurry out to where the water laps at the beach.

I haven't ever fished before—that's generally Chug's job—but he's intent on getting enough wood to make two boats. I've watched him fishing, at least, and it seems pretty self-explanatory, so I toss out my line and wait until there's a tug and the bobber goes down. I pull in a salmon, then a cod, then a brightly colored tropical fish, then another cod, then, of all things, a book. It looks like it might be enchanted, so I can't wait to show it to Tok. Still, I'm not going back until I've got at least a few pufferfish. Finally, after two more cod, I pull in a weird little orange fish that gets all puffy, and I keep fishing until I get a second one. By the time I return to Tok's work area, I have enough fish to keep us all eating well for a few days, and my stomach growls as I think about what Chug might cook up for us.

Lenna is back from her walk around the island, and she's brought some eggs and chickens she found on the far side. As Tok works on the boats, Chug makes a fire and sets out the fish to cook before heading out to catch some more pufferfish—apparently we need one for each Potion of Water Breathing—and also because, I think, he doesn't wish to be outdone when it comes to fishing. I show Lenna and Tok the book I pulled out of the water, and Tok freaks out and starts strategizing with Lenna about what to enchant with it.

There's not much for me to do right now, so I sit down on the beach and enjoy the sun and the breeze. I can't see the land we left behind, can't see Jarro and the horses and Poppy and the cats, but I'm sure he's happily building a nice shelter, glad he didn't have to enter the cold embrace of the sea. Chug and Lenna and I have made several runs into the Nether for potion ingredients since our last adventure, and Jarro is always welcome, but he never wants to come along. It's kind of funny—he doesn't really belong in town, but he doesn't want to have adventures, either. I guess Tok is the same way. I'm glad they've both found a happy medium outside the wall in New Cornucopia back home, and I hope the Elders don't make even more rules that make it difficult for us to visit. I definitely don't want to miss lunfast.

Chug comes back with three more pufferfish, enough cod to

feed Lenna's family of twelve, and, of all things, a saddle. We eat the roasted fish, and Tok finishes the boats and crafts more potions, and it's nice, the way nothing explodes. He spent the last year without eyebrows, but now that he's mastered his brewing stand, no one has to get blown up.

As we push the boats out into the water, Chug stops and considers the sturdy wooden vessels.

"Boats need names, don't they?" he asks. "I'm pretty sure I read that in one of Nan's books."

Lenna nods. "People tend to name important boats. And they're all female for some reason." Before Chug can ask an embarrassing question about boat anatomy, she adds, "Or at least, we call them 'she.'"

"I hereby name this boat . . . *Lady MacBoat*," Chug says, bowing dramatically over his boat.

"And this boat is called the *Adventurous Nan*," I break in before he can name our boat something even worse. "May they ferry us to glory! Or, you know, to Efram."

Lenna gets in with me, and Tok and Chug ride together. I take up the oars, knowing that Lenna has the sharpest eyes. We row out into the open water, and my arms are already tired. Lenna leans over the side, squinting down, down, down.

"I still don't see why anyone would live out here," she says.

"Nan said he wanted to get away from people." I shrug as I row. "So it stands to reason he wouldn't make himself easy to find."

"But underwater? That's a pretty weird place to live."

"There are people in Cornucopia who still think we're weird," I remind her. "Just because we like to go on adventures and keep pets."

"And Lars called me Loony Lenna just the other day." For a moment, she stops staring down into the ocean, hunting for signs of Efram, and instead she gazes off toward the horizon, a hazy line where the dark blue of the sea meets the clear azure of the sky. "No matter what I do, they think I'm weird. It's like they completely forgot that we've saved the entire town. Twice. And that if we weren't willing to risk runs to the Nether, Cornucopia wouldn't have a single Potion of Healing."

I sigh and let the boat drift, stretching my shoulders. "The part I don't get is . . . I mean, how long do they think they can control us? Sure, we're kids, but we support ourselves. We can survive anywhere. We keep *them* safe, not the other way around. I can't think of a single reason that we need to be told what to do."

"The Elders run the town, and the Elders make the rules. That's the way it's always been, Mal."

"Well maybe that needs to change. Maybe being old doesn't mean you're smart or wise or caring. Maybe it just means you're old." I take the oars back up and row with renewed vigor.

I'm definitely mad at the Elders, but not Nan. She may be old, but she really is smart and wise and caring. She's the one who sent us out into the Overworld, after all, the first person who believed in us. We're going to find this Efram guy, and we're going to get the enchanted golden apple, and we're going to hurry home and get Nan fixed right up.

And then we'll see about the Elders.

"Wait. Wait," Lenna says, leaning so far over the edge of the boat that she falls in before I can catch her. I'm worried at first, but I don't really need to be—she has the potion, after all, and she knows now what a drowned looks like. She disappears under the waves for a few moments before bobbing to the surface.

"I think I see it!" she crows. "Efram's house!"

9.

TOK

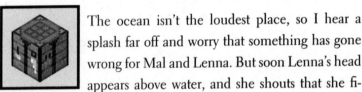The ocean isn't the loudest place, so I hear a splash far off and worry that something has gone wrong for Mal and Lenna. But soon Lenna's head appears above water, and she shouts that she finally found something. Chug rows us over, slightly bummed that we didn't spot it first, but I assure him that the sea turtle eggs we found on a nearby island were just as exciting a discovery.

Our boat thumps gently against the other boat, and I look over the side and see, quite far away still, a big square sort of building, very decorative with lots of layers. It's made of a stone I've never seen before, a beautiful teal that shimmers and seems to move with the sunlight that dapples down from the surface.

"What's it made of?" I ask Lenna, since her family owns the mine and she was forced to work pretty much every job there before they gave up on her.

"I don't know," she says, paging through one of Nan's books. "We don't have that stone in our mine. It's something new, I suppose. We'll have to ask Efram, maybe bring some back home to study and put on display. It's pretty, though."

"I've never seen it, either," Mal says, and she would know, because she's done a ton of mining in the back of her cow farm and in the Nether, too.

"Why are you guys so interested in boring old rocks when there could be all sorts of cool stuff down there that's better than rocks?" Chug complains. My brother has never really enjoyed rocks, unless he was throwing them at Jarro, back when Jarro bullied us on the regular. "Let's go!"

"How long will our potions last?" Mal asks me.

I pass around four fresh bottles, just to be safe. "I'm not quite sure. The books don't give an exact time, but it seems like . . . maybe a quarter of a day? Surely long enough to swim down there and talk to Efram. And he's got to have some way to breathe constantly without having to worry about potions, or else he'd be waking up choking to death every night." I shudder at the thought. I'm not the most adventurous in our group, and I'm slightly dreading swimming all the way down there.

But I don't let the others know that. If Chug's worried about me, he won't be worried about himself, and that tends to get both of us in trouble.

We drink our potions and hop down into the water. I wish there was a way to make sure our boats stay right here, but hopefully they won't drift too far, or a squid won't show up and push them, or whatever. Mal leads the way, swimming straight for the underwater structure. Chug motions for me to go next so he can keep an eye on me, and I take a deep breath, even though I don't really need one, and dive.

It's nice underwater, peaceful and quiet, but creatures move in the periphery of my vision, and I startle every time a turtle or a fish shows up. They're harmless, but my brain doesn't know that. I'm still a bit jumpy after those brigands kidnapped me and dragged me into the Nether. A fish isn't a brigand, but my brain just shouts, "Argh! Attack! Panic!" and I don't really have a choice.

Still, the more I get out and experience life and have good adventures with my friends, the less I'm bothered by those bad memories, so I focus on Mal and keep on swimming, knowing Chug is behind me with his sword and Lenna has her bow and arrow out and ready.

The closer we get, the bigger Efram's house appears. The stone really is beautiful, shimmering like a prism. Tall fronds of seaweed wave around it like trees. We don't see an immediate door, but Mal must be thinking the same thing I am—that it's probably at the bottom of the structure, just like a regular house's door would be. Big fish swim around it, almost like they're on patrol.

"This guy's house is really something," Chug says in his squeaky potion voice. "Like, huge. Really big for one old guy. Don't old people usually shrink?"

"Or you just keep getting taller," I remind him, although technically, he's probably right. I don't think being one inch shorter would change the fact that Efram built a really huge home, though. It doesn't even really look like a house.

It's almost more like . . .

A monument.

Especially now that we're level with it.

A flash of movement makes me startle, but then I realize it's just a fish.

As it swims closer, though, my danger sense starts tingling.

It's bigger than all the other fish I've seen.

Meaner looking, too.

It's almost like a pufferfish, with spikes sticking out all around it, but instead of two goofy, bulging eyes, it's got one huge one.

"What happened to that cod?" Chug asks.

"I don't think that's a cod, bro." I answer. "Lenna, do you remember anything about big, angry fish covered in knives?" I begin to swim backward as I reach for my pocket and probe around for the sword I keep on hand even though I'm not very good with it.

"Nan doesn't have any books on the ocean," Lenna says. "Should I shoot it?" She has an arrow aimed but is uncertain. I pull out my sword and—

Ah!

Fish!

FISH!!!!!!!!!!!

FISH FACE!

Right in my face!

Angry fish!

I scream and paddle backward with my hand, but the gigantic fish is right in front of me, and it slams into me, and it feels like getting run over by a horse covered in knives, and I thrash and squeal and panic, and if I didn't have the Potion of Water Breathing, I'm pretty sure I'd be drowning.

I strike out with my sword, again and again, striking and striking, unable to see anything through the bubbles, and finally the giant fish swims away. I blink until I can see again, and only then do I realize all my friends are likewise dealing with big, angry one-eyed fish of their own.

Chug is screaming, "Die! Die some more! Die a deadly death,

dude!" as he hacks away. Mal is silently fighting, her face bright red against the water's cool blue. And Lenna is having a hard time of it, because she's a ranged fighter and doesn't have Poppy with her to help distract her attacker. I don't know how I think I can help because honestly, this isn't my forte, but I swim over there and start smacking the fish from behind with my sword. Together we take it down, and then Chug and Mal join us.

"Quick snack break?" Chug says hopefully. "Because being spike-smacked by King One-Eye was no fun."

"Eat while you swim," Lenna says, shoving soggy cookies at us. "Their friends are on the way."

Sure enough, more of the fish are headed toward us. One of them swings around to stare directly at me, and my entire body goes rigid. A weird beam of purple wavy light bursts out of its giant eye and straight for me, and I flail and dodge.

"They can shoot wavy light!" I shout. We've got to dodge! Get behind something!"

Nothing bad happened, but maybe it was just charging up. All I know is that I don't want to find out what happens when that purple beam hits me. When Mal dives down toward the base of the building, we all follow her.

"I thought Mom said you weren't supposed to swim within thirty minutes of eating," Chug says, not that it's stopping him from wolfing down his cookie.

"That's so you won't barf in Inka's pond," I explain. "I don't think these fish care about barf. And I only care about not getting hit again."

We reach the bottom of the building, and sure enough, there's enough space to allow us to swim underneath it. Huge pillars hold up the structure, and I can't imagine how much it must weigh. The whole thing looms over me, and I think about how easily it would squish me if those pillars gave out. As soon as I'm under the building, I feel this wave of . . . I don't even know. Nausea and weakness. There's a spooky sound, and a nightmare-like vision of the spiky fish hangs right in front of my face, making me flail around and panic before it, weirdly, disappears. I wobble and blink.

"Did anyone else feel that?" I ask.

"A wibbly wobbly, bibbly bobbly, wimpy gray swirly fish face ick?" Chug says.

Oddly enough, he's described it exactly.

"Yes, but we can't slow down," Mal says. "We've got to get inside and away from those fish guys."

We swim around awhile but can't find a way in. The bottom of the building is perfectly flat and very dark.

"I think we have to look up a little higher," I say.

We swim up and find the blocks arranged like a pyramid, but just a little way away, I notice some interesting designs in the stone that almost resemble a giant arrow, pointing down. Mal must see it, too, as she makes a beeline for it. We're all swimming as fast as we can, and the big fish are angrily swimming right after us. I wish I knew a potion to help us swim faster, but it's too late now.

Mal aims for a series of arches that look very much like an entryway, and we hurry to swim under the arches and into the building, narrowly avoiding a patrolling fish. Mal leads us upward and into a little niche, and the fish swim right past. They're mean but not particularly smart. Because, again, they're fish.

Once they're out of sight, we creep back down into the entranceway. It's deep blue down here, mysterious and murky, and

I'm not a huge fan. Rather than a nice, reasonable, symmetrical design like a woodland mansion, this place appears to make no sense—more like a Nether fortress, if I'm honest. Which I don't really want it to be, because Nether fortresses are confusing, and I don't want to be trapped in a maze underwater. When we're a little farther into the structure, we stop by a series of glowing white lanterns and take a moment to eat more cookies and recover.

"Does anybody feel kind of weird after getting beamed in the face with fish bubbles?" Chug asks. "It felt almost like a potion, but I don't know what it did to me. I'm still breathing underwater. I don't feel weak or sick. It definitely didn't heal me."

"They aren't fish," Lenna corrects. "I don't know what they are, but they're definitely not fish."

Chug raises an eyebrow. "Name something they resemble more than fish."

"Oh. Well. Um." Lenna's face scrunches up as she thinks.

"Then as long as we're underwater and fighting for our lives, for simplicity's sake, let's call them fish," Chug finishes.

I shake my head. "I wish I knew what they are and what those purple bubbles mean. And why I feel so tired in a very specific way. Fish eye beams haven't been in any of my books. Mal, did you bring any milk, by chance?"

"Milk was the last thing on my mind." She swallows her last bit of cookie and holds up her sword. "At least the fish bubbles aren't poison. And they don't work like a Potion of Weakness or Harming. I don't feel damaged, but . . ." She frowns. "It definitely feels like . . . like . . ."

"Like a rain cloud threatening a storm," Lenna says. "It's not raining yet, but it follows you around, looming, and you know you're going to get drenched."

Mal lights up. "Exactly!" She frowns again. "Not that I like that any better." She pulls out her diamond pickaxe and considers the beautiful turquoise stone. "But while we're here, I'm going to take a couple of blocks of this stuff. It's almost like a prism, isn't it?"

"Prismarine," Lenna says. "If it doesn't have a name yet, let's call it that."

"I was thinking waterstone, but I guess prismarine isn't bad," Chug says, a little disappointed that he didn't get there first.

Mal goes to mine the block, arcing down with her diamond pickaxe, something she does probably hundreds of times a day, but . . . the block doesn't budge. There's not a single chip in it. She huffs an angry sigh and slams her pickaxe into a different block of prismarine, and . . . nothing.

"Let me try," Chug says, flexing a muscle. Mal hands him the pickaxe, and he winds up for a hit that would shatter diamond, but the prismarine makes a sound like a kitten slapped it with a paw.

"This is the hardest substance I've ever encountered," Mal says, running a hand over the nearest block as Chug puts every ounce of his strength into trying to mine a single chip.

"Wait." I put a hand on Chug's back, and he stops. I don't know how he can be sweaty when we're underwater, but he somehow is. "Maybe it's not the stone. Maybe it's . . ." I don't know the right word for it. "Like, a potion without a potion, or an enchantment without the enchantment."

"Like a curse?" Chug asks.

I nod eagerly. "Yeah. Those guardian fish did their weird wobble thing, and now we can't mine. Maybe they don't want us to take the blocks. Maybe it's a way to protect Efram's house." Although I'm beginning to get suspicious of that, too. "Or whatever this place is."

Mal eyes me. "So you think maybe this isn't Efram's house, then?"

I look around. "It's not a house. It's way too big for one person. Why would anyone bother building something this big and eye-catching if they didn't want to be bothered? It screams, *Hey, come bother me!*"

"But then why are the definitely-not-fish guys guarding it?" Lenna asks.

I stare into the indigo shadows of the tunnel. "Because there's something in here worth taking."

Mal looks at each of us in turn. "Raise your hand if you think this is Efram's house," she says. I keep my hand down. So do Lenna and Mal. Chug puts his up.

"I'd build a house like this, if I had nothing else to do. But, like, with my face on the side," he explains.

Lenna says, "Okay, so even if it's not a house he built, it's possible he found it and moved in. Like those bastion remnants in the Nether. Or the woodland mansion. There are all sorts of old places in the Overworld that are sitting abandoned and would make a good home for someone who wanted to hide. I still think it's worth going inside to see."

"Old places often have chests full of goodies," Chug reminds us.

Mal's mouth twitches. I can tell that not being able to mine is really, really bothering her. I guess that's how I'd feel if you gave me a big room full of potion ingredients and no brewing stand. "If Efram might be inside, then we have to go in," she says. "But we're going in fully armored and with our best weapons. Those guardian fish were hard to kill. Who knows what else might be in here?"

Chug snorts. "Bring it. Everything we've faced off with has lost. Whatever is in this weird building, we can take it. Together."

He reaches into his pockets and pulls out armor for each of us. We distribute the best pieces so that we each have something of diamond, something of gold, something of iron. Chug has diamond and netherite, which is the best, but we all agree he should keep it, as he's the one that bellows into battle and takes the biggest hits. Lenna pulls out her enchanted bow and arrows, which will set anything aflame, Chug wields his sword that I've enchanted with Sharpness, and Mal trades her diamond pickaxe with its Silk Touch enchantment for a diamond sword that does pretty well on its own.

Before I pull out my own sword, I take a deep breath and reach into my pocket to reveal four new potions.

"What are those?" Lenna asks.

"Potions of Regeneration. They should help us heal faster, if we get hurt. Just a little something I've been brewing lately."

Mal's brows scrunch down. "Do you really think we need to use them now? We might run into something much worse back on land."

"It's not that big of a deal." I swirl the violet liquid around in its bottle. "Just a ghast tear and some Nether wart. Besides, I haven't tried it out yet. So consider this . . . a test run."

Chug shrugs and takes a bottle, and I grin. My brother always supports me, even when it involves drinking questionable substances. After gulping it down, he chuckles and says, "Tastes like salted mushrooms."

Everyone drinks one down, and I hold my sword, hating how

awkward it feels in my hand. Maybe I should've stayed on land with Jarro, or even up in one of our boats so we'd be sure not to lose them. The potion makes me feel strong again—or as strong as I ever feel. But then Chug takes off swimming deeper into the building, and I'm glad I'm here. Someone's got to watch his back.

After all, what if this place isn't as abandoned as it looks?

10.

CHUG

 I love exploring new places and discovering adorable new animals and adding delicious new foods to my recipe box. I would add Tok's new potion to my soup for a little of that umami flavor, especially if it makes me heal faster. I didn't want to admit it to the group, but that creepy one-eyed fish beat me up. I should've asked Lenna for another cookie, or maybe hit Mal up for some fish. I'm definitely not at my strongest. Not that it matters. If we can just get through this place, we'll find Efram and his enchanted golden apple and be back on the surface in no time.

I find an opening in the bottom of the building and swim up. I can see—not great, but well enough—and the moment I'm into the next level, I start—

Ah!

Fish!

Fish in my face!

I beat the fish down with my sword, but it gets a few slams in with its aggressive spikes. I see another fish and run at it, but it turns away from me and pulls its orange spikes in like it's hiding. I take it down and touch my arm, where the other one got me.

I . . . do not like spiky fish.

Someone screams behind me, and I spin to find Mal being targeted by a fish-eye bubble ray. I hit it with my sword from behind, and it spins and comes after me. As I keep fighting it, trying to dodge the spikes, it suddenly feels like my entire body is on fire.

Okay, now I see why Mal was screaming.

I scream, too.

There's an annoying amount of screaming going on.

Tok hurries toward the fish that's frying me with its eye bubbles and immediately gets spiked. I finish the fish I'm fighting and turn to help him.

The spiky fish are everywhere.

Everywhere.

Lenna grunts in annoyance, and I see a fish coming up behind her. "My arrows should be on fire, but I guess the water cancels it out. Nothing works down here!"

"Come on!" I shout. "We've got to get to a better position!"

Maybe this is like a woodland mansion, and we've got to get to a quiet hallway or room and regroup. I lead the way down the tunnel, but it's cramped and dark. When an opening appears overhead, I take it. Mal, Tok, and Lenna follow, and I breathe a sigh of relief as I hurry down the hallway, take the next left, and go up again into a—

Fish!

Fish in my face!

It got me with its spikes right as I swam up. It was like running headfirst into a box of swords. Everything hurts, but I can't stop. I beat at the stupid spiky fish with my sword, but I can tell that my energy is going down, that I've taken a lot more damage than I usually do. Which is weird, because this netherite is the tightest armor we've ever seen. It can usually withstand anything, so why are these fish causing me so much trouble?

This time, when the fish falls over, I notice that it drops crystalline shards made of the same stuff as the beautiful blocks I couldn't break. I pocket them—and I'm desperate enough for food that I gobble down the raw fish meat it left behind.

With that fish gone, I'm relieved to see that we're in a proper room now, with niches and benches and pretty sea lanterns. It kind of reminds me of some of the rooms in Krog's woodland mansion, like someone very talented and thoughtful placed each block in the prettiest way possible. Krog didn't do that—he was just a mouthy villain who found it first—but I have to agree the mansion made a great secret base. This place would not make a good base, I realize now. Too many murderous not-fish. I swim in and look around in awe as my friends join me. Except—

"Where's Lenna?"

I look at Tok and Mal, and they look behind them, and Lenna . . . isn't there.

My heart starts beating like crazy, and I want to ask Mal for some more food, but finding Lenna is more important. I hurry back out of the room and into the hallway, but it's dark and twisty.

"Lenna!" I call.

"Chug, garble barble burgle borgle!" Lenna calls back, or at least that's what it sounds like through all the water and prismarine.

"You guys stay here," I tell Mal and Tok. "I'll be right back."

I swim down the hall, checking all the weird little offshoots and upshoots. Whoever designed this place must've had vertigo and liked messing with people, because it makes no sense, and it definitely seems like buildings should make sense. I take it back — it's nothing like a woodland mansion. It's a horrible place. I guess Efram really, really wanted to be left alone.

A guardian fish appears up ahead of me, but it's facing away with its spikes all pulled inside, so I silently charge it and take it down with just a few hits.

Aha!

If you attack the guardians while they're facing away, they don't hurt you!

This is excellent news.

My usual strategy of aggressively attacking first is actually going to serve me pretty well underwater.

"Lenna!" I call again.

"Chug, borble barble broken!" she calls.

I try to follow the sound of her voice but end up in a weird hallway with blocks at waist height like someone thought it would be a great place for a fence. At least there are plenty of lanterns in here. I backtrack out and swim up, and there's Lenna in a room with two of the spiky fish trying to . . .

Well, it looks like they're trying to eat her.

I roar my rage and charge, beating on the guardians while they're focused on Lenna. Her bow lies on the ground, broken, and I see now how she got trapped. I double down on my on-slaught, even when one of the guardians turns to face me, spikes out and bristling and big eye shaking like he's going to start blow-ing bubbles at me again.

I take a few more hits before the last guardian goes down and immediately snatch up the raw fish and chuck it down my gullet.

I know I should've offered it to Lenna first, but let's be honest—she can't make it out without me, so I have to keep up my strength.

"They chased me in here, and my bow broke," she says in a tiny voice. "I . . . I don't have another weapon."

I can see three books lying on the ground, like she got so desperate she was throwing whatever she had at the fish. I pick them up along with her broken bow and hand them back to her before reaching into my pocket and handing her a gold sword. "Now you've got a great weapon. Tok made it himself. Let's get out of here." I collect the shards and crystals the guardians dropped and lead Lenna out of the room.

The only problem, of course, is that this place is a maze.

And it just so happens I am particularly bad at mazes.

Know who're good at mazes, though?

Tok and Mal.

You know, the two members of our party who are somewhere else, waiting for me to return.

"You wouldn't happen to know the way back?" I ask Lenna with casual coolness.

"Nope. I was running—swimming—for my life."

I turn left, but instead of finding the room with the fences, it's a dead end. That's not the way. Back in the hall, I go right, but that's the way Lenna's room was. Maybe up? Yeah, I guess we go up. The hallway isn't familiar, but it's possible I got confused. I was moving through here so fast. And all the rooms have to be connected somehow, right?

We corkscrew through a claustrophobic hall that reminds me of the stairwells in a Nether fortress and swim up into a big room with multiple columns.

"Okay, so let's rest here a minute—" I start.

But Lenna interrupts me, shouting, "Giant spiky fish! Run away! Run away!"

I take it she means swim, but I don't correct her. I dive back down into the hallway, but not before nearly peeing myself as a gigantic, all-gray guardian swims aggressively at us, the biggest mob we've seen underwater so far.

My only comfort is that it's too big to swim through the only door.

Isn't it?

We're back in the twisty halls, and we're too desperate to really notice where we're going. Down, around, through, right, left. It's dark and twisted and the thought briefly crosses my mind that . . .

Well, Tok's potions are going to run out eventually, and then we'll be trapped in here without a way to breathe. I haven't seen a single pocket of air.

I can feel my breathing speeding up, and Lenna's hand lands on my arm. "It's gonna be okay," she says. "Just keep swimming."

"Just keep swimming," I repeat.

Thankfully, I see a flash of familiar light, and we swim into the lantern fence room.

"I know this place!" I say, and relief floods me as I realize Tok and Mal should be right around the corner.

We swim into the big room I remember, and there are Tok and Mal, sitting on a bench, eating some of last night's fish. Mal hands pieces to Lenna and me, and I tear into it. As it settles in my stomach and my strength begins to come back, I'm more aware than ever that down here, underwater, my armor isn't really doing me any favors. Or maybe it is, and without it, I'd already be fish food. I could eat all day and maybe never feel full or like I was at full strength, but I know we need to hurry. I'm scared to ask Tok how long we have left with our potions, so I just finish up my last piece of fish and burp fishy-smelling bubbles before pointing to another door.

"Everyone ready?"

No one looks ready.

Lenna looks like she's about to pass out, the sword shaky in her hand. Tok's shoulders are hunched up, and I know he's remembering the stone fortress where he was held captive in the Nether. Mal just looks angry, like everything is going wrong and there's nothing she can do about it. She hates that.

"Come on, Mob Squad," I say. "I bet Efram is right around that corner. Let's go find him and get that enchanted golden apple and get home to Nan and throw a party. We can make a cake taller than Elder Stu for her!"

Mal nods. "Yeah, okay. For Nan. We can do this. But for the record . . ." She sighs in resignation. "I hate it down here. Give me a nice cozy mineshaft, any day."

"I actually prefer the Nether," Lenna adds. "At least you can see for miles and miles, most of the time."

"I don't like any of those places, but I don't like it here, either, and let's just say time is of the essence. Hurrying is better than standing still." Tok is nervous, which makes me nervous, but I have a good feeling about things.

Efram is probably somewhere nearby, sitting on a throne of golden apples, waiting to reward some plucky kids for their dedication to his old friend Nan.

At least that's what I tell myself so I won't prove my mom right and throw up.

I lead the way out into the hall and toward the next room because I think everyone understands that this place is brutal, and I can take more hits. Light shines through the archway, and I charge in, and—

It's not Efram.

It's another giant gray guardian, and it's mad.

"Back away, guys!" I say.

Remembering how the smaller guardians got shy when directly attacked, I swim right at this one, screaming, sword slashing down.

Pain bursts behind my eyes and I scream and nearly black out for a second.

These big guys have bigger spikes and more anger issues.

One hit, and I think I broke every bone in my body.

I go in with my sword again, but I take another spike to the sword arm.

My arm is full of bees. Angry bees. And fire. Angry bees that are on fire. I want to cut it off and throw it away. That's how much it hurts.

My body propels itself backward as if the animal in my heart knows that if it doesn't run, it will die, but my brain tells me to stay and protect my friends. Mal darts in from the side and goes for a hit with her diamond sword, but those spikes just won't stop. Her scream feels like an arrow in my soul, and the sword falls out of her hand.

"Get out of here!" I shout. "We have to get out of this stupid place!"

I make sure they're swimming away before I turn to hit the big guardian one more time, hoping it will give us a chance to escape. I land a hit and spin to follow my friends, but the stupid spiky guardian fish monster jerk gets me with one last spiky stab, right in the back.

A cheap move. So not fair.

My entire body is fire, is stone, is iron. I'm heavy.

The sword drops from my hand.

The water is cool.

The ground is soft.

I fall.

11.

JARRO

 Let me tell you, I am living in some kind of paradise. With all the blocks Mal left, I was able to plan and build a beautiful shelter. The walls are matching stone, the roof is gorgeous wood. There's enough room for all our beds and pets, plus space for Tok's workshop. Then again, the weather is so balmy outside that he might like to set up on the beach. I don't have the know-how or equipment to make windows, but I did leave the door facing the ocean so that I can stare out at the mesmerizing waves and wait for my friends to return. The day is breezy, the dolphins are jumping, and I don't have a care in the world.

Well, until my friends are gone a lot longer than I'd anticipated.

I guess I thought they would swim out twenty feet, dive down, and find this Efram guy just standing around, but they disappeared from view hours ago and I have no way to know if they're happily succeeding and stuffing their pockets with enchanted golden apples or if they're being eaten by—well, whatever eats kids underwater. Seeing as how there are dangerous creatures on land and in the Nether, I just have to assume that there are things in the ocean that can do more harm than a squirt of squid ink.

I pace around the shelter a little before heading back out to the fence I set up for the horses. It's a little away from the beach so they have grass to eat, as I'm pretty sure they wouldn't enjoy hanging out in the sand. Speckles, Mervin, Dottie, Bee, and Moo—a horse I bred myself, named by Chug, of course, because he is white with black spots—should be calmly grazing and doing that nice thing horses do where they go kind of unfocused and swish their tails, but . . . they're acting weird. All the horses are turned in the same direction, heads up and ears pricked, staring off into the distant plains as their tails twitch nervously.

"What's up?" I ask Speckles, reaching up to pat her neck. Her skin shivers at my touch, and she gives a nervous whinny.

I squint out where the horses are looking and see something strange there.

Is it . . .

Is it . . .

Fire?

I pull out my enchanted golden axe and run toward the flames, wondering if I need to dig a trench to protect the horses and the area surrounding our shelter. I've seen lightning start a fire before, but the sky has been blue all day, so I'm not sure how one might've started. As I get closer, I stop in my tracks and stare. My mouth hangs open, my hands go numb, and I nearly drop my axe as my stomach does a flip.

There are words there.

Giant words, spelled out in meaty-looking netherrack, rising up from the ground.

Giant words that are literally on fire.

HA HA, the words say.

I swallow around a huge lump in my throat and grasp my axe in both hands.

I wish my friends were here to see this, because I wonder if I'm dreaming. It definitely feels like a nightmare. I long to be back home in Cornucopia, where everything is safe and tidy and tame.

I don't know who's done this, but I know someone did it.

This is not something that happens naturally.

I think back to Lenna and her insistence that we were being followed.

I thought it was maybe just that creeper I saw, but a creeper couldn't do this. Only a person could.

But why?

Ha ha?

What does that mean?

Okay, yes, laughter, but is someone laughing at us? Did someone from home follow us out here to do this, or is it some deranged stranger? Or maybe a message from Efram, who's gone a bit barmy out here all by himself after all these years?

I walk closer to the letters, axe in my hands and scanning the area. Nothing moves except the flowers and grasses rustling in the breeze off the sea. Other than the words, there's no sign that anyone else was ever here, no footprints that I can see—but then again, tracking is not my forte. I wish the others were back. Lenna knows more about the natural world, Tok knows more about netherrack, and Mal and Chug know how to fight pretty much any monster that exists.

But alone, it's just me, and I don't have all their skills. I've grown accustomed to the comfort of working with a team—and let's face it, even before that, I always had Remy and Edd around.

I'm not much of a loner. And just now, I'm really remembering why I've always preferred being around other people.

Because it's terrifying, being alone.

Especially out here.

Far off, one of the horses whinnies, and when I look back, there's a panel missing from the fence and the horses are running away in five different directions.

"Speckles!" I shout, running for my horse. "Stop, honey!"

I know the absolute worst thing you can do about a panicking horse is run right at it while screaming, but I'm so scared and freaked out that I don't know what to do. If we don't have the horses, our traveling speed goes way, way down. With Nan increasingly sick, time is very much of the essence. It would take an entire morning, possibly a whole day, to find and tame five horses, and we don't necessarily have that time to spare.

Plus the fact that the horses got away while I was left in charge of them makes me want to shrink into a tiny ball and die. My mom used to yell at me all the time—for not picking sweet berries fast enough, for not keeping my room clean, for not getting good grades—and it's been an amazing feeling, not being guilt-tripped and marinating in shame all the time now that I don't live with her anymore. But the thought of facing my friends and telling them I lost our horses? Yeah, that makes me want to throw up.

Luckily, Speckles loves me, so she gallops right to me and tosses her head and looks at me like, *Well, dummy, what did you go and do that for?*

Even though I didn't do anything except check out the giant flaming words.

I hop on her back and gallop over to the nearest horse, Moo, who just so happens to be her son. He's bucking and kicking like this is all super fun, but he's easy enough to catch. One by one, I gather the horses and return them to their pen. The fence panel is lying nearby, which is weird, but maybe one of them kicked it down? I didn't know horses could do that, but I learn new things about horses and llamas and mushrooms every day at my little farm. Maybe Moo got a little too excited because of the fire and just ran it right over. He's young and strong, after all, and doesn't always make the best decisions.

Yeah, that must be it. The horses were acting twitchy because of the fire, and then I acted weird, and then it was just too much for a bunch of easily freaked-out herd animals.

That's the only answer I can find.

The only answer that makes sense.

Once all the horses are safely back in their repaired paddock, I throw them some wheat to help them calm down and go around to the front of the shelter to look out at the ocean and see if my friends are on their way back.

Of course not.

That would be too easy.

There's no sign of anyone or anything out on the ocean, just endless blue and a few leaping dolphins. I turn to go inside the shelter, and again, I stop short, my jaw dropped.

My bed has been utterly destroyed.

Seriously, my bed looks like someone took an axe to it. It's in pieces and chunks, the blankets torn. I hear a quiet meow, and Candor and Clarity peek out from under a pillow that's landed in the corner. They look terrified.

I spin around, checking every corner, but there's no one in here.

And still . . . someone *was* here. Someone did this.

The pieces begin to fall into place.

Someone created the flaming words in netherrack to lure me out. I went right out there to investigate, and they were ready. They took down a panel of the fence to release the horses and distract me and then ran inside the shelter to destroy my bed.

The inside of my mouth has gone dry. My tongue is too big and my throat closes up. I thought that I would be safe here, alone, in the shelter. I thought the Overworld was an okay place, as long as you kept out the mobs at night and avoided brigands on the roads during the day.

I was very, very wrong.

Lenna was right.

Someone has been following us, someone who means us harm. They're clever enough to set me up and sneak in without being detected. And they're still out there, somewhere, probably quite near. Probably watching me.

Planning their next move.

Outside again, I blink against the afternoon sun and take a few steps into the ocean. The water is cold and wild, frothing white around the ankles of my boots.

"Come on, come on, come on," I mutter, shielding my eyes as I gaze out at the distant waves. "Come back, you guys. I can't . . . I can't do this alone."

I need Chug's confidence and strength and sword arm.

I need Mal's leadership and optimism and cunning.

I need Tok's cleverness and ability to solve puzzles.

I need Lenna's heightened senses and unique way of looking at things.

So funny to think I used to look down on them, that I thought they were weird and annoying and deserved to be punished. Right now, I'd give anything to see any of them.

I head back inside, alert for any sound, but the lapping ocean waves make it hard to hear. Without putting my back to the open door, I try to put my bed back together, but I can't. It's just smashed to pieces, which makes me think that whoever did this is mad. Really mad. The *ha ha* was definitely sarcastic.

Tok took his crafting table with him, so I can't make a new bed, but then again, I'm pretty terrible at crafting and I don't have any raw materials, anyway. I hate that when the others come back, probably exhausted from all that swimming, they're going to find a wreck and I'm going to have to ask for a bed. At least I got the horses back. At least I have some use.

I go back outside and find a place to sit where I can see the ocean, the front of the shelter, and the horses. I sit and take off my boots and bury my toes in the sand. It would feel nice if I didn't feel so terrible. As I stare off at the ocean, my axe by my side, willing my friends to return, I think about who might've done all this, and I can only think of one person.

Well, a group of people, actually.

Orlok and his brigands.

First they robbed the Mob Squad on their original adventure, stealing everything from llamas to Mal's great-great-great-great-grandmother's diamond pickaxe. They even tried to steal Chug's pet pig and turn him into pork chops. Then they found Cornucopia, stole every potion in the entire town, and kidnapped me and Tok and stole him away to the Nether, where they forced him to churn out potions and weapons for them. We thought that leaving Orlok and his gang in the Nether without a portal was kind of like putting them in jail, but I guess maybe they found a way out? Apparently you can find active portals in the Nether, if you travel far enough, so maybe that's what they did, and then they got reoriented in the Overworld and sought revenge on the meddling kids who'd banished them to a life of lava and hoglin meat.

But if it really is the brigands, well . . . I'm doomed.

There were six of them when we left them in the Nether, and they were all in armor and bristling with weapons. They were mean and angry even before we slipped out of their grasp, stealing Tok on our way through the portal and destroying it the moment we were safely back in the Overworld.

If they're here, and I'm alone, I'm going to end up just the way I did last time, tied up and blindfolded, abandoned in the middle of nowhere. They tied me to a tree and left me to die, alone and without weapons or any of the skills and knowledge needed to survive outside of our walled town.

They are not nice people.

And what do I have at my disposal to deal with them?

An enchanted golden axe, an old iron sword, and knees that are already knocking together.

Tok's cats slink outside of the shelter and mob me, head-butting me for pets as they purr. I scratch their chins and stroke their backs, but now I'm worried for them. I can't keep them safe, and if something happened to them, Tok would freak out. Every time I step out of Cornucopia, I realize, there is a whole world of things that could go wrong. Maybe the Elders have it right. Maybe life is better inside the wall. Maybe things are safer when dangerous strangers can't get in and dumb kids like me can't go waltzing out, rent a horse, and embark on a journey to their own death.

Candor rubs against my cheek, and I realize I'm crying.

"If bad guys come, you two run away, okay?" I tell her. Clarity meows, and I add, "Run away and wait for Tok."

I startle as both of the cats hiss and bolt into the shelter. I'm on my feet in a heartbeat, golden axe in hand, wishing I hadn't taken off my stupid boots. It takes me a minute to find what has frightened the cats, and my innards go all cold and runny.

Running directly for me is the thing I've been dreading all along. A creeper.

12.

LENNA

 My entire body is both on fire and made of iron. I'm a thousand miles under the ocean, trapped in a maze full of, yes, fine, murderfish, sleepy and hurt and heavy and helpless. Utterly helpless. Usually Chug and Mal swoop in to save me, but Chug is unconscious and floating toward the prismarine floor. Mal is still fighting, but she looks as damaged as I feel. Tok is shaking Chug, begging him to wake up.

"The potions are going to wear off soon, you big lug!" he shouts. "Just wake up and swim to the surface, and you can have all my cookies for the rest of your life. Ow!"

The big gray guardian fish hits Tok, and Tok gasps and flails. He turns and meets my eyes. For once, I don't look away. "Get out of here," he says. "Swim to the surface. Now."

I shake my head and join him by Chug. "No way. We'll pull him out together. Come on. At least he floats down here."

Tok and I each take a leg, but Chug is still wearing armor and it's clunky and it's hard to maneuver him, even through water. The gray guardian—the elder guardian, I guess, since it's big and gray and mean, just like our Elders—focuses its eye bubbles on Tok, and Tok lets go of his brother and squirms in pain. Its spikes briefly disappear, and Mal lands a hit, but that only makes the guardian more furious.

We're losing this fight.

For the first time, I don't see how we can escape, much less win.

Ow!

One of the regular guardians hits me, just rams right into me with all its stupid orange spikes out, and I feel like it punched a hole in my lungs. I let go of Chug's foot and let myself fall to the ground beside him. It's peaceful down here, and I twine my fingers with his, holding his much bigger hand.

"You were a good friend, Chug," I say, bubbles flittering out of my mouth like little birds.

"Do not give up!" Mal orders me. "Don't you do it! You stand right back up this moment, and we're going to get out of here."

"I can't stand," Tok says weakly. "Too many hits. Barely awake."

He's on Chug's other side now, holding his other hand.

Mal swims over, diamond pickaxe out, and swings hard at the guardian coming over to ram us again.

"I don't care. We're the Mob Squad, and we keep going, no matter what. Come on, Tok!"

But Tok, like his brother, is no longer conscious.

We can't do this much longer.

They're barely breathing.

"I can't, Mal," I say, almost begging. "I can't."

"You can! You have to!" she says, and I don't know how she's crying underwater, but she is. "We're going to get out of here, and we're going to get that enchanted golden apple, and we're going to save Nan."

"So swim away and do that," I say. I can barely make my mouth move. I can't even feel my hands anymore. "It's okay."

"No! No, I'm not leaving you! I'm never leaving you!"

There is a terrible beat of silence, and I'm about to tell her she has to leave, now or never, but it's so much work, moving my mouth.

"What if you all left?" says a new voice, and I manage to make my eyes open.

There's an old man beside her, and . . . no, this must be a dream. He's in netherite armor and holding an enchanted trident. There's—really? A turtle shell on his head instead of a helmet, and I can feel tons of potions radiating off him. He must be using a Potion of Water Breathing, too, as he's all the way down here and talking.

"Who are you?" Mal says.

"I'm the guy who's here to save you," he says gruffly. "Now let me kill this big beamer, and then we've got to hurry."

I blink, and the big gray guardian is gone, leaving a sponge behind. The old guy stuffs it in his pocket and grabs Chug under one arm and Tok under the other.

"You get the girl," he tells Mal, and I realize from far away that he must be talking about me.

Water is moving past me, and when I open my eyes again, Mal is pulling me along through the twisty tunnels and oddly lit rooms. It feels like a dream, except my lungs are burning and my whole body hurts. I blink again, and we're swimming through a sea of water plants. They're so beautiful as they undulate through the deep turquoise water. I trail my fingertips through their waver-ing green leaves. It must be evening, I think, or maybe I'm just really, really hurt and everything seems dark.

"Hold your breath," Mal says, and I do.

My body feels oddly light, and I'm rising up up up toward the surface. My head breaks through, and I gulp in a huge lungful of air. It tastes sweet and salty and pure and good, but then I have to breathe out and I'm pretty sure all my ribs are broken.

"Get her into the boat," the old man says, and Mal tries, but it's awkward, thanks to the armor. I help her, clawing up over the side, feeling the rough wood scrape my waterlogged fingertips.

I flop into the boat and land on my back, looking up at a blue sky going dusky with evening.

"Give her this," the old man says, and a potion bottle touches my lips. I gladly drink it down.

"Team Floor Potion," I murmur, and when I try to chuckle at my own joke, salty water comes out of my nose.

Oh, the potion feels so nice, the warmth seeping out of my middle and down to my fingers and toes. The aches in my ribs fade away, and it's almost like I was never pummeled into mush by angry one-eyed fish monsters on the bottom of the ocean. As soon as I can sit up, I do.

"Are Chug and Tok okay?" I ask.

Mal is drinking her own potion, so I look to the old man. He's in a third boat with Chug, supporting him as he pours a potion down his throat.

"This kid's in a bad way," he tells me, as if it's my fault.

"He does that from time to time," I say, still a little out of it.

Tok sits up and looks around him dazedly. "Did I dream that, or did we almost die? Like really, seriously, for real almost die?"

"It wasn't a dream," Mal says, her voice haunted. "That could not have gone worse."

"Yeah, you fools nearly died down there. First time I went in that ocean monument, same thing happened," the old man says as he tosses that potion bottle into the ocean and pulls another one out of his pocket. "Didn't get as far as you did. Definitely didn't try to take on a big beamer. But at least I had the good sense to keep drinking Potions of Water Breathing. What happened— did you run out of potion? Or are you just stupid?"

"We didn't know how long it would last or how we would know when to drink again." Tok bristles, arms crossed. I know Tok, so I know he's both deeply concerned for his brother and deeply embarrassed that he messed up in the realm of potions.

"Well, now you know." The old man cracks his back with a grunt and stares at Chug, head cocked thoughtfully. "And knowing is half the battle."

Chug is deathly still, his skin a pale, cold blue. It doesn't look like he's breathing, but the old man got the potion into him, so he has to be okay, right?

As we all watch, holding our breath, the old man punches Chug right in the stomach. Tok gasps and stands in his boat, but the old man just growls, "Wait."

After a long moment, Chug spews a fountain of water and sits up, his eyes wide, asking, "Did I beat it?"

"Did you beat what?" Tok says, smiling through his tears.

"The one-eyed spiky gray jerk fish."

We all stare at him.

"No. It beat you. Bad. We thought you were dead, bro."

Chug swallows hard and tries to step from his boat into Tok's boat. He fails and falls into the ocean, and Tok helps him drag himself into Tok's boat, and they hug each other and beat each other on the back and sob.

"I was trying to save you, bro!" Chug wails.

"I know, bro! I was trying to save you! But that fish guy—"

"I hate that fish guy!"

"He was too much for us. For all of us."

"Then how did we get out?"

Tok points to the old guy, and Chug's eyes fly wide as he notices him for the first time.

"Bro, who's the old dude?"

"That's Efram," I say.

Because, let's face it—that's the only answer.

We came here looking for a really, really old guy with lots of clever tricks who lives far away from everybody and everything, and it's not like there could possibly be two guys who fit that exact bill floating around in this part of the ocean.

Probably.

"How'd you know my name?" he barks, immediately defensive. "Who sent you? What are they paying you? I'll double it."

"No one sent us. We're here because Nan is sick, and she said you might have an enchanted golden apple."

We all turn and look at Mal. Her potion has taken its effect, but it's easy to see she's been pushed to the edge. Her red braid has come undone, her sopping hair straggling down over her eyes. Tear tracks wriggle through her freckles, and there's exhaustion in every line of her body.

"Nan, huh?" Efram strokes his chin. "Little thing, about this tall?"

He holds up a hand to a spot that would be correct for a six-year-old.

"She's my great-great-great-grandmother, and she's short, but she's definitely grown a bit since you knew her." Mal spits out a little seawater and wipes off her face. "So do you have the apple? Because . . ." She sighs. "We just need that enchanted golden apple. It's the only thing that might help her. She can't last much longer."

I can immediately tell by the look on Efram's face that we're not going to like the answer.

"Funny story," he says glancing away. "I ate it. The first time I tried to storm this ocean monument, in fact."

Mal tries so hard not to show how upset she is, but she fails. Her shoulders droop, and she takes a shuddering breath.

"Okay. Thanks. Sorry we bothered you." She takes up the oars of her boat. "We'll leave you alone now. Thanks for saving us." As she rows us away, I stare back in confusion. I've known Mal my whole life, and she's never given up this quickly, but . . . well, it's been a pretty terrible afternoon. I think we'd all like to be back on solid ground.

Chug takes up his oars and starts rowing, too. "Sorry, Mal," he murmurs.

We're not that far away when Efram calls out, "Wait. Don't tell me a descendant of Nan's gives up that easy. You know it wasn't the only enchanted golden apple in the world, right?"

Mal stops rowing and stares at him. "You know where we can find more?"

Efram sighs and scratches his belly under his armor. Now that I'm fully awake and he's not rescuing me from an underwater grave, I can see that he really is older than Nan, and I wonder how many potions and apples and enchantments it took to get him strong enough and fast enough to save us. He looks sad and exhausted, like he's constantly on the verge of fading away.

"I have a map," he allows.

"A map?" Mal prods.

He huffs a sigh. "Well, I was saving it in case I ever needed it, but today's little adventure has convinced me that I probably couldn't fight my way to it, even if I needed to. If I wasn't using twenty different potions and enchantments, you'd all be fish food. You might have trouble believing this, but I'm not as young as I used to be. Enchanted golden apples can work miracles, but even miracles have an expiration date."

"Where is it?" Chug asks.

"That map? Oh, it's hidden. Hidden real good."

Chug shakes his head. "Nan was right. He is paranoid."

"Of course I'm paranoid!" Efram barks. "After what happened to—" He clears his throat and closes his eyes, trying to calm himself. "Look, I stayed here because the world out there is dangerous. If you're Nan's descendant, that means the rest of my old buddies followed through, right? They settled down and founded their own town?" Mal nods confirmation. "See, after I lost Cleo, I couldn't do that. Couldn't just pick some new girl like an apple off a tree and settle down somewhere new. Couldn't live with people who would always remind me of her. So I stayed behind and built me a compound."

"An underwater compound," Chug says, nodding knowingly.

Efram snorts. "Underwater? Kid, are you a moron? Of course I didn't build a house underwater. I picked out one of those little islands. It's got everything I need. So if you'll follow me over there, I'll give you the map, and then you can go away. It's the least I can do for little Nan. Nobody needs to know what it feels like to lose—" He clears his throat. "Just come on, then."

He rows toward the island just beyond the one where we stopped to build our boats, and I slap my forehead.

"He built a home *out in the middle of the ocean*," I say. "On an island in the middle of the ocean. Not underwater. Nan never said it was literally underwater."

We all exchange sheepish, rueful glances.

"I can't believe I could've just skipped the nearly dying bit if I'd checked out a few more islands," Chug says.

"I can't believe I didn't ask Nan exactly what she meant or consider other interpretations of her words," Tok moans.

"I can't believe we thought you lived in a monument," Mal finishes.

"Yeah, there was definitely something fishy about that." Chug grins, and I grin, too, because if he's making bad puns, he must be feeling a lot better.

"Now listen," Efram says, his voice stern. "When we land on my island, you stay right with me. Don't take a step out of line, you hear?"

"But why?" Mal asks.

"Because it's full of traps, and if you step one foot off the right path . . ." He pins Mal with a sharp glare. "You'll die for real."

13.

MAL

 At first I think we're going to the same island we stopped at to build the boats, but then Efram directs us around it. There are at least two more islands out here that I can see, and Efram rows to the more heavily forested one behind the one we used. I nervously scan the area for any sign of habitation, but I can't see any evidence that Efram's been hiding out here. I guess that's why we missed him the first time around.

We hop out of our boats and pull them up onto the sand, and I worry that I won't have enough energy to stand, but that potion must've been really well made because I feel great. The moment he's out of his boat, Efram takes off his armor and shoves it all in his pocket but leaves on his turtle shell hat.

"Is that a turtle on your head or are you—?" Chug starts.

"Made this baby out of old turtle scutes." Efram knocks the helmet with his fist. "Lets me breathe just a little longer underwater. You kids might not've been in such dire straits if you'd had a good shelmet. Now come on. Walk only where I walk, and don't touch anything."

"But—" Chug starts.

"ANYTHING," Efram roars, sending a flock of colorful parrots screeching into the sky.

"I think he means anything," I whisper, and Chug giggles.

Efram heads into the forest, walking the trail with confidence. I motion for Chug to go right after him so I can keep an eye on him, because the moment he sees a piece of low-hanging fruit, he's going to get us in trouble. Then it's me, Tok, and Lenna, and we carefully follow Efram's exact path.

"First trap," Efram says, pointing at a beautiful pie sitting on the forest floor in a clearing between two blocks of wood. "Take the pie, get crushed."

"But it's pie," Chug whines.

"DEATH PIE!" Efram barks.

A little farther into the forest and we pass a tidy little shelter, exactly the place a tired traveler might wish to spend the night.

"Second trap," Efram says. "Pit full of lava. Open the door, fall into the pit."

"Nice hospitality," Chug mutters.

Next we pass a trail that branches off. I can just see a sign nailed to a tree. The top line says *Read Me*, but the lower lines are so small that even if I squint, I can't make them out.

"Third trap," Efram informs us. "Step up to read the sign, trigger the redstone, and a piston-loaded trap catapults you into the air."

Tok perks up. "Wait, you know about redstone?"

"I'm so old I know about everything."

"Will you teach me?"

"Ugh. No. I want you to leave as soon as possible. You can have my book."

"Those are the most beautiful words I've ever heard." Tok sighs blissfully.

Efram points out his fourth trap, and I ask, "So you really, really don't want to be bothered, huh?"

Efram shakes his head firmly, the turtle helmet rattling around. "Nope. I didn't come all the way out here and set up all these traps just to be bothered."

"So why did you save us?" Lenna asks, cutting to the chase as usual.

"Yeah, how did you even know we were here?" Tok adds.

"I keep a lookout. Saw you coming."

"Oh! Were you following us, back before we reached the ocean?" Lenna asks. "Because I sensed we were being followed but couldn't quite prove it."

"Nope. Haven't set foot on the mainland in nearly fifty years. I have everything I need out here. You'll see. I heard someone crafting and spotted you on the beach. There's no sound in the world like crafting, you know. Watched your boats go out and immediately knew you were diving down to the ocean monument like a bunch of knuckleheads. When you didn't come back up in time, I figured I had to go down and get you."

"So you are a good guy!" Chug says.

"I wouldn't say that. I just don't need abandoned boats and child-sized skeletons choking up my bit of the ocean."

"When I grow up, I want to be just like him," Chug whispers in my ear.

"Here we are." Efram moves some branches aside to reveal . . .

An island paradise!

Seriously, it's like a miniature version of Cornucopia. He's got a little cow pen, a little sheep pen, neat little plots for pumpkins and sweet berries and melons and carrots and potatoes. In the center is a one-story shelter, simple but well built, and it even has a small overhang like the one at Tok's workshop so he can work outside no matter the weather.

"Sweet setup," Chug says.

"Don't even think about staying. It's a one-man sort of place."

Chug snorts. "Thanks, but no. I have a pig to get home to."

Efram takes a few steps toward his house, and we follow exactly behind him. "No traps inside the clearing," he says. "But I like my privacy, so wait here." When we stop, he goes into the house and slams the door.

Chug steps gingerly to the side, as if the ground might explode, but of course nothing happens. It's a relief, to be somewhere that seems vaguely safe again, but the sun is going down and I realize with a sinking feeling that it's not going to be safe outside much longer.

"Anybody else notice that night is falling?" I say nervously.

"I noticed my stomach growling for dinner." Chug rubs his belly. "And I noticed a pie sitting unattended in the forest."

"We were in that ocean monument way longer than I'd planned," Tok admits.

I know he feels bad about his miscalculation, so I tell him, "I don't think anyone could've anticipated what we faced in there."

"Hopefully I can change that for the next adventurers." Lenna already has her book out and is scribbling madly. "Does anyone remember how many spikes those guardians had?"

"Too many," Chug mutters. "Just, way too many."

I reach into my pockets and pass out the rest of the leftover fish, and Chug complains that it's not a cookie, and I tell him that I'll be sure to make cod cookies for him next time, and he makes polite barfing noises. Lenna stops drawing long enough to eat her fish and then pass out cookies when she hears Chug mimicking the way Poppy whines when she's hungry. I keep glancing back at Efram's door, but it remains closed.

Night falls, and we're in darkness. Chug pulls a few torches out of his pocket and places them around us in a circle. He takes out his sword and stares off into the darkness, where birds call and rustle in the leaves. Thanks to the light of the torches, I can see his blade shaking, throwing glints of flame against the shadows of the trees. Chug's my best bud, and this might be the first time I've seen him less than courageous.

Ah. Because this is the first time he's faced a foe and lost.

He's grown accustomed to being our hero, and . . . well, I guess he feels like he let us down. I definitely feel like I let my friends down. They look up to me as their leader, and I led them right into a death trap. After Krog and the woodland mansion and the bandits and the Nether, I guess we all began to feel like we could vanquish any foe, tame any beast—except for hoglins—and survive no matter what.

Today we learned that there are still things we can't beat.

It's a hard lesson.

And it wasn't just Chug—it was all of us. I led my friends into danger and wasn't able to lead them back out. Tok made our potions, but he didn't keep us topped off, and now that he's met Efram he knows there were potions and enchantments that might've helped us but weren't in his books, or maybe he didn't know that they might help. And Lenna—well, she got lost, probably trying to sketch something for her book, and that distraction was the beginning of the end for Chug. If Efram hadn't heard us crafting boats and kept a close eye on us, it's very likely we'd all be dead.

I shiver and long for walls and a bed. I wouldn't even mind being behind the big wall at Cornucopia just now. The Overworld feels scarier than ever, even if it was the ocean that tried to claim us.

Finally Efram's door bursts open and he tosses a map to me and a book to Tok, as if he doesn't want to get too close to us again. Tok immediately starts flipping through the book, muttering to himself about redstone. I unroll the map and try to figure out which way is up.

Efram takes the map and turns it upside down before pointing to a symbol on the far right. "This apple's too far out of my range, but the map is good. I don't know the area, so I can't give you any tips, but at least it's not underwater. You kids are good with caves, right?"

"Caves, cliffs, mountains, valleys, the Nether," Chug says, puffing out his chest. "Pretty much anything other than exactly where you found us."

"Clearly." Efram raises an eyebrow. "Or else I guess your skeletons would be clogging up someone else's backyard."

"Did anyone ever tell you you have a real way with people?" Chug asks.

In response, Efram makes a sound that's all too close to a growl.

Before Chug can insult him further, I break in with, "Thank you so much. This is exactly what we needed. I know Nan will appreciate it so much."

"Most people appreciate not dying," Efram offers.

"Just a stunning amount of charisma and charm," Chug mutters, and I elbow him in the gut.

"But where do we sleep?" Lenna asks, looking up sleepily from her drawing.

Efram seems genuinely confused. "Sleep? Why should I care where you sleep?"

"Because you brought us into the middle of your creepy, booby-trapped hermit island and it's pitch-dark outside and if we try to get back to our camp, we're gonna die in a pie pit," Chug explains.

Efram sighs and rubs his face like this is the most exhausted he's been in a hundred years. Which, in all honesty, it probably is. Chug just does that to people.

"You can't camp here. I got real used to silence and I'm glad to help Nan, but I seem to remember that children are noisy and messy. I'll take you back to the boats. Then you can go back to your camp or sleep on the beach. But you can't chop down my trees. Those are my trees. Mine!"

The longer we stay here, the more I realize that living alone on an island for a century probably isn't great for the human spirit. Efram was kind enough to save us but hasn't offered us food or beds or explanations. He was generous enough to give us the map to a lifesaving apple but doesn't seem to like us very much. He actually reminds me of some of the Elders back home, and I wonder what it is that makes some old people end up like Nan, fun and curious and kind, while some people end up boring and closed-off and grouchy.

Whatever it is, I want to be more like Nan.

Instead of explaining further, Efram marches us back out toward the beach. He doesn't even remind us to be careful, so I whisper, "Remember—stay on the path and touch nothing! Not even pies!"

"Don't forget your weapons," Efram says, pulling out an enchanted sword. "I assume you know how to fight on land?"

"On land," Chug affirms. "We're great on land."

As we wind through the trees along a path only Efram can see, a groan erupts from the right. Efram dispatches the zombie in a few quick slashes and moves on. Then an arrow twangs at us from the left, and Lenna takes it down with a few arrows of her own before it comes into sword-fighting range.

"Good shot," Efram notes.

Everyone is jumpy and on edge. My brain keeps feeding me images of those guardians just appearing in front of me as if out of nowhere, slamming me with their face bubbles and spikes. The night's darkness allows my imagination to run all too wild, and I'm on high alert for any sound other than our feet on the path. It feels like at any moment, something could jump out of the forest and right into my face.

As the noise of the waves grows louder, my heartbeat settles back down. There's the water lapping up on the beach, our three boats right where we left them. Efram stops at the edge of the whispering starlit forest.

"Stay on the sand and you'll be fine. Go into the forest and you'll probably die a terrible death. Tell Nan I hope she feels better. She was a good kid. Bright little soul," he says.

"We'll tell her. Thank you so much—"

"You say thanks too much. Good luck finding the apple."

And with that, he's gone.

"Charisma, charm, and manners," Chug mutters. "That's Efram."

We stare down at our boats by the light of the moon. From all the way out here, we can't see the far shore, where Jarro has likely built a cozy shelter and is waiting for us to return.

"So we have two choices," I say. "We can get in the boats and try to find our way back to the shore . . ."

"Do we know where the shore is?" Chug asks.

I stare out into the endless black. "That way . . . ish."

"I thought it was more this way-ish," Lenna says, pointing slightly to the left.

"Okay, so no boating tonight." I put away my pickaxe and rub my temples. "We're not allowed to cut down trees, and I left all my stone with Jarro for the shelter. Tok, do you have any spare wood? Enough for a door?"

He feels around in his pocket and nods. "On it."

I take my pickaxe right back out, go to the spot where sand becomes dirt, right in front of the forest, and start digging. "Efram said we couldn't cut down his trees, but he didn't say anything about digging out a shelter."

When I see that Chug has his sword ready and is glaring into the dark, I'm free to focus on digging. It's nice, actually. I know how to do this. It feels right. I know my friends will have my back if anything nasty shows up.

Nearby, Tok fixes Lenna's bow before starting on a door. Glad to have her weapon again, she stands between him and the ocean, ready to defend us from anything that might crawl up from the depths. I smile. It reminds me of old times, of our first adventure. Maybe we can't raid an underwater ocean monument, but we can survive with almost nothing. We can fight anything on land. Sure, we'd all rather be cozy in Jarro's shelter, but it's nice knowing he, too, is safe. Worried about us, maybe, but cozy in his bed with Poppy guarding the door and Candor and Clarity asleep on his feet and purring.

I hack the smallest shelter I can out of the ground, barely enough room for our four beds. As I dig deep, Chug asks if water is about to come flooding in, and I stop.

"I never thought of that," I say.

"If water comes in, that means the islands are floating, and they can go anywhere they want. Like giant horses!" Chug says excitedly.

"I think they're probably attached to the ocean floor," Tok says. "Because they clearly don't float away. We should be safe from water, thank goodness."

Lenna sits down by a torch with her book spread out in her lap. "Good point," she says. "I'll include that."

When the shelter is done, Tok attaches the door, and we drop down inside. It's crude and quick but functional. We pull out our beds and place our torches and get as comfortable as we can. Lenna hands out some chicken and potatoes, and I'm barely done chewing before I'm horizontal. I've never been so tired in my life—except for that time I was poisoned, maybe. Or on the floor of the ocean monument . . .

But I can't let myself think about that now.

We wake up some time after dawn, stash our beds, and head back outside. Our boats are right where we left them, and there's a disturbing number of zombie and skeleton footprints in the beach sand.

"Glad we didn't try to camp under the stars," Chug says.

Tok takes his door, and I fit a block of dirt over the hole I made so that Efram won't think we've ruined his view. After a few bites of breakfast, we're back in the boats, and Chug and I row toward the shore, which is just a misty smudge of green on the horizon.

"Well, at least we found Efram and got the map," I say.

"Ah, Efram. What a delight. So personable. So friendly," Chug quips.

"If he lived in our town, he would totally be an Elder."

"The Eldest Elder! Because he would've been a Founder!"

The thought of Elder Stu's face if an actual Founder showed up and took charge makes me cackle.

"Hey, what's that?"

I look where Lenna is pointing.

What I'm seeing makes no sense. Everything should be green, but it's . . .

"Fire!" Tok shouts. "Jarro's shelter is on fire!"

14.

TOK

 I can't believe what I'm seeing.

I was expecting a nice shelter of stone and wood, a paddock for the horses, a smiling Jarro with my cats and Poppy by his side waving from the shore.

But all I see is a shelter on fire and an open paddock.

No horses. No cats. No wolf.

No Jarro.

Something terribly, desperately wrong has happened.

"Can you row any faster?" I ask Chug.

"Kinda almost got killed yesterday, bro," he grunts. "Doing my best here." Then he sees it. "Oh, no! Jarro!"

Mal looks up, gasps, and puts everything she has into rowing. Her boat pulls alongside ours, and Lenna has her bow and arrow ready. Good. I'm glad she feels the same way I do.

Whatever has happened on the shore—it wasn't an accident.

We have an enemy. Possibly many enemies.

Finally the boats scrape on sand, and we leap out, weapons

drawn. Chug hefts his sword aloft as he runs for the burning shelter.

No—he's running for the lump lying just beyond it in the grass.

It's Jarro, and he's not moving.

Mal is faster than Chug, though, and she gets there first. Kneeling by Jarro's side, she gently rolls him over. His face is so messed up it looks like a sweet berry pie. He blinks through two black eyes, sees us, and sags in relief as Lenna and Chug stand guard.

"Jarro, are you okay? What happened?" Mal asks as I dig through my pockets for a Potion of Healing.

"It came out of nowhere," Jarro says through fat lips.

"What did?" Chug growls.

Jarro swallows hard and his eyes fly wide.

"Creeperhead," he whispers.

The word makes me shiver.

"What's Creeperhead?" Mal asks, but Jarro just blinks and shakes his head like he can't bring himself to say any more.

I move closer and pull the stopper out of the potion. "Jarro, open up. Drink this and you'll feel a lot better." His mouth opens just a little, and I help him drink the potion in careful sips. By the end, he's gulping it down, the bruises and cuts receding to leave fresh tan skin and tear tracks.

As soon as he's done drinking, he realizes that he's half in Mal's lap and looks utterly scandalized. He sits up on his own and moves away a little, dabbing at the muck on his torn shirt.

"What's Creeperhead?" Mal asks again. "Is it still here?"

Jarro shakes his head. "I don't know. I think it's been here all along. Following us." He looks to Lenna ruefully. "You were right.

And when we thought we saw the creeper—it was really Creeper-head."

Lenna scans the area around the shelter, an arrow at the ready. "Back when I lived with my family, I loved getting a chance to say 'I told you so,' but this time, I hate saying it." She zeroes in on Jarro. "Have you seen Poppy?"

His head drops. "Not since . . . well, you should probably hear the whole story. Do you have any food, though?"

Lenna and Mal hand out food while Chug walks a circle around the burning shelter. He asks Mal for a bucket and uses it to throw seawater on the burning wood, putting out the fire and filling the air with the scent of salty smoke. I call for my cats and breathe the Overworld's biggest sigh of gratefulness when they come running out from under a nearby bush. They swarm over me, purring and head-butting me, and my heart is about to burst with relief. Unfortunately, when Lenna calls for Poppy, the wolf doesn't appear.

Jarro eats for a few minutes, but the air is tense with worry. Even though it's clear he needs to eat more, he wipes his mouth and sits up a little straighter, and we gather around him. Lenna stays on her feet, her back to the ocean, keeping watch.

Eventually, Jarro recovered enough to tell us what happened.

When he gets to the creeper, I think about the close calls we've had with them before. How one nearly got Chug on our first adventure. But then the story gets weirder. And even scarier.

"The door burst open, and I thought it must've been you guys, but all I saw was a creeper's head. At first, I didn't notice that the body wasn't a creeper body. In that moment, I just saw the head, and I freaked out, and I grabbed my axe and ran to hit it before it could explode."

I frown. "A creeper wouldn't come near the cats . . ."

"I know!" Jarro wails. "But you know how when you're panicking, your brain forgets that sort of thing? All I could do was run at it with my axe so I wouldn't get exploded again. I didn't see that the creeper had a pickaxe in hand. That it *had hands*. And that it wasn't a creeper at all."

"What was it?" Lenna asks.

Jarro's face is haunted as he says, "A person in a green cape wearing a creeper's head. Like, he straight-up killed a creeper and wore its head like a helmet. It's the scariest thing I've ever seen in my life."

Mal puts her pickaxe across her knees. "What did it say?"

"Nothing," Jarro whispers, his voice hoarse. "He didn't say anything. Now that I think about it, I think it was a guy—I heard him grunt. He just hit me, again and again. I could hear him grunting, but he didn't say a single word. I kept asking questions—what do you want? Why are you doing this? Who are you?—but there was no answer. Poppy tugged on his cape, and I got in a few hits with my axe, but Creeperhead was brutal. Shorter than me but stronger. Angrier."

He breaks off and stares at the ocean, drawing his knees up to his chin.

"Poppy bit him, and while he was dealing with that, I ran outside. The night was pitch-dark, but the shelter roof was already on fire. The horses were gone. I was going to try to gallop away, and I just stood there, staring at the empty pen. And then Creeperhead hit me from the back, and . . ." He looks down at his hands, flexes them into fists and releases them. "I lost the fight. I thought I was a goner. I guess I've been unconscious ever since."

Chug puts an arm around him and squeezes. "It's okay, buddy. We lost our fight, too. It happens to everybody."

Jarro's jaw drops. "You lost—what fight? I thought you were just going to find Efram? Did you have to fight him?"

"We found an ocean monument full of giant spiky fish who wanted to blast us with their eyeball rays, and they nearly killed us, but Efram saved us. He didn't have an enchanted golden apple, but he gave us a map to find one. But—well, bud, I was on the ground underwater, trapped in a maze, and I was toast. So don't feel like you did something wrong, because then we'll all have to feel that way, and I don't like feeling that way. So don't."

Jarro leans into Chug, and I put Clarity in Jarro's lap, and he starts purring, and for a moment, we all just sit there in silence, feeling the weight of the last day sink in our bones like gravel. We all got lucky. Incredibly lucky.

Except . . .

"So this Creeperhead person is still out here, somewhere?" Lenna asks before I can. "Do you know which way he went?"

"Nope." Jarro draws the shape of a horse hoof in the sand. "But you and I saw those hoofprints, back when we thought it was a creeper. So I'm guessing that's how he's keeping up with us. He must have a horse, too."

A thought has been bubbling up inside me, and I want to squash it back down because just saying it out loud makes me want to throw up, but we're the Mob Squad, and we don't lie to one another or hold our tongues when speaking up could keep us alive.

"Do you think it might've been Orlok?" I ask. "Or his brigands? It kind of bothers me, the way we just left them in the Nether. I've always felt like maybe one day they would get out and come find us for revenge."

Jarro stands and shakes off the sand, then inclines his head out to a shape up on a hill. "Come look at this." He starts walking, and we follow.

What he shows us is super creepy.

Someone has used meaty netherrack to spell out the words *ha ha* and set it on fire.

"Creeperhead did this yesterday," Jarro says. "I saw the fire and came to investigate, and while I was over here, he let out the horses. At the time, I thought maybe the horses just knocked down a fence panel, but now I have to guess that Creeperhead was messing with me."

"But why?" Mal asks.

"Intimidation." Lenna looks off into the plains. "He's antagonizing us. Playing with us."

"But why'd he have to beat me up?" Jarro asks in a small voice.

"Because you were here. Because now you're scared, and now we're scared. We know there's someone out there, and he wants us to think we can't do anything about it."

"How do you know that?"

Lenna looks at Jarro like he's an absolute goofus. "Because I've been bullied most of my life."

Jarro blushes, and Lenna gives him an apologetic smile. "Not just you, before. My family, too. My brother Lars used to prank me all the time, and not nice pranks. No wonder they picked him to guard the wall. He loves to make people feel small."

"So what do we do?" I ask.

Mal stands. "First, we look for Poppy and the horses. They probably didn't go too far. Let's salvage what we can of the blocks from the shelter and stock up on fish and any other food in the area. According to Efram's map, the enchanted golden apple is several days away, so it'll take us even farther from Cornucopia. Creeperhead or no Creeperhead, we've got to hurry."

"We can take precautions, though," I say. "I mean, we can't go

Full Efram, but I can probably figure out some traps that will make it harder for him to ambush us at night. I've been reading Efram's book on redstone, and I finally understand why my machines weren't working before."

Far off, we hear a familiar bark, and Lenna's face utterly transforms. "Poppy!" she screeches and takes off running.

The rest of us follow, and it's cute how Lenna yells for Poppy and then Poppy barks for Lenna. I keep expecting to see Poppy running toward us, but I don't. Her bark gets louder, though, so we must be getting close. I'm more aware than ever that I'm not the greatest runner, and I'm soon huffing and puffing as I fall behind the others.

"Wait, are those the horses?" Mal says, and I'm relieved to hear that she's a little out of breath, too.

Brown and black and gray shapes appear in the tall grass, and Poppy finally runs at Lenna at full speed and leaps all over her, yipping and jumping and slobbering joyfully.

"She was keeping the horses together for us," Chug says, impressed. "So wolves may never be as great as pigs, in my mind, but that's a pretty cool trick."

Sure enough, all five of our horses are here, grazing and looking at us like we're fools. Jarro gathers them, since he's our horse expert, and we mount up and ride back to the shelter. Lenna rides last, and she's looking back over her shoulder so much that I'm worried she'll get a crick in her neck. I feel it too, though—the constant, twitchy sense that someone is watching us. If what Jarro says is correct—and I can't see why he would lie about it, or, if he is lying, why he would make up such a weird, elaborate story—then there is someone out there somewhere, probably nearby, following us for the sole purpose of terrorizing us.

It's an unsettling thought.

Sure, back in Cornucopia, in the old days, we were always waiting for Jarro and Remy and Edd to ambush us every time we went downtown, but that was just kid stuff compared with this. I think about what it would feel like, if this mysterious figure cornered me and whipped off its creeper mask to reveal Orlok, the head brigand who kidnapped me out of my bed, and I shiver until my teeth chatter.

I don't want to be followed.

I don't want to be kidnapped again.

And that means I have to think up some really, really cool traps.

15.

CHUG

 Sitting on the beach with my bud Jarro while we fish is really very nice. The sky is blue, the breeze is gentle, and the non-spiky, non-cyclops, non-bubble-ray-shooting fish are biting. Mal is breaking down the shelter, Tok is laboring over his crafting table, and Lenna and Poppy are keeping guard. It's funny how on one hand, Lenna is a mob fighter and master archer with keen eyesight accompanied by the wild wolf she tamed while she single-handedly defends us from an unknown enemy.

But on the other hand, and in the eyes of her parents and our town Elders, she's just a weird little girl who's about as tall as my armpit that most of the town calls Loony as a joke.

Then again, the town thinks of me as the big, loud kid who would fight a stone wall, and no one ever stops to ask if I make the best mushroom stew around, which I definitely do. Not only does the outside not always match the inside, but the person you were two years ago isn't always the person you are today.

And sometimes your outsides don't match your insides because you're some weirdo who wears the head of a dead creeper as a hat to terrorize children.

Jarro is pretty messed up about it. His eyes flick to Lenna every few seconds, then bounce around the beach, then resettle on his bobber. The fish are stealing more of his bait than they should, but that's okay. He's got to get used to being safe again. That's why I'm settled in next to him, trying to send chillness out in waves. I know how it feels to be jumpy. After our last adventure, which began when Tok got kidnapped out of his bed right across the room from where I was sleeping, it took me a while to sleep through the night. I had trouble getting to sleep, and then I had trouble staying asleep. Every little sound woke me in a panic, every dream forced me to relive some horrible moment over and over.

It took time for things to feel normal again. Time, and taking thoughtful, reasonable precautions so that strangers couldn't just bust into our house while we were asleep.

We're going into that mode again—self-protection. I'm not sure what Tok is hammering away at on his crafting table, but he can come up with some really cool machines when he needs to accomplish a goal. It looks like some weird stone slab, but considering how Efram gave him that book on redstone I bet it's going to be something a lot more interesting and dangerous than that. My brother is so smart and talented that it just blows my mind. He was trying to make stuff before he'd even heard of a crafting table, not that it ever worked.

"Jarro, you've got a fish!" I cry, pointing at his rod, which is bent directly down into the water.

He startles and refocuses, reeling in the salmon.

"Woohoo! That's another one for supper!" I pound him on the back and add the salmon to the fire.

"I didn't even feel it tugging on the line," he says softly.

"Yeah, you're a little distracted. That's normal. It's okay. I'll watch the bobber for you. Two fish heads are better than one."

That seems to make him feel a little bit better, and he tosses his line back out.

Mal finishes breaking down the shelter, and Tok finishes his crafting, and I distribute the perfectly roasted fish and make sure everybody knows that Jarro caught most of them. You can barely tell we were ever on this beach. All we leave behind are footprints and some black ash mixed in with the sand. I still can't believe this Creeperhead person set our shelter on fire. At least it was mostly stone, so we only lost a few blocks of wood from the roof.

We mount our horses and Mal consults the map and leads us in the opposite direction of home. I don't know how, but my brain sort of forgot that finding Efram is no longer the main goal of our quest. We still have to go get the enchanted golden apple that can save Nan. When we nearly died down there in the monument, it wasn't even for a reason! We just made a bad decision and were quickly reminded that the Overworld can still kick our butts.

We ride alongside the ocean, and it would be delightfully peaceful if we weren't constantly looking in every direction, waiting to see a creeper's head staring back at us. Lenna rides last, and I know she feels partially responsible for what happened to Jarro. She knew we were being followed, but . . . well, who could've expected what happened? You can't expect things that have never happened before. We've been attacked by a lot of mobs, but not like this. Krog sent illagers after us and threw poison potions at us, but he never ran at us with an axe. Even the guys who kidnapped Tok didn't physically hurt him.

When I think about what I would do if I met those guys again—

Well, I can't get too riled up. I need to stay calm. For Jarro.

It's an easy day. We don't encounter anything new or terrible, and we find plenty of sheep in the meadow, which means plenty of delicious dinner—plus a bed to replace the one Creeperhead apparently hacked to bits. We even find some wild pumpkins, and I start drooling when I think about making a pumpkin pie.

We have to stop earlier than usual because we have to build a strong shelter—and Tok has to set up whatever trap he's devised. Tok whispers with Mal for a moment, and she begins building a stone wall facing the ocean. It's almost twice as long as the walls of our shelters usually are, but I don't question that, because, let's face it, they're both smarter than me, and explaining it to me would only waste time. Lenna is patrolling the area with her bow and arrow, concentrating on everything that isn't the ocean— I guess since we know Creeperhead has been on horseback before and is probably still following us.

Jarro starts setting up the paddock, but Tok tells him not to bother, and when Jarro asks why, Tok just chuckles and asks Jarro to please just keep the horses together for a while.

I make a fire and get to cooking, but Mal asks me to come help her. I'm not the best builder, but we're not exactly trying to win a Prettiest Anti-Creeperhead Emergency Shelter Award. She just hands me a stack of stone and tells me to keep going, and I do. It's kind of fun, actually, and it reminds me how exciting it was when Tok and I chose the site for our home and shop in New Cornucopia and started building. Mal gave us the stone, but we planned and completed the design ourselves, and it's been a vast improvement over the farmhouse where we grew up, if only because we added more windows and cats and I got to decorate by hanging armor and weapons on the walls.

I begin to see the shape of the shelter, and I'm confused, because it's at least twice as big as the ones we usually build. The whole idea, when we're adventuring, is to create the fastest, easiest shelter possible, and we're definitely not doing that.

Then I put two and two together and figure out why, and it makes a lot of sense.

Once Mal and I have built up the walls, she tells Jarro to bring the horses inside and wall them off with his fence panels, and I can see the relief on his face when he realizes Creeperhead won't be able to scare them again. The smell probably isn't going to be great—five exhausted kids, five exhausted horses, and a wolf—but then again, I've fallen asleep hugging a pig, so clearly I'm not that sensitive. As Mal and I build the roof, the horses look up at us, eyes wide, and make nervous noises.

"Don't worry, Mervin," I tell my horse. "I'm not going to drop anything on you. Probably. Except maybe a carrot."

And then I do drop a carrot down for him, because otherwise it would feel like I just got his hopes up for nothing.

After we set up our beds in the shelter and place torches on the walls and floors to make it homey and keep out hostile mobs, we take a few moments to sit outside and watch the sunset as we eat dinner. I can feel the tension among us, everyone's eyes going all shifty and our shoulders all hunchy. We're all waiting for Creeperhead to attack. Poor Jarro looks as nervous as a rabbit. I offer him one of my pies, and it seems to calm him down a little. At least, for a few minutes, he looks at the pie more than he looks over his shoulder. He is kind of forgetting to chew, though, which is a recipe for an upset tummy.

We all go inside at dusk except for Tok. He's arranging things just outside the open doorway, placing things on the ground and laying slabs of stone.

"What are you doing, bro?" I ask from just inside.

"Don't come outside," he warns me. "Not even a step. If I can make this work, it's going to keep us safe."

"So . . . do you think you can make it work?"

It may not sound entirely supportive, but it's a valid question. On his quest to create new tools and machines, Tok has blown up my bed, singed my leg hair, and once collapsed the roof over our dinner table back home, destroying a very nice cake.

"It's going to work," he says, as sure as I've ever heard him. He jumps into the shelter and fits a thick metal door into the remaining open space. "Iron." He knocks on it, and it sounds like the sturdiest door that's ever been made.

Mal looks up from her bed. "So how is this going to work?" she asks.

Tok flops on his bed with his cats and grins. "If Creeperhead leaves us alone, nothing will happen. But if anyone tries to get in the door, they're going to get a big surprise. Believe me—as long as none of us go outside, we're totally safe."

As if she understands that Tok's inventions don't always work the first time, Poppy leaves the foot of Lenna's bed and gets up to go lie in front of the door. Just in case.

We settle down, and this is one of my favorite parts of adventuring in the Overworld. We had a hard day, we're tired, we're well fed, and now we're super cozy. I like it when all of my best friends are in the same room and I know without a doubt that they're safe. Tok's bed is always next to mine, and I can tell by the way he falls asleep easily, his cats on either side of him, that he is confident in whatever he's designed. His confidence gives me confidence, and I'm just about to fall asleep when I hear the softest sound of snuffling from my other side.

I roll over in the torchlit darkness to see Jarro's back. He's facing the wall, his back quivering as he tries with all his might to cry silently.

Not that you can do anything silently in a stone shelter at night, even with horses gently snorting and stamping.

"Hey, bud," I whisper. "You okay?"

"No." It comes out strangled.

"Was the fish at dinner that bad?" I ask, trying to lighten the mood. "Undercooked seafood definitely gives some people the toots—"

"Stop. Please. I feel stupid enough."

I sigh. "I thought if I made myself seem stupider, it might help."

A little chuckle. "Well, it's not like you have to try very hard."

It makes me smile, knowing that he's proud of that one—and that he doesn't really mean it. "Jarro, bud, look. Another person tried to end you today. It's pretty normal to feel messed up after that."

"I know. I mean, I wouldn't say there's anything normal about it, and I'm aware it's not unreasonable to be upset. But . . ." Jarro takes a shaking breath. "That's the thing. I don't think Creeperhead was trying to—to end me. I think he just wanted to scare me. I didn't fight back—I couldn't. I just curled up in a ball until it was over. I feel like . . . it was a warning, maybe. That's what made me so upset. It was so random."

"Random is scary," Lenna says softly. "Fighting a zombie or a skeleton makes sense. Even fighting a brigand makes sense. But if you don't know why someone is doing what they're doing, you don't know what they'll do next. Or how to stop them."

"I guess I thought that I would be ready for anything this time around," Jarro says.

I snort. "Yeah, so did I. I was wrong. You got beat up by a person in a costume. I got beat up by a one-eyed fish."

"Things change," Lenna says. "And you can't stop it. You just have to figure out how to go on. I used to think I hated change, but then all the changes that happened were for the better. Getting out of the mine, getting away from my family, going on adventures, finding Poppy, meeting Nan. It was all just so much better. But you can't expect things to stay the same. Every adventure is going to be different."

"But what about Creeperhead?" For a big guy, Jarro sounds really small just now.

"Like everything else, we'll deal with it together," I say. "With Tok's traps protecting us at night and Lenna keeping watch during the day, we'll be fine. We won't leave anyone alone again."

I hear a creak on my other side, and Tok gets out of bed and picks up Clarity. He carries the cat over and places him on Jarro's chest.

"Cats keep creepers away," he says, half asleep. "So snuggle the cat and go to sleep. Some of us had a tiring day."

Jarro can't help laughing, but just a little. He doesn't want to disturb Clarity, who's already purring. In between the purring and the gentle snuffles of the horses and the slow, measured breaths of my friends, I'm soon asleep, too. All night, it's like I'm still on high alert, waiting for something to happen, but nothing does. If

Creeperhead came anywhere close to the door, I'm pretty sure Poppy would bark her head off, and then we'd hear Tok's trap spring.

But the night is quiet and nothing happens, and when we wake up in the morning Tok tells us to stay inside while he heads out to pick up the trap first thing. Whatever it is, by the time I stumble out the door and into the misty gray morning, it's gone. Bow in hand, Lenna walks all around the perimeter of the shelter, but she can't find anything to suggest Creeperhead has been in the area. We eat breakfast, and I help Mal break up the shelter, and we mount up and leave. It was pretty smart, building a shelter with enough room for the horses. I know if Thingy was here, he would definitely be sleeping inside.

Mal tells us that the map has us following the ocean for a long time. We should reach the cave we're looking for in two days. I settle in for a long day in the saddle and think about asking Tok to invent some sort of saddle cushion, or maybe armored pants with a pillow attachment.

At lunch we stop for a quick bite, but I can tell the time thing is getting to Mal. Her Nan might already be—well, I'm not going to say it out loud—but we know she can't stick it out forever. The horses are speedy, and I know it would take ten times longer on foot, but I think we all feel like we're not only in a hurry, but also being chased. This is not a relaxing trip. Lenna spends so much time looking over her shoulder that I'm afraid her head will stick that way, like my mom always said my face would stick if I kept making funny faces at the dinner table.

The afternoon stretches out, gray but with the sun almost peeking through the clouds. The ocean shimmers to our left, and it's funny how just a few days ago, I'd never heard of an ocean, and now it's just this big thing over there that goes on forever. If I stare too far out for too long, I start to think I'm imagining things, grand ships stuck in the sand and terrifying sea monsters and odd sticky-uppy things that look like towers.

But then I see something so ridiculous that I know the stress and rump aches must be getting to me.

"Um, are you guys seeing this?" I say, rubbing my eyes.

"Seeing what?" Tok asks. "I was daydreaming."

I point out into the ocean.

"On that island—are those . . . cows? Or mushrooms?!"

16.

JARRO

 Chug is right on both counts, and I am so confused right now. It's misty and far away, but I'm pretty sure I'm looking at an island covered in red mushrooms bigger than a house, and I'm also pretty sure I hear plaintive mooing.

"Can we stop?" Lenna asks, looking excited for the first time since she began to suspect we were being followed. "I've got to do some sketches, and those cows look really, really weird."

"I can stock up on mushrooms for stew." As if in punctuation, Chug's stomach grumbles. But then again, his stomach is usually grumbling.

"And think of the breeding possibilities if that's a new kind of mob," I say, because yeah, I'm always thinking about my animal empire back home.

Mal looks off into the distance, the ocean and meadow seeming to go on forever. "We shouldn't. Every moment we waste, Nan is in pain and one step closer to—" She shakes her head. "We need to hurry."

"But . . . wouldn't Nan want us to stop?" Lenna asks. "Her favorite thing in the whole world is hearing about new discoveries. She always says, 'Nothing ventured, nothing gained.'"

And, yeah, I've heard Nan say that. Maybe Mal is Nan's's descendant, but Lenna is her assistant, and she spends the most time in the little cottage in the woods.

"She can't hear about new discoveries if she's dead." As Mal says the D word, her voice is hard, her eyebrows drawn down.

"What if there's a new plant or potion out there?" Chug says, shielding his eyes with his hand. "Maybe there's a chest with an enchanted golden apple hidden on that island. You never know."

Mal sighs. "Wishful thinking. We have the map. We just need to get the apple."

"A quick trip," Chug begs. "I just have a feeling this place is gonna be worth it."

"And Nan always says to follow your gut," Lenna adds.

Mal looks out at the island, frowning. "Really quick," she finally says. "We need to be a lot farther by nightfall. It's all galloping, after this."

Chug shifts in his saddle. "It's a sacrifice my butt is willing to make."

We dismount and I put up fences for the horses. We only have two boats, and we don't want to waste time making another boat, so we have to consider who gets to row over to the mysterious island. Lenna has to go so she can record what she finds in her book and look for plants that might be useful. Mal should go because we definitely hear mooing, and she grew up on a cow farm. Chug wants to go because he likes cute animals and is also our resident expert on mushroom stew. That means it's down to Tok and me.

"You should go," Tok says. "You're the one who tamed horses. If it's some new kind of animal, you'll probably have an affinity for it."

"But don't you want to, I don't know . . ." My eyes flick to Chug, and Tok knows exactly what I mean.

"Just keep my brother in line for me, okay? If there's a mean cow, don't let him try to hug it. I'd rather stay here and try to make this new potion I just remembered."

"But what about Creeperhead?" Chug says, which I appreciate, because it's my main concern but I don't want to look like a coward by bringing it up too much.

Tok looks out into the meadow. It's flat and empty, just sweeping grass for miles. "There's nowhere to hide. You won't be gone long. I'll have Poppy to keep watch. And I'm not without my defenses." He pulls a sword out of one pocket and an evil-looking bluish gray potion from the other. "I'll be fine. As long as he can't sneak up on me—and he can't—I'll be fine. Now that we know he's out there and can be on the lookout, the element of surprise is gone, and he's just a jerk in a dumb mask."

I step into the boat with Chug and sit down, pleased to be included and glad to be just a little bit farther away from Creeperhead. I still can't get over the fact that I have a valuable skill, that they want me to come along. My mom always told me I was useless and did everything wrong, but now my friends think I can do something they can't, which makes my heart feel like it's too big to fit in my chest. And I can contribute something, so it's not like the Mob Squad is just dragging me along. No matter how many times they remind me that I'm one of them, that I'm their friend, it's hard to silence that mean old voice in the back of my mind that says they'll one day realize I'm a fraud and kick me right back out.

I've never been in a boat before, and I'll admit it makes me a little queasy. As Chug rows, I look down through the glimmering turquoise water and see all sorts of interesting animals just going about their business down below. I keep an eye out for the one-eyed spiky fish Chug warned me about, but all I see are cod and salmon and little colorful fish that wink in the dappled sun filtering down through the blue. It would be nice, if my breakfast wasn't threatening to come back up.

As we get closer and closer, the island goes from misty and shadowy to very real . . . and very weird. I would say it's impossible, except I'm living it. The land rises up from the water, almost like steps made of dirt, but here and there, huge mushrooms with red or brown caps sprout, as big as trees. A few cows gambol about, including one really adorable baby, but they don't look like Mal's cows back home. She introduced me to her herd after I mistook horses for cows and looked like an absolute fool. And, yeah, I do like horses better than cows, but I wouldn't say that to Mal or her cows.

But these cows aren't brown—they're red with white spots and wet black noses and . . .

Oh wow.

Mushrooms growing on their backs.

"Mushmoos!" Chug cries gleefully as he rows.

"I was thinking mooshrooms," Lenna says. She's already sketching.

"But mushmoo is so much fun to say," Chug argues.

Lenna grimaces. "Sorry, Chug. I already wrote it down as mooshrooms. And it was in pen, so it's not like I can just change it."

Chug pouts. "Aw, I was gonna call the babies mushmittens."

Then, quietly, to himself, he mutters, "And I'm still gonna call 'em mushmittens. Let's see your pen try and stop me."

Our boat scrapes up onto the island, and we hop off. The mooshrooms—wow, that is catchy—don't really seem to care about us, and I notice everyone kind of hanging back and staring at me. It takes me a minute to realize they're waiting for me to make the first move. I always have wheat in my pockets because of the horses, so I pull out a sheaf and hold it out to the nearest cow. She moos and waddles over and eats the wheat and nudges me with her head, and I pat her and run a hand down her back. I still can't believe she's growing mushrooms right out of her hide. Chug sidles over as quickly but nonthreateningly as he can and giggles while he pets the cow. The baby trots over, its big eyes curious, and soon Chug is on his back with a baby mushroom cow standing on his belly. The parents, luckily, don't seem to mind.

"Yeah, so it's just a different kind of cow, I guess," Mal says.

With Chug overcome by cow snuggles, she collects a bunch of mushrooms and then wanders around until she finds a spot that looks good for mining.

"Five minutes," she says warningly before hacking in with her pickaxe.

Lenna sits down with her back against a mushroom stalk and alternates between scribbling and sketching. I feel like I need to do something useful and animal-related, and it occurs to me that, well, the mooshrooms have udders.

"Hey, Mal. Got a bucket?" I ask.

"Always." She tosses a bucket to me, and I approach the first cow I met, who's still a little blissed out by the wheat. I've never milked a cow before, but I've watched Mal do it, and it doesn't seem difficult.

Soon I'm holding a full bucket of milk, and to be honest, I'm kind of surprised—maybe even disappointed—that it isn't mushroom juice or something more bizarre.

"Aw, it's just milk!" Chug says, echoing my thoughts.

"But milk has uses," Mal says, joining us with her pickaxe over her shoulder and a smile on her face. "I'm all loaded up. Jarro, can you carry the milk? We should get back."

"But—" Lenna starts.

"No buts, no witch huts," Mal says. "We have to get going. We can come back some other time, once Nan's better."

Lenna reluctantly stands while still drawing, and Chug extricates himself from a pile of mushmittens and joins us, covered in red fur. We're navigating the hill back down to the beach when we hear a sound that makes my blood run cold.

Tok.

Screaming.

"Tok!" Chug bellows. He leaps into the boat and is about to row off without me, but Mal jumps in right before he pushes off into the water. That's probably for the best—if something is wrong, she's a much better fighter than I am.

I get into the other boat and take the oars while Lenna sits across from me. She puts her book in her pocket and pulls out her bow and arrows and faces the shore, leaning forward as if she can make the boat speed up through sheer will.

I've never rowed before, but again, it's pretty obvious, if exhausting. Chug is already way ahead of us, but I put everything I have into moving the boat. I heard one scream from Tok and then nothing else, which is not a good sign. I'm pretty sure I was hollering the entire time I was facing off with Creeperhead, hoping my friends would hear me and come save me.

The beach comes into focus, and . . . oh no.

Tok is gone.

His crafting table and brewing stand are there, but he's not. Neither is Poppy.

The horses are in their paddock, whinnying nervously and stamping their feet, and the cats sit by Tok's workstation, twitching their tails and meowing plaintively like they're confused.

"Creeperhead took Tok!" Chug bellows. "I'm gonna rip off his head! His creeper head and his real head! And then I'm gonna— find something else to rip off!" He runs out toward the meadows, sword drawn, and screams, "Bring him back and fight me, you jerk!"

"Wait." Lenna is pointing at the sand. "I only see one set of footprints. If Creeperhead kidnapped Tok—if anybody did— there would be signs of a scuffle, or at least multiple footprints. But these are just the ones from Tok's boots."

"And the cats are calm," I say, struggling to think of a reasonable explanation for what I'm seeing. "And the horses are nervous, but they're still here. And horses are nervous most of the time, anyway."

Lenna whistles for Poppy, and we hear a faraway bark but can't see any sign of the wolf. Mal is out by Chug now, and they've both spread out in the meadow like they're going to find Tok curled up asleep in a patch of grass, or maybe discover Creeperhead carrying him away in a chest. Lenna and I walk out into the meadow, too, but there's nothing to see, no flaming letters or destroyed shelter. Just a missing boy and a mystery.

"What's that?" Lenna asks, pointing at some animal running across the green.

"A horse, maybe?" I squint. "But it's faster than a horse."

She pulls a book out of her pocket and pages through it intently. "An ocelot, maybe? But they live in jungles, not meadows. And it's bigger than an ocelot."

Poppy barks, closer this time, and we see her bounding through the grass toward us. Her tongue lolls out, and she looks like she's laughing, not like she's been in another tussle with Creeperhead.

"Where's Tok?" Lenna asks her wolf.

"Woof!" Poppy responds, leaping up excitedly.

Lenna sighs. "That's your answer to everything. Poppy, go find Tok."

Poppy turns around and runs deeper into the meadow, barking excitedly at us over her shoulder.

"That's her *come play with me* bark," Lenna says, her eyebrows drawn down. "Definitely not her *something is wrong* bark."

We all edge deeper into the meadow, our weapons at the ready. I can feel my heart thumping, my fist tight around the handle of my golden axe. If Creeperhead comes for me again, he won't escape unscathed. Whatever he's doing to Tok, we're going to make him pay. I'm scared, but surrounded by the Mob Squad, working together to save one of our own, I have the strength to keep going, anyway.

"Woooo!" someone yells, and the animal we've seen running back and forth charges right for us in a blur.

We all drop into a defensive stance, and Lenna takes careful aim and lets her arrow fly.

"Ow! Ow! What? Why?"

Tok stands before us, an arrow in his shoulder. He's out of breath and sweaty and looks like we just ruined his birthday party.

Lenna is freaking out. "Oh my gosh! Tok! I'm so sorry! We just saw something moving at us way too fast, and I assumed it had to be Creeperhead, or maybe a really fast creeper, or—"

"It was me. And you totally shot me," he says simply, yanking out the arrow and handing it back to her with a wry grin that says he'll never, ever let her live it down.

She hands him two cookies, which he immediately gobbles up, sighing as his wound fades away and moving his shoulder around to test it.

"Explain yourself, bro," Chug says, trying to look stern but failing completely because he's elated that his brother is okay.

Tok reaches into his pocket and holds out a potion as he walks back toward the ocean. Poppy gambols beside him, nipping at his heels.

"I mostly make the potions our town needs," Tok explains. "Boring stuff. As you know, the ingredients are hard to come by, and I never want to waste them. We need Potions of Healing more than almost anything else, so that's what I focus my time and resources on. But I remembered that one of my books has a recipe for a Potion of Swiftness. I figured that if we used it on our horses, we could go twice as fast and maybe get back to Nan earlier. But I had to test it first." He grins. "So I tested it on myself."

Chug hug-attacks him. "You glorious idiot! You stupid genius! You're not supposed to test things on yourself, but whooboy golly, you were moving so fast! I'm so proud of you and mad at you at the same time!"

Tok takes the hug in good humor. "Well, I wasn't about to use it on one of the pets. Besides, it was pretty fun. I've never been particularly fast—"

"Remember that time we had field day at school and you tripped on literally nothing and fell down and broke your nose and—" Chug clears his throat. "And made me promise to never bring it up again?"

"I remember," Tok says slowly, one eyebrow raised. "But I

guess now I understand why people like to run. I've set up the potion so we can just pour it on the horses and it should really help our time."

"I'm glad we don't have to feed it to them," I say. "They tend to slobber a lot."

We're all relieved as we head back to the beach, where everything is exactly as we've left it. No one has seen a sign of Creeperhead since yesterday. Maybe beating me up satisfied him and he's done tormenting us.

It's a nice thought, but I know it's not true.

Creeperhead is still out there, waiting—and we don't know why.

17.

LENNA

 The Potion of Swiftness works even better than anticipated. The world is flying by in a blur, and I realize that even if Creeperhead has a horse, he won't be able to keep up with us anymore.

With the ocean on the left, we all keep our eyes peeled for anything unusual on the right. It's gratifying to know that my instincts were correct—we were being followed, and it wasn't by a pig or a wolf or some senseless, hungry mob but by what appears to be a person who wants to hurt us, if not kill us, for some reason of his own. The words "ha ha" don't really hold any clues to the motivation behind our enemy. At least now I know what to look for—a creeper and a horse—and at least now we're moving faster than our pursuer can. Of course, that doesn't mean I'm going to relax for even a second. If something moves in my line of sight, I'm going to shoot first and ask questions later.

Which—oops. I'm glad Tok is forgiving.

He doesn't even blame me.

But I feel terrible about it, anyway.

Not that I would do anything different if put in that position again.

The horses ahead of me are kind of hilarious, their legs moving at double time and my friends bouncing along. Tok had to make a potion for Poppy, too, and she loves racing across the meadow grass, her tongue hanging out as she grins. Tok's cats are on his shoulders, and I don't envy what it must feel like to have their claws sunk in like that. Maybe he'll invent cat armor for himself with leather pads over the shoulders for them to cling to.

We're headed directly toward craggy, dark gray mountains, and the day is getting progressively darker. The sun pops in and out of the clouds, the shadows shifting across the meadow. I look back over my shoulder constantly but see no sign of Creeperhead.

That evening, Mal stops us a little early and builds our double shelter by the shore. If we push, we could maybe reach the cliffs tonight—but not in time to dig out a shelter. Up ahead, the ocean ends and the mountains begin, and I'm glad we'll get one more night by the pretty blue water and the soft song of foamy waves lapping at the shore. There's nothing like this back home, but being here makes me feel calm in a way I never do there, like maybe since the ocean is constantly moving, my mind can finally be still. We dismount and each turn to our usual preparations. Mal and Chug build the shelter while Jarro watches the horses. Tok would usually be crafting, but I guess his pockets are full and he's satisfied with whatever trap he's rigged outside our door, as he borrows Chug's fishing pole and sets out to catch supper.

The world feels like it's moving so slowly now that I'm off my speed-enhanced mount. Poppy, on the other hand, is still influenced by her potion, so she's darting here and there like a bee, terrorizing the local rabbits in the meadow and shearing flowers from their stalks. Bow and arrow ready, I walk in increasing arcs around our campsite, all my senses on alert. I take down a sheep once I'm pretty far out, but I don't hear or see anything worrisome. It's almost worse this way—before, I knew we were being followed, but now I don't have that same feeling. Most likely, we left Creeperhead in our dust, thanks to the Potion of Swiftness, but if he's here, he's likely working harder to stay hidden, now that we're on the lookout.

Far off, I hear Mal calling my name, and Poppy and I return from our scouting. I give Tok the wool for the next time we need a new bed and offer Chug the mutton, since he's our best cook. Several kinds of fish are already prepared and steaming hot, along with bowls of mushroom soup. I sit in the circle with my friends but position myself with my back to the ocean so I'll have a full view of the meadow and anything that tries to approach. Jarro and Tok are extra jumpy, and I don't blame them a bit.

As the sun sets, we lead the horses into their side of the shelter and line up our beds. Tok goes outside to fix his traps and reminds us all not to set foot out there. I curl up under my blankets, thinking about how things used to be, back when I shared a room with two of my sisters and was convinced I could hear scratching and groaning through the wall of our house, which backed up to the wall around Cornucopia. Now I know it was probably zombies bumbling around outside at night, but back then, my sisters laughed at me and said it was my own imagination gone wild.

I never really believed them, though. It felt like so much of what other people told me was wrong, or at least not true for me, that I've never had a problem just following my heart and ignoring what the crowd says. When the noises were especially bad, I would take my blankets and pillow and sleep under my bed.

I don't have to do that anymore. I know that the zombies outside can't get in and that, thanks to the torches we always place carefully around our shelter, they can't spawn inside. We're perfectly safe.

So why do I want to sleep under my bed?

Not that I actually do it. The floor in here is dirt, and it's not nearly as comfortable as the stone I'm used to back home. Dirt is just too . . . dirty. There are some textures I just don't like, and that's one of them.

I fall asleep in my bed with Poppy finally slow again and breathing gently at my side, and I wake up to a noise I can't immediately identify, followed by Poppy barking like mad at the door.

"My trap!" Tok says, bolting out of bed. "Get your weapons!"

I whip out my bow and arrows, and Mal and Chug each have a sword in hand. It takes Jarro a moment to remember his axe, but even if he's scared, he's still on his feet with the rest of us. Tok has his own sword as he creeps to the door. I grab Poppy's collar and move her out of his way. He motions to Chug, indicating that he should be ready with his sword when the door is open. Chug nods and creeps forward, his face grim under his helmet.

Tok holds up three fingers, then two, then one, then throws open the door.

What we see outside is totally confusing.

A sheep stands just beyond our shelter, utterly still.

Wait. No.

Not utterly still.

It's just moving very, very slowly.

Weird little gray whorls wiggle through the air around it, and there's broken glass on the stone Tok has placed before the door.

"This isn't good," he says quietly.

"I mean, there are worse things than sheep," Chug says.

"Shh. Stay inside."

Tok leaps over the glass-strewn stone and puts it in his pocket.

"That was a pressure plate," he says. "If anyone tried to open our door from the outside, the pressure plate would activate two Potions of Slowness. The idea was that if Creeperhead tried to hurt us, he'd be as slow as that sheep."

We look at the sheep, but it's barely moving, a look of horror on its face as it says, "B-a-a-a-a!" with infinite slowness.

"So I would hear the trap, we'd run outside, and Creeperhead— or any trespassers—would be easy to catch and tie up."

"I still don't see why you hate that sheep so much," Chug says.

Tok shakes his head at his brother. "Because sheep don't just walk up to a shelter's doorstep on their own. I'm guessing that Creeperhead knows about pressure plates and redstone or guessed that the door was booby-trapped, so he put the sheep here to spring the trap." He looks everywhere, nervous as a rabbit. "Which means he might still be close."

Chug barrels out the door with Mal by his side, and I follow with my arrow nocked. It's pitch-dark outside, and the only sound is the ocean's endless shushing. The night is cloudy with neither moon nor stars, so I can barely see anything. Creeperhead could be standing twenty paces away and we wouldn't know.

"Poppy!" I call. "Smell anybody?"

My wolf sniffs the air and excitedly runs a few steps before she realizes she's no longer superfast and sighs in frustration. She sniffs the sheep, sniffs the ground, and follows a trail a bit into the dark before returning with a disappointed look on her face.

"Show me the trail," I ask, but she just thumps her tail sadly as if in apology. "I don't get it. She smells something, but she won't follow it."

"Then she probably has a reason." Tok goes into thinking

mode, his eyes vacant and his sword hanging useless at his side. We know him well enough to give him time and space, but then there's a groan from somewhere nearby, and the hairs on the back of my neck prickle.

"Let's get back inside," Mal says.

"Yeah, I can deal with sheep delivery but I don't want a bag of rotten meat," Chug says.

We head back into the shelter and close the door, but no one goes to their bed. We cluster by the door as the horses stamp and snort in annoyance at being woken up. Horses, it turns out, don't make great roommates.

"I should've laid more traps—" Tok starts.

Chug interrupts him. "Don't beat yourself up, bro. We thought we were way ahead of Creeperhead, but I guess he kept traveling when we settled in. Or maybe—"

"Creeperhead has potions, too," Tok finishes dejectedly. "Ugh. I hate this! I keep thinking I've got the answer, but nothing seems to work."

"Then we go back to basics." Mal sits with her back against the door. "We sleep in shifts. I'll take first watch and wake up Chug when I feel sleepy again. Whoever is on watch, just sit here with your weapon." Poppy hurries over to snuffle around Mal before flopping down on her side by Mal's knee. Mal smiles. "And it looks like whoever's on watch will have prime company."

We settle back in our beds, but it's clear no one is comfortable. We toss and turn and rustle and sigh. I finally fall asleep, but I stir a little when Mal wakes Chug and then nearly punch him in the nose when he gently shakes my shoulder to wake me. The spot he's vacated by the door is warm and smells a little fishy, which tells me Chug has been eating the leftover fish. I put my back to the door and my hand on my wolf as the ocean tries its best to sing me to sleep. Nothing happens while I'm on watch, except at some point the Potions of Slowness must wear off the sheep, as it gives a surprised and insulted "Baa!" and runs off into the night. Poppy lightly woofs at this like it's part of her job but she's too polite to wake the others. When I can't keep my eyes open a second longer, I wake Tok, and he trudges out of bed and over to the door after carefully covering his sleeping cats with his blanket.

When morning comes, we all look like we got run over by a minecart. We yawn and stretch and stumble outside with our weapons drawn. Nothing really feels safe anymore.

"Oh no," Jarro says, horrified, and we all look where he's pointing.

The words *Nice Try* have been formed of netherrack and set on fire for us to find.

"So I guess the sheep wasn't an accident," Chug says darkly.

"Creeperhead is still following us." Jarro's eyes flick everywhere, desperate. "How is that even possible?"

"He must have potions, too. It's the only answer. So we've got to get on the road now. If we hurry, we'll reach the cave by nightfall. I have some obsidian, so maybe we can block up the entrance to . . . wherever we go. I don't know." Mal rubs her eyes. "I just wish I knew what Creeperhead wants."

"I think it's Orlok and the brigands," Jarro says. "And they're mad at us for basically jailing them in the Nether. I mean, who else could it be?"

"Maybe the Elders sent Jami and Lars after us?" I say. "Although I don't think either of them has ever traveled in the Overworld . . ."

"I've never rented a horse to either of them." Jarro pats Speckles. "I wouldn't, not after what they pulled at the gate. But if they didn't rent my horses, they probably didn't go farther than New Cornucopia."

"Maybe they stole horses after we left," Mal says.

Tok shakes his head. "That wouldn't explain the potions. I don't think Lars and Jami are smart enough to brew a Potion of Swiftness. No offense, Lenna."

"None taken. I completely agree. They couldn't brew mud."

And I mean it. Lars is my second least favorite sibling out of nine, which is saying a lot. He's one of those people who sees everyone as a threat and faces the world with defensiveness instead of curiosity. I kicked him in the shin when I was three and he's never forgiven me.

"So it has to be the brigands." Tok taps his chin. "But we're being followed by one person on one horse, from what I can tell, and there were six brigands."

"Maybe they didn't all survive," I say. "Remember how you can't sleep in the Nether? If you can't sleep, you can't live. And that would explain why whoever it is is acting so unhinged. If it's Orlok, maybe the lack of sleep and watching his friends die sent him over the edge."

"And drove him to revenge," Chug says in a gravelly, dark voice, staring off toward the mountains. "A broken man, an angry man, a man who's reached the point of no return and will stop at nothing to punish the—" He clears his throat and in his normal voice says, "To punish the cool kids who ruined his life."

"It doesn't really matter who it is," Mal says firmly. "We have to keep going. We have to reach that cave before dark."

I pass out cookies and bread, and we mount our horses and wait for Tok to apply the Potions of Swiftness. Soon we're galloping across the meadow toward the mountains, leaving the ocean's tranquil beauty behind. It's a bright blue day, and I would be loving every minute if I didn't know that Nan was dying.

And that Creeperhead is out there, whoever he is, and a lot smarter than we'd hoped.

18.

MAL

 The ocean isn't my favorite place in the Over-world, especially after I nearly died there, but I'll admit I kind of miss the scenery—and the fact that while we traveled alongside it, we could only be attacked from three sides. These mountains are more my style, but they're tall and looming and definitely don't give off a tranquil vibe. Still, there's nothing I like more than mining in new places . . . except reaching my goals and saving Nan.

Thanks to Tok's potions, we're going to reach the cave by nightfall. The maps we get from village cartographers may not be detailed, but they're accurate, and I can tell by the scale that we're on the right track. I'm guessing this cave will contain a stronghold like the one near Cornucopia, but the map just shows an entrance at the base of the mountain, a yawning black hole. At least we'll be back on familiar ground. Between me and Lenna, we know everything there is to know about everything underground. And if I can use my obsidian blocks to make it harder for Creeperhead—I'm assuming it's Orlok— to follow us, then maybe we can . . .

No.

It's not going to work.

Even in the best possible situation, he'll just be waiting outside the cave for us.

And if we leave our horses outside, he'll drive them away . . . or worse.

If we take the horses into the cave, he'll still be able to see their hoofprints. He'll know exactly where we are.

Tricky.

A plan begins to take shape in my head. I don't like it—it's not what I want to do—but my job is to figure out how to get that enchanted golden apple to Nan, and that means I have to strategize around the dangerous creep who's dogging our every step and who sincerely wants to do us harm.

When we stop for lunch, I accept my fish, but I don't eat it. As the others stand in the meadow grass—because we're all sick of sitting and the Potion of Swiftness means we only get our butts bumped more—I pace a little, trying to find the right words.

"So we all agree Creeperhead doesn't show any signs of giving up," I begin. "We all believe he's still on our trail?"

"He has to be," Tok says around an apple. "That sheep did not place itself on our doorstep last night for fun."

"And we have to assume that he has his own Potions of Swiftness and is on horseback, since Lenna saw his hoofprints and he's able to keep pace with us?"

"I really hate this guy," Chug grumbles.

"Then it follows that when we go into the cave, he's either going to follow us inside or wait outside to ambush us, right?"

"But I thought you had the obsidian to block him out—" Chug begins.

"I do. But with enough time, he'll be able to mine it and get into the cave. Or—like when we broke through the wall, maybe he'll just mine around it. And if he's trying to hurt us, he might drive the horses away. Or worse." Chug has a soft heart, so I don't elaborate, but the look of horror on his face suggests he understands.

"So we can't let him follow us in, but we can't leave him outside," Jarro reasons.

"I have an idea." I stop pacing and face them. "What if we get up into the mountains and ambush him? We can hide the horses and climb up into the rocky cliffs. Lenna can shoot him with flaming arrows, or we can throw potions at him. Or maybe set some kind of trap, like the one Efram had with the pie."

Tok shakes his head. "We won't have that kind of thick tree cover. It would be too obvious."

"And I'm not giving up any pies," Chug growls.

Lenna is looking back the way we came, always scanning for any sign of our enemy. "I hate fighting people," she says. "I don't mind mobs, but I don't know if I could release a flaming arrow knowing that it could kill someone."

"After what he did to me, I could," Jarro says, his voice rough.

"No, I don't think you could. I've seen you choke up in a fight before," Lenna says with that somewhat clueless honesty she's known for. She looks around at each of us. "I don't know that any of us could do it."

"Then we're going to need a different kind of trap." I look to Tok. "We're counting on you to think of something. I know last night's trap didn't work, but . . ."

"But this one has to." He looks both determined and slightly terrified. Ever since the brigands kidnapped him, Tok has been a little jumpy under pressure, so I know this is going to be a challenge for him. "And to be clear, the trap did work. He just knew what to look for, so I'll have to do a better job of disguising it."

"You can do it," I say, looking directly into his eyes.

"You can do anything, bro," Chug agrees.

"Well, I do have some interesting ideas after reading Efram's book . . ." Tok trails off, staring into the meadow as if he's going to find answers there. "I'm going to need some moss. And if we can stop in a place that's a little busy, visually speaking, it will help. Closer to the cliffs. We need him to be distracted. It can't just be a sparse patch of dirt."

"So we lure him," I say. "Maybe we can find a pass like the one where the brigands ambushed us on our first adventure. We don't give him a choice."

Tok's smile is slow and diabolical, and I'm glad he's on our side. "I'll figure it out."

When we mount back up and pour more potions on our horses, Lenna keeps looking behind us. She's right—we're kids, and we can't just attack a person with weapons, or at least we don't want to unless it's a last resort. That sort of thing would be hard to live with on my conscience. When Orlok and his cronies had Tok, all bets were off, but this situation isn't as clear. If the trap reveals it's Orlok again or any of his crew, Lenna's mind will likely change. I hope we won't have to find out.

The cliffs loom higher and craggier the farther we go. The meadow flowers give way to trees, including strange ones I've never seen before. As we rush by, I pluck a bright pink bloom and put it behind my ear.

"What are these trees?" I ask Lenna.

She pulls out a book and pages through it before saying, "Huh. They're called azalea trees. Pretty flowers. I wonder why we don't have any back home?"

"Maybe the wood's not as pretty, or maybe they only grow in rocky places," Tok says. "I mean, giant red mushrooms don't grow back home, either."

"And we don't have islands crawling with mushmittens!" Chug reminds us.

Lenna sighs. "I think this is what I miss the most, when we're not traveling. We don't see anything new."

"We also don't get stalked and beat up by creeps in masks." Jarro has been pretty quiet since he was attacked, and the only way I know to help him is to make sure Creeperhead can't follow us anymore.

The light is golden and the shadows are stretching out long and purple when I finally see the cave opening up ahead. My heart speeds up, knowing how close we are to the enchanted golden apple.

Tok halts, and when we stop our own horses and backtrack to where he's waiting, he says, "Here. Let's do it here."

It's a good spot. On our left, the cliffs rise up starkly with several outcroppings wide enough for trees, bushes, grass, moss, and boulders. The ground below is a bit jumbled, the meadow fully giving way to forest and the oak trees thick and leafy. And the open cave mouth ahead is just the sort of distraction we need, because it's going to be pretty obvious that the cave was our goal all along.

"What can we do to help?" I ask.

Tok points forward. "Jarro, walk the horses in that direction and see if you can find a place to hide them where they won't be visible or too noisy. Take the cats and Poppy, too. We need them to stay out of the fight." He looks around, head cocked. "I'll need a few blocks of stone and some moss. Lenna should find a place to hide on a high ridge and have her bow and arrows ready, and Mal and Chug should stay on the lower ledge with me. If the trap works, you'll need to jump down quickly and tie Creeperhead up as soon as they take effect."

"As soon as what takes effect?" I ask.

He grins. "You'll see."

We dismount, and Jarro leads the horses away, softly explaining to them that they need to be quiet. It's pretty cool, the way they seem to understand him; I just can't make that kind of connection with animals. The cows back home are sweet but share one brain cell among the whole herd, and I'm pretty sure Moo only puts up with me because Jarro gives him carrots. Half of the time I'm pretty sure he's going to bite me when I'm not looking.

Moo, not Jarro, just so we're clear.

Lenna tells Poppy to follow Jarro before she scrambles up the steep cliff wall. She finds a place to hide high up, right behind a bush and near a grazing goat, and as I squint up and shield my eyes with my hand, I can't see her at all. I give her a big thumbs-up, but I don't know if she can see it. Probably not. I'm betting she's scanning for Creeperhead back the way we came, bow and arrow ready in case he somehow gets here before the trap is ready. She may say she doesn't want to hurt a person, but if he threatens any one of us, I have no doubt she'll do whatever she can to keep us safe.

Chug and I stand and watch Tok at his workbench. It's beautiful, really, to see him in the zone. When he's crafting or brewing, he does things I don't even understand, dreams of things no one has ever dared to envision. And then he makes it real, even if it fails the first hundred times. I try to figure out what he's planning, but all I see are potion bottles and a slab of moss.

"Go hide," he says without taking his eyes off his crafting table. "I get self-conscious when you guys watch me."

Chug and I share a look and start climbing up the scrubby cliff. To look at Chug, you wouldn't think he was an agile climber—and, honestly, he's not—but he decided at a very young age that apples taste best when "borrowed" off a neighbor's tree, so he's learned how to drag himself up, even if it's difficult and slow and involves a lot of grunting. Lenna is way up high on her outcropping, higher than the roofs of the houses in the Hub back home, but Chug and I stop at the first ledge that has enough room for us both and a convenient boulder to hide behind. We're maybe ten feet up, high enough that you wouldn't expect us but low enough that we can jump to the ground if necessary. We might need a cookie afterward, but I don't think Chug would complain.

"Who do you think he is?" Chug asks me.

"Who, Creeperhead?"

"No, that freaky guy in the teal shirt and dark blue pants with the dead, white eyes that Lenna said she saw skulking around the mine one night," Chug says. "Of course I mean Creeperhead!"

"I think it has to be Orlok. Who else hates us and would want revenge?"

Chug pulls a fish out of his pocket and munches thoughtfully. "I mean, there are plenty of people in town who hate us. Jarro's mom can't stand us and thinks it's our fault she lost all of her sweet berries. Elder Gabe, Elder Stu, and Tini are furious that

Tok takes all their business and charges more reasonable prices. And you saw Jami and Lars at the wall. They'd lock us outside it forever, if they could."

"There're also the brigands who work for Orlok, I guess. Whoever made it out of the Nether . . ." I trail off, because it feels too final to say *whoever made it out of the Nether alive.* "And Krog, but he's still in jail, thank goodness." I sigh and rebraid my hair. "Although I haven't gone to visit him in a while to make sure here's still there. I guess we've made a lot of enemies."

Chug throws a rock at a nearby tree. "Which is weird, because we're not even trying to make enemies! Jarro's mom—and Jami and Lars, too, I guess—they don't like us just because we're different and the Elders don't like us because we stopped them from ripping people off."

"And also because we left Cornucopia against their rules, and now they've had to open the wall. I guess they have more reason than most to hate us. But it's not like Elder Gabe or Elder Stu could do all this traveling just to torture us. Jarro's mom definitely wouldn't do this to him—she's not that cruel, and she's also pretty lazy. And let's face it—Jami and Lars are incompetent."

"I doubt either of them knows which end of the horse goes in front!" Chug laughs, a little too loud, and I put a finger to my lips. We're laying a trap, after all.

"But Orlok and his crew have reason to hate us, they can travel and fight, and they would probably emerge from the Nether a little nutty because they couldn't sleep the whole time they were trapped there. So it has to be one of them." I pull my pickaxe out of my pocket and lay it across my lap. I don't say it, but I really hope it's one of the brigands, because I don't know how I would feel hurting someone I'd grown up knowing. I don't like Lars or

Jami or the Elders or Krog, but I don't want to hit them with a sword, either.

From overhead, Lenna whistles like a bird, and we go quiet and hurry behind our boulder, weapons drawn. Tok hears the signal, too, as he packs up his crafting table and brewing stand and runs behind a tree. I can't see the trap he's built, but I do notice that he's placed a book on the ground, like maybe it just fell out of his pocket. I cross my fingers and toes, hoping that whatever he's done, it will work. His inventions don't generally perform flawlessly the first time, but anything that can give us an advantage over Creeperhead will help.

I look back the way we've come, but I can't see anything, thanks to the trees and bushes. We chose this place because you couldn't see far, and now it's punishing us, too, because we can't see what's coming toward us. Chug and I wait in silence, tense, barely breathing, to see our prey appear.

But no one comes.

Instead, the sky goes dark as night, coal-gray clouds hurriedly building. There's something weird about the air—some sort of pressure I can't explain. A deep, ominous chime rings out. I look to Chug, who shakes his head and shrugs. I don't know what's going on, but I have a bad feeling about it.

Just out of view, something explodes, and Chug and I step out from behind the boulder just in time to see the most terrifying monster I've ever beheld.

19.

TOK

 I was so excited to see if my trap would work. Just positively giddy, giggling to myself behind that tree. But then I felt something in the air change, like the calm but dangerous heart of a storm. The sky went dark, like the sun had died. And now my blood runs cold as I watch the monster approach.

I've never seen anything like it, nor read anything about it in Nan's books. It's like a flying three-headed skeleton with no legs, floating on a bone torso as its coldly glowing eyes lock onto me. On second thought, the three skulls look a little familiar—like those weird skeletons we saw in the Nether—but that's not a comforting thought. I don't know what I'm expecting, but having flying skulls lobbed at me by a floating rib cage is not it.

The thing—which almost seems to have withered, puckered skin around its heads—focuses on one of the goats jumping around the cliff and spits a black skull.

Boom!

The goat is now a charred smear on the rock.

A twisted black rose sits on the ground where the goat once innocently frolicked.

My jaw drops.

"Tok, run for the tunnel! Get Jarro!" Mal shouts at me, because let's face it, any hope we had of ambushing Creeperhead is dead. We have to deal with this—this thing first.

I do exactly as she says, running as fast as my legs will take me—which honestly isn't that fast. Thank goodness I already packed up my traveling workshop. This monster looks like it's going to offer new challenges, and I don't need to be the only person on the ground with it. Jarro and I are the worst fighters, so getting us out of the way is smart while the others figure out how best to fight it.

Maybe it's weaker than it looks.

Maybe it'll go down without much of a fight.

That's what I tell myself as I run away from my brother and friends and toward the safety of the caves.

Even as I think it, I know it's wrong.

See, my brain likes puzzles. It likes to find connections. And my brain knows that it's not a coincidence that this monster attacked us right here and right now. We were waiting to ambush Creeperhead, and right when he should've arrived, we got a terrifying hostile mob instead. Since what I've seen of Creeperhead so far suggests he's smart and knows a lot of tricks, I have to assume that he somehow brought the monster here. That he summoned it to hurt us.

I'm out of breath by the time I reach Jarro. He's just outside the entrance to the cave, patting Poppy on the head and telling her what a good girl she is. He's already put up the paddock for the horses, but they look nervous, like they can tell something dangerous is happening nearby.

"What's going on?" Jarro asks me.

"We've got to get the horses inside the cave," I say. "This thing can kill mobs."

Jarro's eyes go wide. "What thing? Kill what? What?!"

But he's been with our crew long enough to know that you work while you question impossible things, so he's already opening the gate to lead the horses out. I'm not as comfortable with animals as he is, but I know that Bee is kind and won't bite me or anything, so I lead him and Mervin into the cave after Jarro with the cats twining around my legs and meowing worriedly.

"What thing are you talking about?" Jarro asks. "Creeperhead? I heard some kind of explosion—"

"Not Creeperhead. A new mob. A monster. That's what made the explosion—when it arrived. It's like all the wrong parts of three skeletons smashed together and flying right at you while trying to kill you with exploding skulls."

Jarro starts jogging. "I don't want to see that. I don't even want to know that that exists."

The cave entrance has plenty of room for the horses with a long, narrow tunnel extending into the darkness beyond. We pull out our torches as we lead the nervous animals down the hallway, and then, thankfully, the cave opens up properly into a big, roomy space. As Jarro sets up more fence panels, I take out my pickaxe—because I always carry one of everything—and mine some blocks from the stone walls inside. I carefully place them in the cave mouth, building them up until the only entrance is just big enough for one person. From the outside, once those last two blocks are placed, it will look like just another cliff. As long as the withered-skull monster isn't terrifyingly intelligent, we should be able to escape it.

"Stay here with the animals," I tell Jarro.

"Where are you going? Not back out there with the monster, right?" I can tell Jarro doesn't want to be left alone in the big, dark cave, lit only by that tiny door and a ring of torches, but if I don't go tell the others my plan, Jarro and I might be alone forever.

"I'll bring everybody back. Just put up some torches and be ready for the regular mobs that spawn in caves. Wait! If you have some spare fence panels, maybe you could block off the rest of the cave so the mobs can't get to us. And then have your axe ready, just in case. I'll be right back."

Jarro nods, one hand on Poppy's head, doing his best to stay cool, and I pull out my sword and run outside.

Or, more accurately, I peek out the door and then skitter behind a tree. As soon as I'm sure the Wither—that's what I'm going to call it, just to save time, because its skull looks withered and seeing it makes my heart feel withered—as soon as I'm sure it's not in the immediate area, I zig and zag back toward my friends, hiding behind trees and rocks. I can hear the battle raging, hear explosions as the Wither's skulls explode against cliffs and hopefully not too many goats. Hopefully not against my brother and my friends. The last time something like that hit Chug, it was as if he'd been poisoned, and I'm not ready to watch him lose another fight.

A skull smashes against the ground a few lengths ahead of me, and the shock of it sends me reeling back. That's close enough. I peek through the tree's branches and see that the Wither is high up, near Lenna. She's shooting it with one of her enchanted bows, and each shot she lands seems to enrage it. I've never been more grateful that I learned how to make bows, fix them, and enchant them—and that Lenna can deal so much damage with my creations. Chug and Mal are still up on their ledge, but there's not much they can do, seeing as how the Wither is out of reach and Chug only has a sword. Mal has her bow out, but for every three shots Lenna lands, Mal maybe gets one. She's been practicing, but not enough.

I whistle, and Chug zeroes in on me. His eyes fly wide, and he makes a frantic *get out of here* gesture. I shake my head and point at the cave, then point up at Lenna and make the same gesture. We have to figure out how to tell Lenna that we need to make a run for it.

Chug scrambles down the cliff first, jumping the last few feet and landing hard, sword in hand. He runs behind the tree with me, and the Wither must not have noticed, as it's still focusing on Lenna.

"Bro, what are you doing? Get back into the cave!" he rage-growls.

"We can't fight this thing," I tell him. "Lenna is absolutely pelting it with arrows, and it's barely wounded. Plus Creeperhead is somewhere out there, waiting for us to get our butts kicked. We've got to get into the cave and hide. I blocked up the front entrance so it just looks like a cliff. We just need to get away."

Chug looks back to Mal and Lenna, where they're shooting arrow after arrow at the Wither while dodging its stupid exploding skulls. "How do we tell them?" he asks. "Because I'm pretty sure if we shout, it'll get mad."

"And then Creeperhead will know what we're doing, too." My heart sinks, because I just realized the answer, and I hate it.

"Give me your armor," I say.

"Bro, no," Chug starts.

"I have to climb up and tell Lenna. I'll go around the other side of the cliffs and approach from the back. There's plenty of cover. You get Mal, I'll get Lenna. If you keep running that way, you'll see the cave entrance. It's small, but it's there. Jarro is inside with all the animals. Tell him the plan. Have your weapons ready in case it follows us on the way in. And get ready to place those last two blocks before it can see the entry. That might be the difference between us winning and losing this fight."

Chug puts his hands on his helmet. "There has to be another way—"

"I ran all the calculations. This is the best plan I can think of. If only someone could invent a device that would let you talk to someone over long distances . . ."

My brother snorts a laugh. "That's crazy, dude. But it would be nice."

The thing about Chug is that he trusts me. Me and Mal and Lenna and, yeah, even Jarro. Chug knows his limitations and he knows our strengths, and even though he seems like the kind of guy who would have an ego problem with that, Chug doesn't. That's why he just hands me his helmet, then starts pulling off his chest plate, pants, and boots. He knows I'm the smartest, and he knows that I'm a faster climber than he is. And he knows that if I'm volunteering to do this, it's the only way.

I switch armor with him and am soon decked out in netherite. Chug is in diamond armor now, scratching at his armpits because I made that set a little smaller to fit my frame.

"Be careful," he warns.

"I'm always careful," I reply.

He hugs me, pounding me on the back, and then turns to jog for Mal's ridge.

I hurry past him, and once I'm around an outcropping, I start climbing up the cliffs. There are plenty of little goat trails and lots of handholds, and I'm glad I didn't let Chug attempt this. I'm about half his size and pretty agile, so as long as I focus upward and keep on climbing, I feel confident. I can't see Lenna from here, but I think I'm high enough, so I creep around the ridge, hurrying from rock to bush and trying to stay hidden. I finally see Lenna, but once I get to where she is, there isn't much cover.

I really hope this works.

Sword drawn, I hurry to Lenna, running, and—oof!

I trip and—

Skid across the stone on my belly.

The armor helps cushion the blow, but now I'm gasping for breath on my hands and knees without any cover.

"Tok?"

Lenna shoots her bow and stares back at me in confusion before reaching for her next arrow.

"We have to escape to the cave," I wheeze, most of the breath knocked out of me. "I've got it all set up. This is a plan. Come on."

"If I stop shooting it, it's going to kill us all," she says, to the point and unemotional.

"Then we need to distract it."

"I hoped shooting it a hundred times would distract it, but I was wrong," she snaps, never missing a shot.

A black skull zooms toward us, and I roll out of the way. It hits the ground a few lengths behind us and detonates, and I'm showered in rock dust. I have to think. That's what I do. Chug's weapon is a sword, and Lenna's weapon is her bow and arrows, and my weapon is my brain, but it's hard to think when a floating torso is trying to explode you.

But how do you distract a monster that's directly focused on you?

Right.

Make it focus somewhere else.

"Do you know where Creeperhead is?" I ask.

Lenna doesn't turn to me as she speaks. "Yeah. He's on the ground. Little green lump. Thinks he's hiding, but I can see him."

"Do you have any flaming arrows left?"

I can't see her grin, but I can hear her chuckle. "I was saving them for our moment of need, but this sounds like something we need. Hold on—he's gonna try to get us while I dig around."

She zips around a boulder and digs through her pockets, and the Wither glides toward us and releases one of its skulls—a blue one. But this one is a lot faster than the others, and I don't know how to stop it. It's headed right for Lenna, and without telling my body to do anything, it's sprinting toward her, sword out. As the skull nears us, I swing my sword, and it whooshes right past my blade and smacks me in the chest, and the world explodes around me in a flash of white against the dark sky. I slam into the ground on my back, ears ringing, mouth tingling like I've been chewing on gravel. I can't hear anything, and the sword falls out of my hand.

"You okay?" Lenna asks—or at least, that's what her moving mouth seems to say. I can barely hear anything.

I can only shake my head. Something is very, very wrong, but I don't know what.

"Just . . . hit . . . Creeperhead . . ." I grind out.

Lenna sends a flaming arrow at the Wither, nocks another, then aims downward and releases the string. There's a scream, and she grins in triumph, which tells me her arrow flew true. Focusing on Creeperhead now, the Wither glides down toward the ground, releasing another skull, and Lenna pulls me to standing and tugs me along the ridge. We keep low and take advantage of every boulder and bit of scrub we can find to avoid recapturing the Wither's attention.

It seems pretty focused on Creeperhead, so I decide to stop focusing on it. Just moving takes all my attention. My body doesn't seem to want to work. My arms are weak, my legs exhausted like I've already run a mile. My head hurts, my mouth is dry—am I sick? This is so—

I don't even know.

That's how bad I feel. I'm forgetting words.

Me. Tok. The genius.

There's something familiar about this, though.

We've experienced this before.

Or—Chug has.

"Can you make it down?" Lenna asks, pointing to the little goat trail I used to get up here.

I nod and start climbing down, but I feel clumsy and stupid. My fingers will barely hold on to any rocks. I nearly fall at one point, and Lenna catches me by my sleeve. The goat trail becomes the biggest challenge of my life as I struggle not to give up and just roll off the mountain to get it over with. I fall the last few feet and land in a heap.

Lenna skids down and hitches me up under my arm.

"'Sa good thing I'm not Chug," I mumble. "You couldn't carry him."

"Shut your piehole," Lenna says, struggling to pull me along.

"Are you guys talking about pie?"

I could weep with joy when my brother appears and picks me

up like a wayward cat. As he runs for the cave entrance, I watch the Wither shooting skulls at the ground. I can't see Creeperhead, though. I hope he loses this fight, whoever he is. I hope the monster he created or brought or found or whatever destroys him, because I've never felt this terrible in my entire life and it's all his fault.

The cave entrance is so narrow that Chug can't carry me through. I wobble in on my own feet and then collapse forward onto the cold stone. Chug drags me in to get me out of the way as Lenna bounds in. Mal is ready, and she fits two dirt blocks into the entrance, making the cliff face look like there was never an opening there at all.

It has to work. It has to trick the Wither, and maybe Creeperhead, too.

I flop on my back and close my eyes.

It's ironic that I called that thing a Wither when it's me that's withering away.

20.

CHUG

I don't know what's wrong with my brother, but it's bad. He looks as terrible as Mal did when she got hit with that Potion of Poison.

"Was it a potion?" I ask Lenna.

She shakes her head. "The monster—"

"Wither," Tok splutters, because of course he's got to be a know-it-all while he's dying.

"I was going to call it a tri-skull," she says.

"Argue about it later!" I bark. "What got him?"

"One of the skulls hit him. He was trying to shield me. He went downhill pretty fast."

"Yeah, totally fell down the hill," Tok mumbles.

I make a garbled yelp. "He's making puns. That means he feels really terrible."

"I feel like death."

"No! Bro! No! We're gonna get you better. Can you reach your pocket? Get me a Potion of Healing?"

Tok's hand is pale and wrinkly as he reaches into his pocket and pulls out a Potion of Healing. I'd know that swirly magenta color anywhere. I help him drink it, because he can't even lift the bottle, and he gulps it down through lips gone blue and cold. Mal and Jarro are with us now, too, and we all wait breathlessly to see the fast healing his potions provide, but nothing happens.

If anything, he looks worse.

"It's not working. Tok, do you have a better potion? A super potion? Maybe you feel better and just look—"

"Wither effect," he murmurs through lips that barely move.

"I know the Wither affected you, but what do we do about it?"

"A Potion of Regeneration, maybe?" Mal prods.

Tok flaps a hand. "Wither effect. Won't work. Can't remember . . ."

"What do you mean, it won't work? Your potions always work!" I know I sound like I'm begging, and it definitely feels like I am. I can feel my eyes tearing up.

"If one potion won't work, another probably won't, either," Lenna says.

"But potions always work!" I roar.

"Tell that to Nan," Tok whispers. "Wither effect . . . drink . . . need drink . . ."

Mal snaps her fingers. "Tok's right. Potions don't always work. When I was sick, remember what Nan said to give me?"

I gasp. "Milk! It's the same thing that happened to me when that withered skeleton hit me in the Nether. Why didn't you say so, bro?"

Tok weakly raises an eyebrow. "My brain is withered."

"But we don't have milk," I say, the terror of it landing heavily on my chest. "Somebody go grab a goat! You can milk a goat, right? When they're not ramming you in the rear?"

Jarro has been a little outside the circle all this time, listening but not really contributing, but now he digs around in his pocket and pulls out a bucket. "Might taste a little bit like mushrooms," he says. "But I milked all the mushmoos on that island, just in case."

"You're the best, bud! I'm so glad you went to the mushroom island with us! And you called them mushmoos!" I want to hug Jarro, but first I need to keep my brother from dying. I take the bucket of milk and dribble a little into Tok's mouth. He sputters before he starts swallowing, and I sigh in relief.

It's working.

It's working!

The change is almost instantaneous. His skin pinks up, his eyes open, and all the gross wrinkles and puckered bits melt right back into normal, healthy Tok.

"Cookie?" he grumbles, and Lenna hands him one, and he devours it in two bites. My stomach grumbles, but now is not the time to beg for cookies.

"Bro, are you good?" I ask.

Tok sits up on his own and rubs his eyes. "Yeah, I feel fine now. But that . . . that was terrible. I've never felt anything like that in my entire life. Like my soul was just draining away, and my brain leaked out my ears. Let's definitely not go out the way we came in."

Mal has her pickaxe in hand, and now that Tok is out of the jaws of death, she heads farther into the cave, past where the horses are nervously milling in a puddle of light cast by a circle of torches.

"I think—" she starts, but then she says, "Ah! No! No! Absolutely not!" and I realize this is because a spider has skittered out of the darkness right at her. I leap to my feet to help, but she takes it down with a few quick swipes of her pickaxe.

"As I was saying," she continues, unflappable, "Our first priority is getting the enchanted golden apple, but we can't just leave that Wither thing hanging around. What if it finds our town, like Krog's vexes? Or just shows up randomly to kill some travelers? I know we didn't unleash it, but it feels like we need to end it."

"Well, if the place we're going has loot in chests, it stands to reason that there might be better armor or weapons or enchanted objects," Tok says. He stands up, and I reach to help him, but he grins and swats my hand away. "We can load up with everything we have and take it by surprise. We know that ranged weapons are the best attack against it, so we need as many enchanted bows and as many arrows as possible. And we need that trident, too. I bet I can find an enchantment that will make it return after you throw it."

"That would be so cool," I say, pulling the trident out of my pocket and enjoying the way it glows in the torchlight. I tug at my chest plate. "And speaking of armor . . ."

"Let's switch back. Because I'm guessing armor that's a little too small is a lot more uncomfortable than armor that's too big."

I try to take a deep breath and fail. "I feel like an overripe pumpkin."

Tok and I trade out our armor, and I sigh in relief as I feel the cool press of netherite again. I'm glad he was wearing it when he got hit by that Wither's skull, but now that we're inside a cave where we know how things work, it's better if I'm outfitted to run directly at any mobs that want to tussle with us.

We know how caves work. Yep, any cave is like any other cave. Nothing tricksy like an ocean monument. Just stone, darkness, hostile mobs, random bats in your face, and the occasional stronghold. Easy peasy. No more nasty surprises.

Once Tok is certain he's back to normal, we fill up on food and say goodbye to the horses before heading deeper into the cave. Poppy and the cats go with us. Lenna's wolf is a great fighter, and Candor and Clarity keep the creepers away. If only they kept Creeperhead away, too. I hope the Wither takes care of him for us. We can still hear muffled explosions from outside. Going deeper into the cave and farther from the Wither definitely feels like the right idea.

"Do you still feel like we're being followed?" I ask Lenna.

She shakes her head. "If Creeperhead didn't follow us in through the entrance when it was open, he's not in here. He might not even know there's a cave. Maybe he'll think we just ran."

"Maybe," I say.

I don't think so, though. I'm worried that Creeperhead will see the horses' hoofprints going right into the cliff wall, but I'm not going to say that. Either it's a dumb idea and I'll sound stupid, or I'm on the right track and it will make everyone panicky. Wherever Creeperhead is, our job is clear: Go into this cave and find the enchanted golden apple.

As we venture into the big, echoing cavern, Mal and I go in front in our armor with our swords while Tok and Jarro hold torches to light the way. Lenna goes last with her bow and arrow ready, and it's not long before she's taken down a skeleton and collected its dropped arrows. The cave seems natural, not like someone mined it. The walls are rough, the ceiling is jagged, and the floor isn't particularly flat. It's big and open, at least, and quiet enough that we can hear the mobs before they get anywhere close. Cobwebs hang from every craggy corner, and there's not a single sign that anyone has ever been here before.

But they must've been, because we have a map, right?

"Does that map say where the stronghold is?" I ask.

Mal puts away her sword and pulls out the map, and I dart forward to take down a zombie that was shuffling too close.

"Nope. It shows the cliffs and the opening, but then there's just a little symbol that kind of looks like the one for a village."

"Is there an underground village?" Lenna asks, perking up. "I didn't know they existed."

"Maybe," Mal says. "But it's kind of an odd color. Light teal. Maybe that's just the symbol for a stronghold."

A slime appears, and Mal and I work together to take it down. Lenna shoots another skeleton and grabs its arrows. Jarro and Tok carry their torches. A bat swoops in out of nowhere, and Jarro shrieks and drops to the ground. Once upon a time, I might've made fun of him, or at least joked about it, but I can tell he's more twitchy than normal. I can't imagine what it would be like to be attacked by some random stranger in a mask, and I wish I could tell him how brave he is without making him feel even weirder. Instead, I just silently hold out a hand and pull him up.

The cave isn't particularly exciting. It leads us this way and that, up and down through twisting hallways like caves do. I'm about to complain about how boring the cave is when I notice a weird glow up ahead.

"Is that a torch?" Mal asks, seeing the same thing.

We speed up, and when we go up over a little hill, the cave opens up into . . .

Whoa.

This cave is just built different.

Caves are usually gray and black and dark and filled with scary dudes that want to kill you, but this cave didn't get that message.

It's beautiful, with vibrant green vines trailing down from the ceiling to the ground, speckled with glowing fruit. Huge pink flowers hang from the ceiling like lamps, sprinkling golden pollen through the air with the haze of a glittering rain. Soft green moss coats the rocks and ores underfoot and climbs up every surface like fuzzy fur. Flowered bushes sprout here and there on the floor, giving everything a pop of pink amid the gently swaying grasses. I don't normally pay any attention to things I can't fight, eat, or hug, but the plants in this cave are just . . . lush.

"Am I hallucinating?" Tok says. "Did the Wither potion coat my eyeballs? Because caves are usually dead and this place is very, very alive."

Lenna has already traded her bow and arrow for her book and pen. "A new biome! I've never seen anything like this in Nan's books. A lush cave. We discovered something new! And I think I hear water somewhere nearby . . ."

She leads us deeper into the cave, her pen speeding across the paper as she tries to capture every detail of this amazing new find. Me being me, I pluck one of the glowing berries from a vine and pop it in my mouth before anyone can stop me.

"Chug!" Mal hisses.

"Tastes like sunshine," I say, eyes rolling back as the berry bursts on my tongue. "Probably not poison."

Jarro slips a few berries in his pocket, and judging by his evil grin, I know exactly what he's thinking—the look on his mom's face when she sees that he's growing a new kind of berry back home will be absolutely priceless. Lenna takes a few berries, too, as well as samples of all the plants we pass. She can't reach the giant flowers near the top of the cave, but I'm sure she's trying to figure out a way to get one. Mal is watching us all like a disapproving teacher, and keeps muttering about how we need to hurry, but then she notices some weird ore on the wall and hurries over with her pickaxe.

"You guys, come here!" Lenna calls. "Chug, you're going to die!"

"I don't want to die," I tease, but I do hurry over, because if she's calling me in particular, that means it's either food or—

It's a cute animal.

And yes, I am dead.

Dead of cute.

"What are they?" I ask as I watch two little pudgy goofuses swim around in a pool. One is pink and one is yellow, and they look like—I don't even know! Like an adorable turtle without a shell, or a fish mixed with a kitten who accidentally grew his whiskers on his head.

"Axolotls," Lenna says, like that explains anything.

"That's probably the worst thing you've named something yet," I tell her. "You should call them cavepuppies. Or fishkittens. Or nakieturtles."

"I didn't name them. I read about them in one of Nan's books. Apparently people in cities sometimes keep them as pets. They have to live in water, but they're not dangerous."

"Axawhatwhats," I murmur, reaching into the water to try to tickle one under the chin. "I love them."

I sit down with my feet in the pool and watch the axolotls play. A little waterfall drips musically down from somewhere overhead, and big, flat leaves that look broad enough to stand on spread over the crystal blue water.

"I wonder," I say to myself.

I look around. Lenna is sketching, Mal is mining, Jarro is harvesting berries, and Tok has pulled out his brewing stand to work because that's just the way he is. No one is paying attention to little old me.

"Sorry if this doesn't work," I say to the axolotls, and then I take a running leap and successfully land on the big, flat leaf.

"Chug, what are you doing?" Lenna asks.

"I'm discovering dripleafs. Because they drip. And I sat on it first, so I get to name it."

She blinks at me and says, "It does look drippy. You can have this one."

I hop from dripleaf to dripleaf and swing from a vine, but then a skeleton shows up and I have to stop playing and get back to business.

The sound of sword on bone seems to wake up the others, as Mal stops mining and turns to us, horrified and . . . ashamed? "Oh, no. I got distracted. I can't believe I let myself do that. Nan is waiting, you guys. We need to hurry."

"To be fair," Lenna says carefully, looking up from her book, "The last time we took a little break to explore on the mushroom island, we found the milk that saved Tok's life. If we hadn't stopped there, and if Jarro hadn't been curious about the new mob, we might've lost Tok for real. Even when we're in a hurry, it's still beneficial to take a moment to look around."

"After a fight like that, we need moments like this," Tok agrees; it's so good to see him upright again. "The good to balance out the bad."

Lenna nods. "The magical to cancel the terrible."

"The pie to remove the taste of the beetroot!" I add. Yes, I'm thinking about pie again.

Mal sighs and nods. "Okay, that's fair. But we've had enough pie for now. There's nothing made by people here, so the enchanted golden apple must be deeper in the cave system, and we need to get going."

Tok packs up his workstation, Jarro stops picking berries, and Lenna reluctantly puts away her book just in time to take down a baby zombie with her bow. I tell the axolotls goodbye and wish I could take one with me, but I'm pretty sure they need more water than I can carry in my pocket, plus I wouldn't want to jostle them if we got in a fight.

Mal takes the lead again, and we follow her past vines and pools, waterfalls and lavafalls, flowers and mosses and ores. This lush cave might be the prettiest place I've ever seen, and I wonder if it will just go on forever. I sure do hate to leave it behind. I'm always on the side of more pie, whether it's real or just a metaphor—and yes, I know what a metaphor is. It's when you say a thing is another thing but really it's the original thing but it's *like* another thing. Duh.

As we leave the lush cave and the tunnel begins to narrow and darken, and as we begin to descend deeper underground I realize I have a very, very bad feeling about wherever we're going next. We had our pie. So where's the next big, bad beetroot?

21.

JARRO

 I wish we could just stay in the lush cave forever, because it's calm and pretty and bright and no one is trying to kill me. Well, except the zombies and skeletons, but Lenna and Chug take care of them before they can get remotely close. I feel safe in this cave, much safer than I did in the Nether. And I'm really excited about the berries. People back home will be overjoyed to have a new fruit to try, and my mom is going to freak out when she has yet more competition for the sweet berry empire she's in the process of rebuilding by stealing from me.

But of course we can't stay. We're on a mission, and we've already lost too much time. Mal's Nan might even be—

Well, I'm not going to say it, but she's super old and very sick. We have to hurry.

As we walk, the cave stops being beautiful and friendly and goes back to being a normal cave. If not for the torches we carry, the darkness would be impenetrable. Mal might enjoy mining and being underground, and Lenna might've grown up in a mine and find it cozy, but I feel deeply uncomfortable down here, no pun intended.

In the way of caves, the route twists and turns and leads us up and down. Every time a zombie moans or a skeleton's arrow thwacks, I startle and cringe, but Lenna, Chug, and Mal make quick work of them. Tok and I walk together with our torches, almost like we're being escorted by the more powerful fighters.

"Doesn't this make you want to scream?" I ask him, right after a bat dive-bombs us.

"Not really," he says. "It's not as bad as the Nether, so I tell myself I can get through it. It's just discomfort, and discomfort can't kill me."

"It feels like it can," I say after a skeleton's arrow whistles by so close I feel my ponytail twitch.

"But it can't. I think maybe that's something I learned through all my years of failed crafting. Discomfort is what stands between the mundane and the great. If you're not willing to be a little un-comfortable, you'll never do anything truly satisfying." He chuck-les. "And you also have to be willing to go without eyebrows for a while, in my case. Everything I want to do somehow seems to in-volve gunpowder."

So I try to play Tok's game. I tell myself that the cold, clammy darkness isn't frightening, it's just uncomfortable. The weight of a million pounds of stone overhead isn't a threat, it's a promise of better things to come. The reaching claws of zombies and flap-ping wings of bats aren't dangers, they're obstacles.

I don't believe a bit of it, but at least trying to believe gives my brain something to do besides internally scream.

The cave narrows to a twisting, turning tunnel and leads us

down, down, down, and I lose all sense of which way we came. There are no turnoffs, or at least there's no point at which we're forced to make a definitive decision that could very well be the wrong one. Mal leads us unceasingly into the dark, the first to meet every mob that comes at us, and Lenna follows, arrows pinging off into the darkness behind us. We begin to see strange blocks appear here and there, black with glowing flecks of teal that seem to pulse like they're alive. I don't want to touch them—they just look . . . wrong. Lenna stops to mine one, looking a bit guilty but needing a sample. I'm surprised that it doesn't scream when the pickaxe hits it.

Time loses meaning. Is it day or night? Are we up or down? There's no way to tell. It's just an endless nothingness, and I want to lie down and cry.

And then the cave widens out again, and we all breathe a sigh of relief. I hope for more glow berries or the welcome signs of another lush cave, but this cave seems less natural and more . . .

Planful.

The light of my torch shows me an even floor, and when Chug says, "Yeah, stronghold!" I nod along.

This is good. Things built by people are logical. They follow rules. At some time in the past, a person said, "This would be the smartest, safest, most reasonable way to do things," and then they directed a bunch of other people to build according to that effective design. That makes sense to me.

But as we get farther in, something doesn't feel quite right.

It's not just the blue-speckled blocks, it's everything.

There's a structure down here, but it's not a stronghold. The lines are straight and planful, but it's not like the outside of a house. It's like . . . the outline of an entire city, but so old that everyone who even knew it ever existed has died. Chunks are missing as if it's so ancient they've crumbled away.

If I squint, I can see it stretching out before us. There are walls, hallways, channels of water. Cold, cyan lanterns are placed here and there, glowing with eldritch power, and odd blocks here and there on the ground almost seem to wave floating tentacles that remind me of both squid and seaweed. Mal leads us down the main—promenade? Road? Hallway?—and it's hard to tell what this place must've looked like, long ago. This might've been an arch, once. There are no roofs, no furniture, no people, but the structure of their ancient city remains, the lines perfectly straight and lit at intervals by a light so cold and alien that I'd almost rather just have the darkness, thanks. At least torches are warm and feel vaguely alive. This light, on the other hand, is like burning ice. It's oddly silent, and I realize that the ground we're walking on is made of tightly packed wool or covered with a carpet, which is . . . very peculiar. It's almost like this place wants us to be quiet. Our feet barely make the slightest shushing noise. It's eerie.

"A chest!" Chug says.

As if in response, there's a weird, otherworldly shriek. Chug freezes. The world goes dark for about ten seconds, and my head goes tight, like a fist is squeezing my brain.

"Ow!" Tok says, hands on his temples.

"You felt that, too?" Lenna asks.

Mal is looking at us, brow scrunched down. "I think we all did."

"Well, if it's over, let's see what's in that chest." Chug darts into a side room, flipping open the top to see what loot is inside.

But his glee is short-lived.

The shriek happens again, and I immediately close my eyes and grab my head.

Not that it helps. There's that fist again, squeezing.

Chug holds out his hands to show us what he's found.

"Why is this chest full of books and balls of snow?" he says glumly.

"Shh!" Lenna whispers. "Please stop making noise."

Chug tries to talk, but Mal puts a finger to her lips and shakes her head in warning.

Tok darts past me and silently grabs the books, and Chug holds up the snowballs as if to ask if anyone wants them.

Lenna shrugs and reaches in to take them, which makes sense. She often collects the things we don't quite understand. She slides a bunch of snowballs into her pocket, and I know she's glad for Nan's clever pocket trick, because otherwise, she'd just have wet pants.

Tiptoeing over to the chest, Mal peers in and frowns. I know she's looking for an enchanted golden apple, but the chest is empty. Chug might like pranks, but he wouldn't pretend it wasn't there if it really was. We all know time is of the essence.

I can tell that Chug is pretty bummed. Even if he's not supposed to talk, he's a pretty expressive guy, and his whole body is slumped over like he doesn't have any bones. I guess he was hoping for enchanted weapons and armor instead of books and snow, or at least to find the very thing that brought us here.

I point to the next opening in the arched hallway and give a smiling shrug as if to say, "Maybe in the next chest," because someone has to stay positive even if they're freaking out on the inside.

We head back out into the grand hallway and continue through the darkness. After that weird shriek and whatever it did to our eyes and heads, we're sneaking carefully, trying to walk on the wool or carpets. Stairs go up to nowhere and windows open onto dark vistas, and I keep seeing this same shape everywhere, almost like a head with horns? Maybe it's a statue of some long-gone hero, or maybe they just liked that particular design.

Mal motions us over to a wide carpet. "Is it just me, or is it really weird that there are no mobs here?" she asks in the tiniest whisper. It doesn't set off the shrieking, thank goodness. "I keep waiting to hear zombies or skeletons, or for a spider to drop out of the sky, and nothing happens."

"It's almost *worse* that nothing happens." Tok is kind of hunched over, a torch in one hand and his sword awkwardly held in the other. "When the mobs come, we know how to deal with that, but when there aren't any, it makes me wonder . . ."

"Who killed them all?" Chug whispers.

"Or what they're so afraid of," Tok finishes.

I didn't think of that, and my level of panic goes up a notch. What's so dangerous that zombies and skeletons and slimes are terrified of it?

But that can't be it. Maybe they can't spawn here because of the weird lanterns, or maybe it's not good hunting since there clearly hasn't been any fresh meat around in a thousand years. Or maybe whoever built the city was as clever as Tok and invented hidden machines that keep the bad guys out. Maybe that's what the shrieker is for. After all, we grew up in Cornucopia, which has torches every seven blocks in every direction, but we never questioned whether those torches were weird and wouldn't naturally be there. Maybe whatever mechanism keeps the bad guys out of this place is as obvious yet mystifying as the torches were when I was a little kid, back before I was forced to go on an adventure into the Overworld and learn what spawns in a place without light.

"Whoa," Mal and Lenna say at the same time, stopping suddenly.

As if on cue, a shriek rends the air, and we all double over, hands over our ears.

When my eyes work again, I look beyond them and see what they're seeing, and—

Whoa is right.

There's a ton of that weird stuff growing on the ground and surrounding structures, that creepy but beautiful deep greenish black substance with glowing cyan speckles. It's almost like the opposite of netherrack, like some kind of deep, dark moss. It pulsates like it's alive, and I can't figure out if it's a plant or an ore or what.

"What is it?" Lenna whispers as Mal takes a closer look.

"I don't know, but I've never seen anything like it. Maybe Nan will know."

"I don't think Nan knows anything about any of this," Lenna says. "She knows about mining and caves, but not about the lush caves, and not about this—this ancient city in the deep dark. It's not in any of her books, at least, and she's never mentioned it in all her stories from when she was a girl. I need to sketch it—"

"We can't stop." Mal pockets the block and keeps walking. "We're so close. We just have to find the right chest."

She jumps down onto the lower floor and laughs. "Speaking of which—a chest!"

But she wasn't quiet enough, and the shriek goes off. I'm almost getting used to it. At least the viselike headache goes away as soon as the darkness recedes. Maybe it's just a temporary sort of thing.

We follow Mal, and I don't like the way the dark green blocks feel under my boots, spongey like a living thing. She quietly opens the chest that was hiding under a ledge and hands some snowballs to Lenna, some books to Tok, and a bunch of wool to me—but I don't have room in my pockets, so Lenna takes that, too.

We hurriedly sneak through the little underground room and up some stairs, then cross a bridge over some lava. Up ahead, there's some sort of giant portal glowing with creepy blue fire. Mal hurries up to it and starts trying to mine a block of the weird, dark stone, but it won't budge. The shriek starts up, we all double over, and then we can see again. Mal looks down at her diamond pickaxe, confused.

We huddle around her, and she whispers, "This stuff is harder than obsidian. When those guardians in the ocean monument blasted us and made it impossible to mine, it felt like something was wrong with me, but this feels like the stone is just unbelievably hard."

"Harder than diamond?" Tok asks, skeptical.

"Harder than anything. Like it's been reinforced somehow. And the fire—why is it blue?"

"Why is anything anything?" Chug asks. "Why does netherrack look like meat, and why do baby zombies like to ride stuff? Who knows? Let's just find the next chest, get that enchanted golden apple, and get out of here before something worse happens. I'm getting real sick of all that shrieking."

He's clearly bored and would vastly prefer an attack to exploring an abandoned city. Not me. I'll take quiet boredom over enemies, any day.

Around the other side of the flaming structure, we find torches everywhere, but they're not quite torches. They smell a little like beeswax, and I'm the first to pick one up because I have to know if I'm right.

"Wax torches!" I say, delighted, and of course, one of the shriekers goes off. I can see it, this time—it's a block with four big teeth poking up and a mouth of swirling greenish black. It almost looks like an animal in the ground, mouth open to eat unsuspecting travelers. It doesn't seem alive, at least. As soon as my head stops pounding, I take the wax torch and stick it in my pocket. I always wondered if bees had a use besides honey, and now I can think of all sorts of uses for this new invention. I bet one would look really festive on top of a cake.

On second thought, I stow a few more of the wax torches in my pocket—after extinguishing the flames, of course, because pocket magic is great but flaming pants are not. We continue sneaking through the abandoned city, past walls and lanterns and lava, and not a single living thing stirs. The farther we go, the worse I feel. We could explore this structure for a hundred years and never see every inch of it.

We go down some stairs, and Chug does a little dance and points at a chest. He and Mal tiptoe over and silently open it.

"Yes!!" Chug shouts, triggering another ghastly shriek.

When we can see again, Mal holds up a big, round apple, golden and glowing, and I can't help grinning with her. Hope and joy bloom in my chest, not only because we have what we came for, what we need to heal Nan, but also because now we can get out of this horrid place. We all do a silent dance of happiness for a moment, and all is well in the world.

Mal slides the apple into her pocket and hands around the rest of the loot—enchanted iron leggings, a music disc, coal, a bone, more snowballs, and an enchanted book. I actually want the leggings, since they look too big for everyone else, so I drop some mushrooms and tuck the pants in my pocket for later. There's no way I'm changing down here. Even if it seems abandoned, it feels like . . . I don't even know. Not like someone is watching us. More like something is waiting to happen.

"Should we go a little farther and check out a few more chests while we're here?" Chug whispers.

Mal shakes her head. "No way. We got the apple, and now we get out."

She turns to head back in the other direction, and Chug violently flails his arms in silent disappointment, accidentally smacking Tok, who says, "Ouch, bro!"

As if in answer, there's another ghastly screech from the other side of the wall.

"Maybe it's an underground animal that hates noise. I need to sketch it." Lenna hurries down a few steps to peek around the wall and says, "Huh. That's different."

After she says that maybe it's an animal, I'm suddenly struck by the notion that it might be in pain. That shriek it made, whatever it is, wasn't happy or calm. It was tortured and awful. I hurry to join Lenna, and when I peek around the wall, I struggle to figure out what I'm seeing.

There is no animal—at least, nothing that looks like an animal. It's a decently sized room full of that greenish black substance, and several of the blocks with tentacles, and several of the ones that look like hungry mouths. It's almost like a dark garden of creepy blocks.

"What are those?" I ask Lenna.

"I have no idea," she whispers back. "But I almost feel like they can hear me."

Chug leans in with us, takes one look at the room, and says, way too loudly, "Oh, gross!"

As if in response, all of the tentacle blocks start waving madly, and the mouth blocks glow with eerie green light. We hear that horrible, grating shriek again, and the entire world goes dark.

22.

LENNA

 I want to sketch these weird, mouth-like blocks, but nothing that makes a sound that terrible can possibly have my best interests in mind. I again wait for the darkness to recede and for my head to stop squeezing itself; I'm almost getting used to it. As I reach into my pocket for my book, I realize that something is very, very wrong.

We've heard that shriek several times already but now . . .

Something changed.

I grab my bow and arrow instead.

"What's happening?" Chug whispers in the darkness.

I turn toward him. "I think you made it mad."

"Made what mad?"

I frown. "I don't know yet. But we're going to find out."

The darkness fades, but my head doesn't feel any better. There's a pressure there, like something sitting on my skull. Mal, Tok, and Jarro join us, and Mal gasps when she sees the creepy garden. "What are those things?" she whispers.

"I don't know, but I think they're reacting to our noise, or maybe vibrations."

Mal gingerly steps down into the field of speckled blackish green, the blocks squishing underfoot. She pulls out her pickaxe and tiptoes up to the waving tentacle block, but before she can get there, we hear a horrible rumbling from the wide patch of green-black ground beyond.

"Mal, get back here," I say, but she's Mal, so she's already trying to mine the wavy tentacle block, which just makes the other blocks gurgle and shriek. I want to put my hands over my ears, but I have to be ready with my bow and arrow. Whatever's happening definitely doesn't feel friendly or safe.

"What . . . is that?" Jarro points past Mal, and my blood runs cold as ice.

The ground is buckling, folding in, grumbling and rumbling. Mal sees it, too, and runs back to us, forgetting the tentacle block entirely.

Something begins to break through the crack in the ground— something big. Huge claws tear at the stone and sharp horns appear, ripping their way free. The beast crawls up from underground, roaring and clicking, and slowly turns.

My entire body goes numb as it faces us.

I can barely see it, thanks to this strange darkness that's clouding my vision. This thing—it's enormous, with a massive head and shoulders and long arms tipped in talons. Its chest—is it open? I can't tell, it's not right—turns toward us, the ominous thump of its heart filling the cavern. I think I see a flash of teeth, but I don't see any eyes.

"In case anyone is wondering, I don't plan on trying to hug it," Chug says, and in response, the beast turns directly toward him with an inquisitive growl.

Beside me, Tok grabs my hand, the one holding the bow, and raises it while pointing at the beast, but I shake my head. This creature, this warden guarding the darkness, is not a normal sort of mob. It's bigger, stronger. We woke it with noise. It has no eyes.

It must track by sound.

Maybe if we're quiet enough and don't engage it, it will leave us alone.

I give Tok a significant look and point at my ear. Understanding dawns on his face, and he nods.

Chug raises his sword to go fight, but Tok and I both grab his shirt and pull him back.

This thing is huge.

There's no way we can beat it.

"Sneak away," I whisper.

"No time for sneaking. Run!" Chug shouts.

And now we have no choice.

Tok is the first around the wall, then Mal and Chug and Jarro. As always, I go last, but as I take off running, I hear the beast behind me, stomping wetly as it stalks us. It doesn't seem to run, at least, but it has a relentless rhythm to its gait. It has a strange smell I can't place, and it moves unlike any living thing. As it follows us, its heartbeat speeds up, a pounding threat driving us faster and faster through the ruined city.

We can't beat it with weapons, and I'm beginning to wonder if we can outrun it. Some of us could, but something tells me Tok and Jarro aren't going to be fast enough or have enough stamina. There has to be some way to distract it.

Aha! With noise!

I turn around and shoot, purposefully missing the beast. My arrow clatters on the stone, and I pause to watch as the creature's head swivels toward the arrow lying on the ground.

Yes! It worked! I can distract it with sound. But I don't want to waste arrows, so what can I throw?

As the others run ahead, back the way we came, I reach into my pocket in the darkness and feel around, hunting for something we can spare. If I toss the cookies, Chug will never forgive me, but then again, if this monster kills us, there will be no one to forgive. And then—what? I touch something unexpected, something cold.

Snowballs.

Snowballs!

The monster—the warden, I'll call it—has turned back toward us now—well, back to me, because the others are still running—so I throw one of the snowballs at the wall behind the beast. It roars and spins, lumbering toward the snowball with a rumbling growl, and I take off running down the long stone hallway. I'm glad to be off the greenish black stuff that squishes when I walk and hosts the gross tentacle blocks that sensed us and set the shrieker blocks to shrieking.

Well, I can't call them shrieker blocks. They only shrieked because we were skulking around. So . . . skulk shriekers. I can't believe my mind does this when I'm in danger, but I just need to know what everything is called no matter what. I need to know the rules. Minds are funny like that.

My friends are running up ahead, with Mal and Chug crowded behind Tok and Jarro, herding them forward and urging them to run faster. There's more light that way, as if the warden brings the darkness, so I put on a burst of speed to join them.

Thump, thump, thump.

With each thump of my footsteps, it's as if the warden's heart pulses with—the opposite of light. I can't describe it. It's so much darker than I thought darkness could be.

It's on my trail again, clawed feet squelching and glowing heart beating.

It's faster than it looks, relentless, with a wide stride and an intent posture that suggests it will chase us forever, as long as we make noise, because we can't stop making noise.

If only there were some way to mask our sound . . .

I put on a fresh burst of speed, jogging past Chug and Mal to Jarro. I'm out of breath, my lungs on fire, but I whisper, "Jarro, give me all the wool you have."

The nice thing about Jarro is that he doesn't make jokes like Chug or ask a million questions like Tok—he just does what you tell him to, if he's able. And so he just reaches in his pocket and hands me all the wool he's been collecting while we traveled to add to what I've gathered from the chests down here. Eleven blocks, total. I nod my thanks and stop, letting the others run past me. I throw a snowball behind the warden, and when it turns and lumbers over to investigate the noise, I silently plant two rows of five blocks of wool across the hallway, effectively making a barrier that will also silence our noise.

The warden is done investigating the snowball now, and it turns back toward me, head swiveling like it's trying to find me. I take an experimental step backward, snowball in hand, but the warden doesn't seem to hear it.

Oh, I hope this works.

I throw another snowball, then run a bit and throw another. The warden keeps running after the snowballs. I don't know if it can jump over the wool or break the blocks, so I throw one last snowball down the hallway with all my might and run as fast as I can after my friends.

My legs burn and my breath wheezes, but I know that the

worst thing we can do is stop in this ancient city filled with gloom and wait for the warden to pick up the sound of our hearts beating like gongs. The farther I get from the beast, the more easily I can see again, as if it brings a storm of darkness and we're finally moving beyond its reach. I strain to hear the sound of squelching footsteps and angry roars and a furiously beating heart, but there's no more sign of the warden.

We aren't really sprinting anymore—we can't, and we don't want to set off the shriekers. Tok is limping, Jarro is holding on to a side stitch, Chug and Mal are jogging but clearly suffering. I tag along behind, my body on the verge of giving up. The warden is the most terrifying thing I've ever seen, and I just want to be back outside under the sun or moon or rain. I don't care, as long as I'm not trapped in the darkness anymore. I like caves, but not deep dark ones.

We pass the glowing blue flames and the statue and set off a few shriekers but don't stop to see if there might be more wardens because we just have to get out of here. We finally reach the gate at the edge of the city. It's all dark tunnels from here, but at least our torches work again. No one speaks; we all feel the bone-deep need to be as far away from the warden as possible. Mal takes the lead and sets a less rigorous pace, which is good, because while running down a long, straight hallway is relatively safe, running through twisted, uneven cave tunnels littered with rocks and debris is a recipe for disaster. I'm still in back behind everyone else, and I strain for the sounds of the warden pursuing us further. I am very, very aware that if he catches up, I'll be the first one to feel his wrath.

When I hear the thwack of a skeleton's arrow, I flinch at the sound before pulling out my own arrow and taking it down. I don't bother to go back for whatever it dropped; there's nothing it could drop that's worth getting a step closer to the warden.

It's a good thing that the tunnel is clear and doesn't involve forking paths, because I'm pretty sure we're all about to collapse. I am running through endless night, danger ahead and danger behind, like some kind of terrible dream. It's almost as if I don't draw a complete breath until I see the golden shimmer of glow berries up ahead as we enter the supposed safety of the lush cave.

Mal doesn't stop immediately—she leads us almost all the way back to that first pool we found, where we watched axolotls play and I sat down to sketch. It feels like we've lived an entire lifetime between then and now, and of all the new things we've seen and discovered in our travels, I'm certain that the warden and its ancient city are my least favorites. I'd rather face a monster that's obvious and straightforward than one that requires sneaking around and then makes it impossible to see. The Wither might be terrible, but there's an honesty to it, a simplicity. You know exactly what it's going to do.

Chug immediately collapses down on his back and flinches at the loud clank of armor.

"Can we make noise now?" he whispers. "Is it still following us?"

"I don't think so," I say, voice low and soft, sitting down with my back to a rock. "I stopped hearing it a long time ago. I think maybe it can't leave the darkness. I hope."

"I don't think I ever want to shout again," Tok says quietly.

The rest of us are flopped around the pool, but Mal is pacing and frowning. "We need to eat," she says. "And sleep. We still have to face Creeperhead and that Wither thing once we're back outside. So let's build our shelter in here and pretend it's a normal night."

"Shouldn't we get out of the cave?" Chug asks. "So the ground-grumbler won't get us?"

"The warden," I say. I pull out my book and start sketching it. "That's what I call it. It's like it was guarding that place, you know?"

"But groundgrumbler really rolls off the tongue," he argues.

"But I already wrote down 'the warden.'" I turn my book to show him the entry, and his eyes fly wide when he sees my drawing.

"You're getting really good at drawing, Lenna. It looks even worse than I remember it."

"Well, I got pretty close to it," I say, remembering the scent of its fetid breath and the heavy thump-thump of its hideous, glowing heart.

I hand out some bread, and everyone eats to recover from all that running. Once Mal and Jarro are fortified, they select a good place for our shelter. Mal flattens out the floor while Jarro begins building walls. At least the horses won't be in there with us this time—they have their own paddock near the blocked-up entrance. Which reminds me . . .

I whistle, and there's an answering bark from far off. Soon Poppy is bounding toward me, tongue lolling, her toothy jaws open in a wolfish grin. I pat her and rub her belly and give her a bone while Tok hurries to collect his cats.

"I sure do miss Thingy," Chug says with a sigh.

"Well, you probably shouldn't put an axolotl in your pocket, but you can definitely play with one," I remind him. Soon he's out of his armor and in the pool, swimming around with the flippy little creatures, and Tok is back with both of his cats purring all over him, and everything feels just the tiniest bit closer to normal.

Once the shelter is built and our beds are placed, we eat bread and apples and mutton and glow berries until our bellies are full and we feel completely healed from the rigors of the day. It's so funny how back home, my days are simple: Wake up, bring Nan breakfast, putter around in the garden, practice archery, fuss with books, feed Nan's horse, visit with my friends. Time seems to pass so slowly, sometimes, like I'm just waiting for something to happen. But when we're traveling, it's like an entire month's worth of events and feelings happen in just one day. We have so many experiences, so many sensations. I wish I had a little more quiet time on my own to recover and just space out. I like a mix of both kinds of day, I think. Some slow and sweet and some long and packed. I'm glad this day is over.

As I lie in my bed that night, my wolf at my feet and my friends around me, torches on every wall, I can't stop thinking about the warden. So far on this trip, we've faced three different mobs that we flat-out can't beat. The warden, the Wither, and well, maybe we could beat one elder guardian, but an entire ocean monument full of them? No way. We almost died down there.

When we were little, we didn't know anything existed outside the wall around Cornucopia. And then we went outside the wall and discovered wonderful things—and scary things. Zombies, skeletons, vindicators, witches, evokers, creepers. At first they beat us, but then we learned new skills and collected new loot and they became familiar and beatable. On our next trip, we faced off with humans who wanted to hurt us, and we learned to beat them, too. But on this trip, we're learning a valuable new lesson: No matter how great you think you are, there are still some things that are too big for you to face, and you have to know when fighting isn't the answer. That doesn't mean I think the Elders back home are right to keep the wall up and further restrict our ability to venture out into the Overworld, but it does mean that there's value in teaching children they're not invincible. No matter how tough you are, there's always something bigger than you out there. There's nothing wrong with running away when it's the best choice. Sometimes, survival is enough.

I don't know if I'll ever be able to face a warden, even with my friends to back me up, but you can bet I'm going to make sure that later generations know about it. That's why I carry that book with me everywhere I go and sketch everything I find. Knowledge is always better than ignorance. I always want to be learning.

I guess tomorrow we'll learn if it's possible to fight the Wither and live.

23

MAL

I'm the kind of person who wakes up ready to go. Back home, I hop out of bed and hurry out to take care of the cows because they depend on me and so do my parents. When we're out adventuring, I hop out of bed ready to face the day's challenges, and today, that means we open up the cave to see whether Creeperhead and the Wither are out there waiting for us.

There's an air of foreboding as we pack up our beds and break down the shelter. I think the warden gave everyone a new and unwelcome sense of fear. Even Chug is quiet as he eats and sorts through his pockets. Tok pulls out his traveling workshop and uses the enchanted books we found to boost various pieces of armor so that everyone has enhanced protection. Both of Chug's swords are enchanted now, plus his chest plate and helmet and trident. For the rest of us, it's mostly our chest plates, but for Tok and Jarro, it's their boots—so if they have to run away, they'll do it twice as fast. It's a smart way to do things, but I hope they'll never need it. Splitting up like that is a last resort. We're stronger together.

Jarro stands at the paddock, hands on the wood fence, but he's not breaking it down like he should be.

"What's wrong?" I ask him.

He rubs Moo's nose and frowns. "Well, if we know we're walking into a fight, it doesn't seem like a good idea to bring the animals into it, at least not the horses and cats. If we have to go up against the Wither and Creeperhead at the same time, there might be confusion, and Creeperhead might hurt the horses while we're worried about the Wither, or vice versa. Maybe they should stay here, in the paddock, until we know it's safe." He looks up, hopeful. "Or maybe we could use the Potions of Swiftness. Just break down the door and run, leaving Creeperhead and the Wither behind. They deserve each other."

Now it's my turn to frown. "Well, we don't know if the Wither is the kind of monster that waits for you or wanders away, but we do know that Creeperhead is just going to keep following us until he gets what he wants. We don't want to lead him back to town, in case maybe he doesn't know about it yet. We don't want another Orlok on our hands."

"But what if it *is* Orlok?" I can hear the fear in Jarro's voice. "What then?"

I put a hand on his arm, because he's a lot taller than me and it would be weird to try to put a hand on his shoulder. "Then we take him down. Tok's got splash potions to use on people, so we don't have to . . ."

"Hurt them?"

I nod. "Or worse. But we've got to go out there and give this fight the best we have, or else we risk bringing two very dangerous enemies right back to our home. Can you imagine if the Wither was in the Hub? How many people it could hurt? Including little kids? Not to mention the buildings it would destroy." I shake my head. "We can't let that happen. We have to end it. But you know . . ."

I can't believe I hadn't thought of it yet.

"Since we need to fight the Wither with bows and arrows, you and Tok and Chug should focus on Creeperhead. I think you're right—we should leave the animals in here, locked up, and block up the entrance. Then Lenna and I will get under cover and start shooting. You guys find Creeperhead."

Jarro looks like he's not entirely on board with this plan. "And then what?"

"Tie him up, I guess. Once he's unmasked, we'll know better how to deal with him."

I go tell the plan to Tok, Chug, and Lenna. Tok is using every bit of wood we have to make more arrows and a few spare bows, while Lenna and Chug are sorting through their pockets to make sure they have easy access to their weapons. Chug has already given her his trident—albeit reluctantly.

"So what do you think will work on Creeperhead?" I ask Tok.

He doesn't even look up from his work. "Potion of Slowness with a little extra something thrown in. That's what I used for the first trap—the one that made the sheep so slow it was practically frozen. Then he can't fight back or run, not for quite some time."

"Aw, I don't get to beat the snot out of him?" Chug wails.

"Our main goal is to subdue him and unmask him," I say sternly, because much like Poppy the wolf, Chug needs a firm hand.

"Can I just punch him a little? For Jarro?"

I try to keep from smiling too much. "'Subdue' can mean a lot of things. But we don't want to take any risks. If we can hit him with Tok's potion, we need to take that chance. We need to capture him more than you need revenge."

Chug holds up his thumb and first finger. "Just a little revenge?"

"I think being captured by kids using a potion and then being unmasked and made fun of and trotted into town like a sack of potatoes will be pretty terrible for him, bro," Tok says as he works.

"Well, if an elbow finds its way into his gut, then that's just a thing that happens." Chug shrugs and windmills his elbows for a minute. "Elbows are like that sometimes."

I go to Lenna next and find her sitting on the ground with her book spread across her knees and Poppy by her side.

"You ready for this?" I ask.

"I never know if I'll ever be ready for anything," she says in her Lenna-ish way. "But I'm ready to find out, I guess. When you think about it, my job is just to shoot arrows and throw a trident, and I'm good at that, so that's what I'll focus on."

I nod approvingly. "Good point. Same, except the trident part. Are you bringing Poppy with us or keeping her in here with the horses?"

She strokes the wolf's head, and Poppy rolls over for a belly rub. "I feel like she could help with Creeperhead, but if one of the Wither's skulls hit her, she'd probably . . ." Lenna shivers and shakes her head. "I'll leave her in here."

As she leans over to pet Poppy, I get a good view of the book, and her drawing of the warden is startlingly accurate—and scary. "Wow. You got a really close look at the warden, huh?"

"Too close. I wish I knew if there were lots of wardens, down in the deep dark, or if there's only the one."

Now it's my turn to shiver as I think about the possibility that any cavern, any mine I'm digging, could suddenly open up into a vast, ancient city full of blue fire and tentacled blocks waiting to shriek for their protector—or protectors, plural. It definitely makes me slightly less interested in mining—or at least, mining too deep.

I stand and hold out my hand, but Lenna gets up on her own because she doesn't really like being touched all that much. She puts the book in her pocket and tells Poppy to go in the paddock with the horses. Tok, too, is getting ready to go, packing up his workshop and firmly telling Candor and Clarity to stay here with the other animals.

"Sweetie, you wouldn't like it out there," he says, holding Candor up so they're eye to eye. "That thing shoots *skulls*."

Soon we all stand at what would be the cave entrance if I hadn't carefully fitted two blocks perfectly into place. I don't hear any explosions, but that doesn't mean the Wither isn't out there. Maybe it only shoots skulls when its prey is in sight. Lenna has her bow at the ready, while Chug wields his sword, Jarro awkwardly holds his axe, and Tok clutches a sword in one shaking hand and a glass bottle in the other. Truth be told, he's not particularly good with a sword and he's terrible at throwing, so I guess the hope is that he'll get really close to Creeperhead before attempting to use the splash potion.

"Are we ready?" I ask, and I work hard to keep any doubt out of my voice.

"I'm ready to kick some Creeperbutt," Chug growls.

"I'm ready to throw some bottles," Tok mutters, the glass bottle nearly slipping out of his hand.

"I'm ready to shoot arrows and throw tridents," Lenna says.

"I'm . . . yeah, I'm never ready, but I've got milk if anyone takes a hit," Jarro says in the silence that follows.

Chug bumps his shoulder and says, "Dude, that milk is worth its weight in emeralds. And your axe is super enchanted, and you're covered in armor. You're a tall guy. Very muscly. Just tackle Creeperhead and call it a day. He can't surprise you this time, right?"

Jarro nods. "Right. Last time, he just caught me by surprise." He turns to Chug, one eyebrow up. "You think I'm muscly?"

"Shut up," Chug grumbles. "Let's go already."

I pull out the two dirt blocks with my bare hands and shove them in my pocket, trading them for my bow and arrow. Lenna and I charge out first, one to either side of the cave entrance. She immediately climbs up to a ledge and hides behind a boulder while I climb up a tree and find a steady place to sit. It's daytime, at least, but the sky is dark and cloudy. The Wither isn't immediately visible, though, so I look down and watch as Chug barrels out, sword in hand, looking like he's ready to beat the mountain itself into pulp. Next comes Tok, struggling to keep up with his bigger but faster brother, and Jarro, who looks like he mostly wants to run right back into the cave.

It occurs to me that even though I see Jarro as the scaredy-cat among us, it takes enormous courage to run out and face an enemy that's already beaten you once. Out of all of us, he's the only one who's been close enough to Creeperhead to take any damage, and yet here he is, terrified but still willing to do the right thing. He's come a long way from his days as the bully who lay in wait in the Hub to throw rotten potatoes at us. I only hope the rest of us can manage to keep him safe.

Boom!

I cast around for the sound and find a burned spot on the grass below my tree. I don't think it was a Wither skull, though, which is confusing.

"What was that?" I shout.

"TNT!" Tok calls back. "He's throwing TNT!"

He points to the ridge above Lenna, and I see a green creeper's head hiding behind a bush. Lenna can't see him from where she's positioned, so I take careful aim and am just about to release my arrow and show Creeperhead we mean business when there's another explosion, this one much higher up against the mountain.

A black skull.

The Wither has returned.

24.

TOK

 My ears are still ringing from the TNT when the Wither appears with its own explosives. Mal and Lenna immediately begin a volley of arrows, and I know that since I can't help kill the Wither, I need to focus on Creeperhead. From his current vantage point, he can't really distract Mal and Lenna, since he can't throw TNT that far upward, but I wouldn't put anything past him. We can't expect him to stay in one place like a reasonable person trying to avoid being exploded by a floating rib cage with three heads. The only two things we know about this guy are that he wants to hurt us and that we should expect the unexpected.

Beside me, Chug is running the calculus on how difficult it would be for him to climb up the ridge to where Creeperhead is currently hiding, but he must be coming up with the answer I already reached: He's not a great climber, and he can't get there in time. Not before Creeperhead lobs another block of TNT at him. Chug is our best fighter, but in this fight, he might be pretty useless.

So am I, unless I can get close enough to Creeperhead to hit him with one of my potions.

In a best-case scenario, we would've all been practicing with bows and arrows so we could divide our firepower against both enemies, but that's not what we've been doing at all. Why would we? We've never had to fight on two fronts with enemies best taken out with ranged weapons. Most of our fights before this trip have been up close with mindless mobs. And that means that our only answer is cleverness, because this time, brute force isn't going to get the job done.

"Chug." I tug my brother's shirt to get his attention, and he reluctantly scoots back behind the boulder with me. "Can you throw a potion and hit him from here?"

My brother takes the glass bottle and tests it in a hand before shaking his head and giving it back. "I wish I could say yes, but I don't think so. Jarro?"

Jarro's eyes are huge and unblinking, and he's been frozen since we left the cave.

"Jarro!" I say again, but he just shakes his head.

Chug grabs him around the arms and physically lifts him, moving him into our circle. "Look, bud. You've got to snap out of it. We need you."

"Yeah. Okay. Sure." Jarro looks like his brain is somewhere besides his body.

"Can you throw a potion bottle and hit Creeperhead from here?" I ask.

Jarro looks down at his fingers, bone white where they clutch his axe.

His hand is shaking.

"I don't think I can do anything right now," he says. "I'm afraid to waste a potion. Do you want me to try?"

I look down at the potion bottle. I have one more, and that's it. Who knew I would need a lot of fermented spider eye on this journey?

"No. With just two potions, we can't risk it."

Boom!

Another block of TNT lands close enough that it blows our hair back.

Creeperhead's aim is getting better.

The good thing is that with Lenna higher up than him and Mal up in a tree, he can't hit any of us with his TNT. The bad thing is that with the girls distracted by the Wither, we can't get up to where Creeperhead is and deal with him personally without taking a highly explosive block to the face.

If only we could—

Wait.

I know exactly what we have to do.

"Stay here," I tell Chug and Jarro.

Chug grabs my arm. "Bro," he says warningly.

"Bro, I know what I'm doing."

"Do not get exploded! I hereby forbid you to get exploded. And don't get hit by a skull again. You are to stay in one piece with both of your eyebrows."

I nod. "I promise. Plenty of eyebrows."

He squeezes my arm and releases me, and I shove the sword and potion in my pocket and dart over to Mal's tree. Creeperhead throws a TNT block, but I'm ready for it, making a wide arc to swerve away from him. I scurry up her tree, keeping an eye out for more flying skulls, but the Wither seems to be concentrating on Lenna. The cliffs around her are craggy now and blackened with soot, and she keeps having to change her position.

"Tok?" Mal doesn't stop shooting arrows to turn her head. "What's up? Kind of busy here."

"We need to take out Creeperhead."

"I know. That's up to you guys. I have to keep shooting the Wither."

"Mal, Creeperhead is throwing blocks of TNT."

She's peeved now. "I know that, too."

Thwack, thwack, thwack go her arrows.

She's really been practicing.

"Mal, *he's holding blocks of TNT over his head* while he aims."

Her eyes briefly meet mine as she reaches into her pocket for more arrows. "The next time he lifts one up, you shout *Now*, and I'll do my best. I can give you one shot, but we have to worry about the Wither first."

"You can take Creeperhead out in one shot," I tell her. "But you have to do it now."

"Tok, get out of here!"

Only when I hear the desperation in her voice do I see the black skull headed right for us. I clamber down the tree so quickly I end up falling the last few feet, but I miss the explosion from overhead.

I don't miss the gasp of pain, and I barely have time to look up and do my best to catch Mal as she falls out of the tree.

The Wither skull—it got her.

"Tok—take my bow," she murmurs. It falls out of her hand, and she tosses a bunch of arrows on the ground as I do my best to keep her from falling down.

She's almost limp in my arms. Chug rushes out from behind his rock and takes her from me, carrying her like a baby back toward the open cave mouth.

"Tok, hurry!" Jarro shouts, and I look up to see Creeperhead raising a block of TNT overhead.

I snatch up Mal's bow and a stack of arrows and bolt for the safety of the boulder. The TNT lands behind me, throwing me forward. I land hard on my hands and knees, but I'm safe and not too banged up.

"What are we going to do now?" Jarro asks, voice shaking.

I stand and gulp down a Potion of Healing as I take stock of the situation.

Lenna had to abandon her spot after one too many strikes from Wither skulls nearby. She's climbed up another ridge, hunkered down behind another chunk of rock, firing arrow after arrow at the Wither with deadly regularity, hitting the hideous thing with the trident between stacks of arrows and catching it when it returns to her hand. I can tell that all those shots are having an effect—the Wither looks droopy, and every time she hits it, it makes a pained grunt.

Boom!

That explosion is so big that at first I think Lenna has finished off the Wither, but then I see that it's changed—it looks like it has armor now. I hear rattling footsteps and find three huge Wither skeletons tromping toward us, just like the ones we saw in the Nether. I go cold down to my feet, and Jarro gasps.

"We have to retreat," I say. "We have to get back to the cave and rethink this."

"But Creeperhead . . . he'll follow us . . . he'll never stop . . ." Jarro breaks off, teeth chattering.

"Lenna!" I call, stepping out from behind the boulder and into her line of sight.

She doesn't look down. She's shooting intently at the Wither, but her arrows are no longer doing any damage.

Seriously.

A direct hit, and no damage.

What *is* this thing?

"Lenna!" I scream, voice shredding.

She looks at me, annoyed, and I point at the cave. She shakes her head no.

"Arrows aren't working!" I shout.

Boom!

Another TNT block from Creeperhead explodes, close enough to make me stumble back.

I don't know what else I can do. Either she'll see reason or she won't.

We've got to fall back.

"Jarro, come on," I say.

"I . . . I don't know if I can."

He's plastered against the boulder, eyes shut.

Boom!

A black skull turns a nearby tree into a black smudge.

There are so many explosions I don't even know what to do.

Rattle, rattle.

A Wither skeleton appears, and I grab Jarro's arm and yank him, and he runs with me to the cave.

"Boom!"

But this time it's not a sound. It's a voice.

We look up to see Creeperhead standing over us, a TNT block held over his head. I can't see his face, can't see his eyes, but I can hear his cruel laughter. I was so scared, I completely forgot he was directly between us and the cave.

"Who are you?" I shout.

"I'm—" he starts.

Boom!

The TNT block he was holding over his head explodes, throwing him back against the mountain.

Lenna appears on the ridge overhead, bow in hand from her flawless shot at Creeperhead's TNT. "Run! Now!"

So we do.

25.

CHUG

Mal is really, seriously messed up, and there's nothing I can do to help her.

Jarro has all the milk, and he's still outside. I have no potions, no food. I know I should always have some on me, but then I get peckish and figure we'll stumble upon a river or a meadow of sheep or a glorious buffet full of pies and cookies. That last one has only happened once, but a guy can dream.

"Just hold on," I tell her. "Don't worry. Jarro will be here soon."

"Never thought those words would come out of you," she sputters.

"Never thought you'd get yourself poisoned again. Do you have any food? Something to keep you going? Maybe you can wait here, and I can go get some glow berries, or maybe you could eat an axolotl—"

Mal grabs my wrist, her fingers weak but insistent. "Stay with me. And . . . we both know you couldn't kill an axolotl."

"Maybe I could, to save you."

"You could try."

Yeah, and she knows I'd fail, because she's my best friend, and she knows me better than anybody, except maybe Tok. I'd probably just cut off my own arm to feed her before I went after a cute animal.

I settle down, try to help her get more comfortable, but it's a cave, so it's not like that's possible. "For real, though. Got any food in your pockets, Mal? It might help."

"Food didn't help Tok. Need milk."

"Oh yeah. Right." I look at the cave mouth, but Jarro hasn't appeared. I look at the horses but don't see any udders. "Do you think I could milk an axolotl?"

She giggles, barely a squeak. "It would taste fishy, I bet."

"I've got to go get Jarro," I say, untangling myself from Mal to stand. But it's hard—she's heavy and floppy, like she can't even move her own muscles by herself.

But just then, Jarro barrels into the cave, followed by Tok and Lenna.

"Did you kill the Wither?" I ask. "And get Creeperhead?"

"No and kind of," Lenna says. "You guys need to get deeper into the cave. We have to fight the Wither in here. It has armor now. We need swords. Arrows don't work anymore."

"Arrows don't *what?*" I screech.

"You have to hurry," Tok says, drawing his sword. "It's coming."

The cave goes darker as something blocks the entrance. I stand, cradling Mal against my chest plate. "Jarro, you have to take her. Get her somewhere safe and give her milk." He just stands there, blinking, and I bark, "Now! You can do this!" When he doesn't move, I shove Mal into his arms and say, "I believe in you," before turning back to the incoming Wither and drawing my sword. I have to trust he can do this.

He has to trust he can do this, but that's a bigger ask.

I hear his feet moving, then a sound that doesn't make sense. I turn to see that, while balancing Mal over his shoulder with one arm like a sack of flour, he's managed to pull one piece out of the horse paddock. The big softy—he doesn't want his horses to be cornered when the Wither shows up. They don't move yet because they don't sense the monster coming, but Poppy barks menacingly and bolts out to stand, bristling, at Lenna's side.

The Wither is coming down the tunnel and will soon be in the open cavern, and I realize that I can't let that happen. This is my chance. I take a deep breath and sprint right at the Wither, running it through with my sword. I hit it again and again, so fast and hard that it can't seem to launch a skull. It barely fits in the tunnel, but then I realize that we can use that to our advantage.

"Tok, I need your sword arm!" I shout.

"But I'm not very good—"

"You don't even have to aim, bro! Just hit it quick! I'm gonna make it turn around. Get ready."

When I hear his footsteps pounding toward me, I drop to the ground and stab up as I roll under the Wither and to its other side. The air is different over here, behind it, almost like I can feel the sun trying so hard to break free of the clouds outside. I come up slashing with my sword and the Wither spins to face me.

"That's right, ugly," I mutter. "Keep your eye on the prize."

Up close, the Wither makes my blood run cold. Three huge skulls glare with glowing white eyes, the bone black and shiny as if burned and polished. It smells like mushroom stew left out in the sun for two weeks.

It grunts as Tok lands his first strike against its unprotected back, and I grin fiercely as I realize I now have my own personal punching bag.

Or stabbing bag, really.

I double down on my onslaught, never giving it a chance to launch one of those skulls. On its other side, Tok lands hit after hit. It's perfect for him, really—it can't move and it can't fight back. All it does is groan now.

Boom!

I'm thrown backward as the Wither explodes.

I lie half in, half out of the cave entrance as the dark clouds fade away to reveal a brilliantly blue sky. Something rattles, and I look up to see a tall gray Wither skeleton coming right at me with a sword. Something gray leaps over me, and Poppy lands just outside the cave, growling. The Wither's skeleton minion, much to my surprise, turns around on its bony foot and runs away. I sit up to watch it catch fire and burn, but it doesn't—it just disappears into the forest.

"Bro," Tok moans.

I shake my head and crawl over to him. "You okay, bro?"

He's dazed, his sword on the ground. "I think I broke my promise."

I shake my head harder. "What promise?"

He points to his forehead. "Pretty sure that explosion burned off my eyebrows. But it got yours, too, so . . ."

As Poppy growls and drives away two more Wither skeletons, Tok and I huddle up on the cave floor, laughing madly as if burned-off eyebrows are the funniest thing in the world. There's a weird purple star on the ground where the Wither died, and Tok puts it in his pocket; I'm sure Lenna or Nan will know what it is.

My stomach grumbles, and Tok hands me a piece of cod, and I gobble it down and stand, holding out my hand to help him to his feet. His eyebrows are back now, thanks to the food he was wise enough to keep in his pockets, and I hug him and pound him on the back.

"We killed the Wither!" I say. "We did it! Together!"

And then I remember . . .

"Mal!"

I bolt past Tok and the horses, back to where Jarro is helping Mal to stand. She already looks a thousand times better.

"Milk," she says, her top lip coated in white. "It does a body good!"

"I sure am glad you milked those mooshrooms," I say, thumping Jarro on the back.

"I mean, it was more for curiosity than anything else," he starts, looking down.

I grab both his shoulders and make him look at me. "Bud, you just saved Mal's life. If you didn't have milk, she and Tok would probably both be dead."

It dawns on his face as he understands, and he nods. "Guess I'm glad I milked a bunch of mushroom cows, then. I'm glad it helped."

I know he thinks he doesn't contribute enough and that he's a coward, but I also hope he understands that he has an important role to play, even if it's not played on the front lines of the fight. I don't know how to tell him this in a way that won't embarrass us both, though, so I just pound him on the back some more and say, "Good game."

We're all on our feet now, and Mal hands out a few more bits of food, but Lenna is nervous and Poppy is guarding the cave entrance. That's when I remember—Creeperhead is still out there.

"So what about Creeperhead?" I say.

"Lenna shot a TNT block with an arrow while he was holding it," Tok explains. "And it totally knocked him out."

"I've had enough food. Let's go capture him," Lenna says, a lead in her hands and a determined look on her face. "Chug, Mal? Can you guys bring your swords?"

"Are you okay? Ready to fight?" I ask Mal.

She grins. "Never better. Let's go catch that jerk."

We draw our swords and follow Lenna down the tunnel and out into the sunshine. I'd completely lost track of time inside the cave, but it feels like it's maybe noon, with the sun high in the sky with some fluffy, puffy clouds. Poppy walks before us, stiff-legged and growling. She can still feel the threat, I guess. Or maybe she's the one keeping those scary Wither skeletons away. Everything out here would seem perfectly normal if not for the signs of dozens of explosions where the Wither's skulls landed and left blackened craters, cracked stone, and broken branches.

I don't see Creeperhead at first, but Poppy is sniffing behind a bush under the ledge where he'd been standing to throw his TNT blocks. We run over to find our enemy splayed out, unconscious. His creeper-head mask is still intact, and I look at his clothes for signs of who he might be. Every inch of skin is covered, including gloves and tall boots. His creeper-green cape hides regular black pants and a black shirt. From what I can tell, it's a tall, thin man, but I seem to remember Orlok being pretty short and buff.

"Shall we?" Mal asks.

I point my sword at his chest, letting the tip dig into his shirt so he knows we mean business.

"Lenna, why don't you do the honors?"

With Poppy by her side, Lenna reaches down with both hands and removes the creeper head to reveal . . .

Our neighbor, Krog.

Krog the beetroot farmer.

Krog the know-it-all blowhard who hates kids.

Krog, the guy who tried to use vexes with poison to kill all our crops so that our entire town would be forced to leave, thereby allowing him to take over all of our resources for himself.

Krog, who apparently snores when he's out cold.

"Isn't he supposed to be in jail?" I say.

"He's supposed to be a lot of things," Lenna growls. "Like not a terrible person."

Lenna uses the lead to tie his hands and feet together tightly, and he doesn't so much as blink.

Mal nudges Krog with her foot. "Hey, Krog! Wake up."

"Hey, Kroggers!" Now that he's all trussed up, I put my sword away and squat down, patting his cheeks with little slaps. "Krog-a-doodle-doo! Time to wake up and face the music!"

Krog blinks groggily and twitches like he's trying to run or draw a weapon, but of course he can't do either. He twists and turns, doing his best to loosen his bonds, growling and grunting like a pig in a sack—not that I would ever put a pig in a sack. He looks thinner than he used to and ragged, with a long beard and scraggly, greasy hair.

He looks . . . angry.

"The monstrous Wither I summoned will soon return to wreak havoc on you sniveling degenerates," he thunders. "Untie me, and I'll help you fight it!"

"We already killed it," I say.

His jaw drops, and he goggles at me.

I shrug. "What, like it's hard?"

"Then the Wither skeletons will—" he begins smugly.

"They ran away. They don't like wolves, apparently."

Krog deflates a bit, but then recovers. "Once I get my TNT—"

"You won't. You're not gonna be able to reach your pockets for a very, very long time."

Tok and Jarro hurry over to join us. "Whoa," Jarro says. "That is not who I was expecting."

"Of course not," Krog says, preening. "Because your diminutive mind can't—oof!"

"Sorry. My bad. My foot just jerks like that sometimes," I say.

Mal aims her sword at Krog's chest. "How'd you get out of jail?"

"Why should I tell you?"

The sword digs in a little. "Because you enjoy monologues and not being stabbed."

Krog sighs. "If I must. You see, children, the Elders are fools. They brought me food and water once a day but otherwise left me to my own strategic devices. I used my bowl to dig a hole in the floor, then sat on the hole whenever they came to check on me. That hole led me into their storeroom, where they keep all the rare antiquities and supplies the Founders left behind. I took the creeper's head, the enchanted cape, the unidentified potions, the books, the spare brewing stand, the unusual ingredients. There was a shulker box, too, so it was easy enough to carry everything."

He pauses theatrically, hoping for some sort of response, but we are not particularly impressed by a guy digging a hole in the ground and committing a burglary.

"Okay, so you escaped jail. Why have you been following us?" Mal asks.

Krog looks at Mal like she's grown an extra head. "To terrorize and punish you, of course. You ruined my plan. Killed my mobs. Drove off my brigands. Put me in jail. For these crimes, you must pay!"

"Krog, do you know you're just an absolutely horrible guy?" Lenna asks.

Krog blinks at her. "I'm writing a musical about my life. There's a song about you miscreants. Would you like to hear it?"

"No," I say.

Krog clears his throat and sings, badly, loudly:

"Punish the children; the children are bad.
They took away everything you've ever had.
Chase them and hit them and give them a fright.
Set fire to their shelter while they sleep at night.
Punish the children for putting you here,
Fill them with terror and fill them with fear."

"That's messed up," Jarro says.

"Ha ha!" Krog says with a creepy grin. "Ha ha! Did you get my message? My message was: Ha ha!"

"Oooookay, so let's get this guy back to town," Mal says. "And let's make sure he can't talk, because I didn't like what he had to say before he spent months in jail making up a song about punishing us."

"But won't they just put him right back in jail so he can break out again?" I ask.

They all look to me.

"Well, what else do you propose?" Mal asks.

"We could throw him into the deep dark with the warden—" I start.

Mal elbows me in the ribs. "You don't mean that."

I shrug. "It was worth a try."

"Well, if we leave him to the elements, he'll probably die, and if he gets free, he'll just chase us again. The only thing we can do is take him back home."

We all look down at Krog. He's angrily muttering to himself about all the terrible punishments we deserve, and all I can think about is how glad I am that he's not hidden in the dark outside our shelter at night, torch in hand, waiting for the chance to hurt us again.

26

JARRO

It doesn't take me long to find the horse Krog hid in a meadow. He might be evil, but his horse isn't. He tells us he named her Carnage, but he stole her from my herd from back home and her real name is Lil Miss Honeyfoot. Chug named her, obviously. He explains to Krog that it's because of her golden ankles, and that sets Krog off onto another speech. At least we know how to make a gag.

There still stands the problem of Krog's pockets: He has all sorts of dastardly things hidden in there that we don't want him to have access to. I end up volunteering my new pair of leggings, and Chug, Tok, and I oversee the extremely weird process of making Krog change his pants with his hands tied. Everyone feels much better once there's no way he can access the shulker box in his pocket and pull out more TNT or dangerous potions. We haven't seen one of these boxes before, but apparently it's like a chest inside a chest that can hold tons of stuff. I'm going to miss those new pants, though. They looked cozy.

Thanks to Tok's brewing and Krog's contraband, we have enough Potions of Swiftness for all six horses and Poppy. After Mal checks the map, we mount up and take off. It's faster to cut through the plains than to retrace our old path along the ocean, so we head off in a new direction. According to the map, there shouldn't be anything unexpected out here—no woodland mansion, no dark forest, no village, no ancient ruins that might contain a terrifying monster. The only slightly different thing we encounter is a flower forest, so that's where we stop for a quick lunch break. It's so beautiful it brings tears to everyone's eyes, with so many flowers that they just blend into a riotous rainbow.

I begin to wonder if maybe I should add a cut-flower business to my horse and llama rentals and mushroom farm, but I would need more land to do that, and possibly have to hire someone to help me. New Cornucopia might seem endless, since it's outside the wall, but houses have already gone up all around us, which takes up the land the flowers would require. Still, I look at this place and I see possibilities.

For all the scary things we've faced on this trip, we've seen wonders, too. No one back home, except possibly Nan, has ever seen a flower forest before. Those people are going about their lives in the Hub with no idea that a flower forest might even exist. Yet here I stand, surrounded by beauty and buzzing bees and the overlapping scent of thousands of blooms. I realize that despite everything that's happened, despite the horror and the pain, I'm glad I came along on this journey. I'd rather live the ups and downs of life in the Overworld than spend every day in the Hub looking at the same old houses and the same old streets and the same old people selling slightly different sheep for slightly more than they're worth.

I'd rather be free.

Well, as long as Creeperhead isn't around.

We're running out of food, so that afternoon, we stop a little early by a river. I set out the paddock for the horses and help Mal construct the shelter. We don't make it quite as big as we did when we needed the horses inside, but she does plan it just a little bit bigger than usual. When she adds an interior wall and asks Tok for an iron door, I see why—a miniature jail for Krog. I hate the thought of him sleeping so near me, hate to know that he might be sitting there, staring at us by the light of our torches. Tok must feel the same way, as he crafts a solid iron door with no window. Chug throws Krog a piece of fish after we've all eaten our fill, but after that door closes, we don't hear a peep. I would worry about that—worry that Krog is again trying to escape—except that Poppy sleeps right by the door, guarding it. Krog might be able to get by our elderly Elders, who are all mostly deaf, anyway, but he's not about to sneak past a wolf, and if he starts digging, we're going to hear it.

The next morning, Krog is still in his little room. He grumbles about how uncomfortable he is and how he deserves better and will punish us one day, but Chug just tosses him another piece of fish and slams the door. I don't see him again until Chug and Mal are breaking down that last little room of the shelter. Chug helps him onto his horse, hands tied, and reminds him that if he makes so much as a peep, the gag goes right back on.

I remember what it felt like, when Orlok and his minions gagged me, and I wouldn't wish it on anyone . . . but at the same time, I definitely did not sign up to hear an adult sing a creepy little song about how he wants to set my toes on fire.

The Potions of Swiftness kick in, and the world is a blur. The horses seem to like it—they snort and stretch out their necks and run like the wind. We gallop up and down little hills, past lakes, through forests. We have to build a quick bridge over a particularly large river, but that doesn't slow us down for long. We should stop for lunch, but I can feel Mal's concern for her Nan growing as we get closer to home. She keeps slipping her hand into her pocket as if checking to make sure the enchanted golden apple is still there. I know she's imagining what would happen if we got back to Cornucopia just a few minutes too late and she had to live with the fact that we went to all this trouble and could only blame ourselves for a bad outcome, that we were happily enjoying a flower forest while Nan took her last breaths.

We all feel it, I'm sure. Nobody asks to stop again. Nobody asks for extra food, not even Chug, which is saying a lot. As the sun sets and Mal gallops on, we don't say anything. We're going so fast it's not like any mobs could catch us, anyway. We're almost there, and we know it, and we whisper to our horses and beg them to run just a little faster, please.

"All the wheat you want," I promise Speckles. "Just keep going a little bit longer."

The night stretches on, and my belly grumbles, and my legs go numb. I know I'm going to ache tomorrow, but I'm not going to be the one who asks Mal to stop. Not when we're this close.

"There it is!" Mal calls, and if I squint, I can just barely see our town's high wall rising up from the still grasses, lit every seven blocks by a torch so that it shimmers like the night sky. I hear a groan, and my horse passes close enough to a zombie that I can smell its stench. We keep going. Mal angles the horses toward the wall. I can't see New Cornucopia from here, but I know it's there, and my heart sighs with relief like a long-held fist finally opening.

I want to go home and sleep in my bed and know that I don't have to deal with anything scary at all the next day, but I tell myself that I just need to wait a little longer. Home is within reach. We just have to save Nan, first.

We skid to a stop in front of the gate. There are giant doors there now, which is odd. Lars is up and pointing his sword at us while Jami snores, leaned back against the wall.

"Who—what?" Lars sputters. "Oh, it's you. Going awfully fast, weren't you?"

"We tend to hurry when family is dying," Mal snaps. "Can you open the doors?"

Lars nudges Jami, who startles awake, goggles at us, and holds out his sword, too.

"That wasn't very polite," Lars says.

"Can you *please* open the doors," Mal says, her impatience growing.

"Still seems pretty rude to me, Lars," Jami says with a sneer.

"Oh, Lars, you big, strong man who is definitely not just a gawky teen boy in ill-fitting armor with a mustache that looks like a chocolate stain, would you please be so kind as to do your job and open the door so I can go save my great-great-great-grandmother from dying?"

Lars snorts. "No."

I can't see Mal in the darkness, but I'm guessing her face is as red as her hair right now, which is not a great time to mess with her.

"No?" she asks, slow and deadly.

"No. The Elders enacted new laws after you lot took off. Again. Krog escaped from jail, and you left without permission. We have gates now, and you can't go in or out unless you're on the list." He makes a show of pulling a list out of his pocket and checking it. "And you're not on the list. In fact, no one is."

Mal sighs dramatically. "Don't you guys get it? You can't stop us. You couldn't keep us in, and you can't keep us out. And we caught Krog, so that might be of importance to the Elders."

"Then you can speak with Elder Stu when he shows up with the key in the morning to unlock the gate. As for right now, we couldn't open it, even if we wanted to. That's how laws work."

"I'll show him how fists work," Chug growls.

"No," Mal says. "That's not who we are. We have other ways in." She turns her horse so that a sweaty horse butt is right in Lars's face. "Thanks a lot, you creeps."

Mal leads us away, and Chug says some unsavory things under his breath.

"You're in trouble again," Lars says to Lenna.

"Not with anyone I respect," she shoots back, and I wonder how I ever thought I could bully this girl for a single second. There is no contest in which I think myself superior to her these days, and I wish there was some way to tell her how much I admire her without it being super awkward.

But as our tired horses plod around the wall, their normal gait seemingly as slow as honey, I notice something that makes no sense. We should be seeing the shadows of New Cornucopia rising against the wall, blocking the torches. I should hear my other horses whinnying to welcome us and Thingy squealing for Chug.

Instead, we find silence.

As we get closer, my suspicions are confirmed.

New Cornucopia is gone.

27.

LENNA

 I'm so mad at my brother Lars that I want to throw up, but I can't let him see that. I knew he was awful, but withholding lifesaving medicine from a dying old woman out of spite?

He may think he's the hero, but he's a villain now.

Not that it matters. We know how to get to Nan, and we don't need a gate or permission to do it.

"Uh, guys? Are you seeing what I'm seeing? Or not seeing?" Chug asks.

Lost in my thoughts, I look up to find . . . nothing.

Disturbed ground where New Cornucopia should be.

"Looks like they decided nobody gets to go beyond the wall," Tok says.

"Thingy! Miss Pig!" Chug wails. "They stole my pig! Oh no. What if they eat him? What if they give the baby pigs stupid names! Oh no, oh no, oh no!" He's so upset that his horse is acting nervous, but . . . he should be nervous. Everything he and Tok and Jarro have worked so hard for is gone.

"They wouldn't hurt the animals," Mal reminds him.

"They would if they knew about bacon!"

"I bet Elder Stu confiscated everything in our shop," Tok says sourly. "I bet he said it's for the good of the town. I bet he's charging top dollar for it."

"I bet my mom claimed my businesses." Jarro sounds so defeated. "I bet she's selling my mushrooms and has all my livestock in her garden."

"We're going to get everything back," Mal promises. "Let's go to Nan, and then we'll sort this out. Come on!"

She kicks her horse and gallops around the wall, and we fall in behind her. I have Krog's horse ponied off my own, and somehow Lars and Jami didn't notice him, or maybe they don't believe us. At this point, they'd do anything to keep their authority and make us feel small. If they were smart, they would've turned Krog in themselves—and tried to take credit for capturing him. But no. They were so busy shutting us down that they ignored that part.

After all these days of travel, the wall seems smaller than ever. It's not long before we skid to a stop in front of the only break in the giant circle of stone—besides the new gate. Nan's little cottage backs up to the wall, and she has a window that looks out at the Overworld. She keeps it hidden with a piston system, so it's possible the Elders don't even know it exists. This window provided my first view of the world beyond Cornucopia, and I still love to gaze through it, out at the endless plains of swaying grasses and flowers.

Mal hops off her horse and knocks on the window, but—well, Nan's too sick to come open it. When no one answers, Mal pulls out her pickaxe, chooses a spot in the wall far to the side of the window, beyond the boundaries of Nan's house, and mines two blocks of stone. We walk our horses through it, and she blocks it back up and follows us. We dismount, and Jarro takes our leads to hold the horses while Mal runs inside with me hot on her heels. Nan may be her ancestor, but she's my boss, and between the two of us, I honestly know Nan best. Whatever state she's in, I need to be there for her. Tok and Chug follow us through Nan's front door.

We burst in, and there's a gasp of surprise. Curled up on the couch is Livi, the daughter of our town healer, Tini. As soon as the door opens, she bolts upright like she's just woken up.

"What are you doing?" she asks. "This is a sick room!"

"We're saving my Nan." Mal walks right past her and over to Nan's bed. Nan looks tiny and shriveled and pale, and Mal reaches for her hand and murmurs her name.

"Mara, is that you?" Nan whispers softly, her eyes barely open.

"It's Mal, Mara's daughter. Nan, we found an enchanted golden apple."

At that, Nan tries to sit up but is too weak. Chug helps her, fluffing the pillow up behind her. Mal reaches into her pocket and pulls out the apple. Its golden glow fills the room, and she holds it up to Nan's lips.

"Good thing I still have a few teeth," Nan mutters before taking a bite.

Considering the shape she's in, it takes her a long time to eat the whole thing, but we begin to see its effect almost immediately. Her eyes sharpen, her spine straightens, her hands tighten. Finally she swats Chug away as she finishes the last bite. "Give a body some space," she mutters once it's all down. "Those pillows are too fluffed now."

"How do you feel?" Mal asks, her eyes wet with tears.

"Better. Spry! Like I'm eighty at the most." Nan gets out of bed and hobbles past us to the window. "Someone was knocking, but Livi said it was nothing."

"It was us," I say. "They wouldn't let us in at the gate."

"And New Cornucopia is gone!" Chug wails. "Our homes, our shop, our animals. Gone!"

At that, Nan frowns, her eyes full of thunder. "That's what Livi said—that the Elders unanimously voted to end the experiment of New Cornucopia and close the wall forever. 'For our own good,' she said, the little nincompoop. Why, if I had taken my position among them, and if I hadn't been half dead, I would've given them an earful! It's all Young Stu's doing, I'm sure. Always such a bully, that one. Thinks he knows everything. Harrumph!"

"Livi, do you know—" Mal starts.

But she stops short.

Livi is no longer on the couch, and the front door is open. We were so focused on Nan that we didn't even notice her leaving.

Nan sighs. "Probably ran off to tattle. Never did trust her. Almost wondered if Tini sent her over here to spy on me. The Elders suspect I have a secret stash of valuable items." She winks. "Which, as you know, I do. But I'll die before I let Stu have 'em. Or I'll stay alive just to spite him, I reckon. Now, close that door and tell me all about my old friend Efram."

Chug obligingly closes the door and chuckles. "You're not gonna believe this, but—"

Just then, Jarro comes in from outside, escorting a bound-and-gagged Krog along on his lead.

"Don't bring that thing inside!" Nan barks. "He never did have any manners. And he monologues too much. Makes a body nervous. Nobody likes being monologued at."

"We gagged him," Jarro tells her sheepishly.

"Good. He can sit in the corner and think about what he's done."

As Jarro is still easily spooked by Nan, he walks Krog over to an empty corner and just stands there, waiting for further orders. Krog turns to face the wall and sits, hunched over inside his cloak. He always was terrified of Nan. Most people are.

"Well?" Nan urges Chug.

"So we're out in the middle of the ocean, and we look down, and we see this huge building surrounded by one-eyed spiky murderfish, and we say to ourselves, 'Clearly, a crazy old dude built that and decided to live underwater,'" Chug begins.

"That's the most ridiculous thing I've ever heard, but go on."

"So we douse ourselves with Potions of Water Breathing and swim on down despite all the eye bubbles—" Chug continues to tell the story, and Nan butts in whenever she has a question or Chug's descriptions make no sense. She nods along, acting like she's heard of lush caves and wardens before, but I know darned well she hasn't.

"Ah, yes, the Zither," Nan says, nodding.

"Wither," I say, holding up my drawing.

Nan clutches her chest and tells me not to give her a heart attack when she's just gotten used to not dying again.

The door bursts open, and a whole crowd of people bustles into Nan's small cottage. Elder Stu and Elder Gabe are at the front, along with Elders Tiber, Zach, Karis, Nico, and Joi. Behind them are Tini and her daughter Livi and son Mac, Lars and Jami, and, much to everyone's dismay, Jarro's mom, Dawna.

"There they are!" Elder Stu squawks. "The Bad Apples who brought all this trouble to our town!"

"Pretty sure that was Krog, but go off," Chug mutters.

"The perpetually hungry boy is right!" Nan hobbles over to

Elder Stu and stares up into his furiously wrinkled face. "I see how it is now. You closed the wall and started all the new security protocols because Krog escaped your little jail. But you didn't tell the town that because you knew you'd look bad, so you blamed it on these kids and confiscated their property. All to cover your wrinkly rumps. You should be thanking these children. They've saved the town three times now! And they just saved my life."

"Ahem, yes, well, beg to disagree on that topic," Elder Gabe says, both hands on his walking stick and chin up high. "I do believe it was the diligent care provided by Tini and myself that has kept you in such fine fettle."

"Balderdash!" Nan roars. "I'm of sound mind, and I still have enchanted golden apple juice on my chin to prove it wasn't your 'care' that got me here. All you did was pat my hand and ask me if I had any secret relics squirreled away that I might like to donate to 'the people.'" She points a finger toward Elder Gabe's pointy nose. "That's it! I'm taking my place as the Eldest Elder. Your closed-minded foolishness can't be allowed to run this fine town into the ground."

And then an absolutely terrifying thing happens.

Elder Stu does something I don't think he's ever done before.

He *smiles*.

"Unfortunately, Nan, we've done a bit of restructuring of the town charter recently. We unanimously agreed that only the current Elders could vote in a new Elder, and I'm afraid that doesn't include you. Whatever arrangements may have once been in place, things are a bit more nailed down now, to put a point on it. Of course, you'll be allowed to live out your days here as a valued town member, but I'm afraid you'll only ever be an elder with a lowercase 'e.'"

I hate watching horror come over Nan's face now that she realizes they've outfoxed her. They've somehow managed to take all her power away, and she knows it. Even with the enchanted golden apple, she's not strong enough to fight with anything more than a few cutting words.

There's a building murmur outside, and heads begin to poke in Nan's door and appear outside her windows. I see my parents, Mal's parents, Chug and Tok's parents, Inka and Fred and Remy and Edd and Benn and Robb and Saya and Rhys. The whole town has shown up, it seems, to watch this play out. A few of them spill into the cottage, and someone opens the windows to listen, and I begin to squirm at how many eyes are staring at us.

"You can't do that," Nan says. "The Founders clearly stated—"

"The Founders are long gone, and the world is changing." Elder Gabe spreads his hands. "It's already done and cannot be undone."

Nan is trembling, and Mal puts a hand on her shoulder.

"Where's my pig?" Chug asks, his words so low and deadly that Elder Gabe and Elder Stu draw back as if he's drawn his sword.

"On your parents' farm, where you belong, young man," Elder Stu shoots back. "That's another part of the revised town charter—children must remain with their parents until they are deemed old enough and responsible enough by a committee of Elders."

Chug's jaw drops.

He'll be fifty before the Elders would ever agree he could live on his own.

"You're monsters," he whispers.

"We're doing what's best for Cornucopia. A closed wall, no one going in or out, and children minding their manners. That's what makes a great town. Huzzah!" As soon as Elder Stu says

"Huzzah," a cheer goes up from . . . well, not everyone, but all the Elders.

"And you're coming back home with me, Jarro," Dawna says, bustling over to him. "No more of this foolishness. I need you to tend the bees and grow more mushrooms and sweet berries. The horses and llamas can go back outside the wall—so much manure!—but you'll be so busy you won't miss them, I'm sure." She narrows her eyes at us. "And you'll be too busy to be led astray by these Bad Apples. They're not good for you."

She reaches for his face, but Jarro steps back, nearly stumbling into Krog, who's been just sitting there at the end of his lead this whole time.

"I'm not going back with you," he says.

"It's your home—"

"Not anymore."

Elder Stu raises his voice, cutting off Dawna's lecture. "You children will all return to your parents. No more of this New Cornucopia business. We have everything we need inside the wall. Now, if—" His jaw drops. "Is that . . . Krog?!"

Sure enough, Krog is now facing the room, his eyes wide and filled with hate.

"Yeah, that's Krog. He stalked us for a few days and released a Wither on us, but then we took him captive. You're gonna need an obsidian jail with a better guard," Tok says, stepping into the ring for the first time. "Does the rest of the town even know that he escaped?"

Whispers go up around the room, and it definitely seems like most people didn't know.

Krog escaped?

He got out?

Why didn't they tell us?

Is that why they closed the wall?

Did these kids . . . catch him?

"We've taken steps to keep the town safe," Elder Stu says, pitching his voice to carry. "Clearly no one was in any danger."

"Except for our children!" Chug's mom shouts.

"Yes, well, they defied our laws and left the town illegally," Elder Gabe says peevishly.

"That doesn't make it okay!"

As chaos ensues, Krog fights his bonds and roars his rage and tries to kick Jarro. Jarro shoves him back onto the floor, and Elder Stu walks over to demand the lead.

"What are you going to do with him?" Jarro asks.

"We're going to punish him."

"How can we be sure you're capable of keeping him locked up?"

"Are you questioning me?" Elder Stu's voice is so high and strangled that everyone stops to listen.

Jarro is cowed by the attention, but I'm used to it, and I'm sick of it.

"Yes, we're questioning you," I say. People's eyes crawl over me, and whispers of *It's Loony Lenna* go up around the cottage, but I don't care, because I've finally reached my limit. "We're questioning you because you need to be questioned. You lie to your children about the real world—about the dangerous things out there, but also about the wonderful and beautiful things they're missing. You lock up adults who were born free and should be allowed to go where they please. You pick and choose the rules that keep you in power and that keep your chests full of emeralds. You don't spread skills so that your people will always need you.

And now, now that you're starting to realize you can't control us, you're trying to turn your rules into laws so you can force us to live the life you think is best."

The room is silent, everyone focusing on me, but I've faced down a Wither and a warden and no one here has any power over me at all. I raise my voice.

"Here's the big secret, people of Cornucopia: The wall is a lie. Anyone can chop out two blocks in the wall and walk right on out at any time. No one can stop you. The control of the Elders is an illusion. Any one of you can learn how to use a crafting table or a brewing stand. The Overworld has more than enough room for every one of you to mine, if you want to. There are sheep and cows and chickens just wandering around outside, free of charge. You don't have to live this way. And I don't intend to."

I look to my friends.

To Mal: our leader, our bedrock.

To Chug: our fighter, our heart.

To Tok: our inventor, our inspiration.

To Jarro: our beastmaster, our courage.

I can even see myself in Nan's mirror, and I look tall and strong and certain.

I'm the one who sees what others can't, and I see what's clear. We've moved beyond this place.

"You guys want to go found our own town?" I ask.

28.

MAL

There's a long, stunned beat of silence.

No one has ever left Cornucopia for good before.

"As the Eldest Elder, I absolutely forbid it!" Elder Stu roars.

I shrug. "Yeah, we don't really care."

Nan chuckles, a sound I know well. She only makes that noise when she's plotting something truly devious.

"I'll come, too," she says. "It's been too long since I've been out there, and I'd like to see some new things. This place is getting pretty boring."

She snatches Elder Gabe's walking stick right out of his hands and waves it in front of her like she's herding horses. "Go on. Get out of here. Shoo. Your welcome is rescinded."

"But—"

"No buts, no witch huts. Now get out or I'll rap you on the knuckles just like I did when you were a boy."

Elder Stu and Elder Gabe are forced to back up, step by step.

No one else in town tries to defend them. Jami and Lars have mysteriously disappeared. Dawna is alternately begging and demanding that Jarro come home. He just hands her Krog's lead and says, "Make sure they really use obsidian or he'll just dig his way out again."

The crowd outside is uncertain and loud. I hear some people decrying what ungrateful, awful Bad Apples we are. I heard other people questioning if it really is true they can just open up the walls themselves.

Lenna joins me and Nan and whispers, "I hope you don't mind."

I smile and fist bump her. "I always knew you dreamed things I couldn't, but this is one dream I want to be a part of."

And it's true. I never would've thought of something so audacious, but it really is the only acceptable answer. These people can't hold us back anymore. I'll miss my parents, but . . . hopefully when Elder Stu and Elder Gabe are gone, the next batch of Elders will be more reasonable. Until then, maybe I can sneak in through the wall every now and then to visit. They're welcome to join us, if they want to . . . but we'll have to have a long talk about my independence.

Nan pats Lenna on the back and says, "Not bad, my apprentice. Not bad," and Lenna grins. She'd already moved out of her family's house, and she's bloomed in her time away from them. No one bullying her, no one nitpicking her, no one telling her she's worthless or loony. She's grown so far beyond them. I doubt she'll want to visit.

Movement catches my eye outside the door—my parents.

I take a deep breath and head out to have the most awkward conversation of my life.

My mom's eyes are all red, and she holds out her arms for me.

I rush into the hug, and my dad stands there and coughs uncomfortably.

"So you're really going?" my mom asks.

"Yep. But Nan will be with us, so it's not like we'll be entirely unsupervised."

"At least you'll be with family."

I step back and look from my mom to my dad. "My friends are kind of a family. We take care of one another. You don't have to worry. And I'll come and visit, I promise. Or you could visit us. You might like it outside the wall. Like Lenna said—it's actually pretty easy to leave."

"You want a cow?" my dad asks, gruff as ever. "You want to take Connor?"

Tears spring up in my eyes. I don't mention that there are plenty of free cows just roaming around the Overworld. For my dad . . . this is as close as he gets to giving me his blessing.

"That would be great, if you can spare him."

My dad nods, clears his throat. "I'll bring him around in the morning."

My mom steps closer, tries to arrange my braid over my shoulder but squints and picks at it. "What is this? Ashes? Chunks of rock? Pink flowers? I didn't even know pink flowers existed."

I take the azalea blossom from her hand and nod. "There's a lot out there you don't know about. You should come see it sometime."

My dad stolidly shakes his head, but my mom gets this faraway look in her eye. Just now, she kind of looks like Nan. "Maybe someday. You set up a town, get it settled, and maybe we can come visit."

"That's my Mara," Nan mutters approvingly. "The heart of an adventurer."

After a few more hugs and throat clearings, my parents leave. I feel like I have their blessing if not their understanding, and that's the most I could really hope for.

With the spectacle of my parents gone, gossipy Dawna goes back to fussing at Jarro, so Nan hustles over and smacks her with Elder Gabe's stick until she heads for the door.

"Show's over. Leave that good boy alone and go back to hoarding your stupid berries, you fussbudget," Nan says.

Dawna has no choice but to exit, dragging Krog along behind her like a very poorly trained wolf. "This isn't over!" she shouts over her shoulder.

"It darned tootin' is," Nan growls. "Get out of my house, you harpy!" As soon as Dawna is out the door, Nan turns to Jarro. "Now help an old woman pack all her gear into chests for a journey, will you?"

I look around for Chug and Tok and am startled to find that they're gone. I actually don't remember seeing them for quite some time. There was just so much going on—they must've slipped out. But why?

At first I think maybe their parents forced them out, but . . . well, let's just say that even when they lived on the pumpkin farm, there wasn't much their parents could do to control either one of them.

Aha! The farm.

I know where they've gone, and I can guess exactly what they're doing. I smile to myself and help Jarro and Nan pack up. Lenna goes out to her own little cottage to pack her things with Poppy by her side, calm now that the crowd is gone. We tell Nan more details of our journey, and as always, she acts both knowledgeable and impressed. She finally admits that she's never heard of a warden, which is kind of a big deal, as she always acts like she's familiar with everything we encounter. When she hears about what Krog, in the guise of Creeperhead, did to Jarro, she gives him four cookies all for himself, and I imagine that in that moment, he decides it was worth it.

As I'm packing up Nan's pantry, I yawn so big my jaw cracks. It's been a long day after another long day, after a series of long days, and we need sleep. I know the people back in town don't want us to leave, but I also don't think any of them want us here enough to stop us. My parents know what's happening, Lenna's parents will be glad to be rid of her for good, Dawna is thankfully out of our lives, and Chug and Tok are probably dealing with their own family drama back home.

I pull out my bed and place it along a wall, and Jarro follows my lead.

Nan stops packing up cookies and sighs dramatically. "Smart kids. Can't travel if you're sleepy. Do you think the big hungry one and the little one with burned eyebrows will be back tonight?"

"They'll be back as soon as Chug finds his pigs and talks his mom out of every pie she's got," I say. "Believe me: Their dad learned a long time ago that they can't be controlled. They'll probably be like my folks. They may not like it, but they'll understand."

Sure enough, Chug and Tok burst through the door before Nan has even settled into bed. Chug is giddy, holding three chubby pink piglets in his arms.

"Just look at them!" he crows. "They're perfect! I'm a grandfather!"

"Don't you mean a grandporker?" Tok asks, his cats winding happily around his legs.

Chug groans. "Yeah, that's it. Tok's making jokes again. We'd better get to sleep before he starts in on puns."

Tok grins. "Well, you know me. I'm always punctilious."

Chug tosses his bed on the ground and falls into it with the piglets squirming all over his belly. "Wake me up when it's time to get out of here. Or when there are cookies."

Tok sets up his bed and then commands Chug to return the piglets to their proud parents. Chug groans but follows Tok's orders, delicately placing the babies in the horse paddock along with Thingy and Miss Pig. Lenna will be staying in her cottage tonight, and Nan's mostly packed up, so I settle into my bed and smile.

I can't believe we're leaving Cornucopia.

Now I just have to figure out where we're going.

I know one thing for sure:

The new town we build will never have walls.

TOK

I'm going to make this story short and sweet because we've got a lot of work to do, and I haven't got all day.

We set out at dawn the next morning, just in case anyone from town thought they could stop us. With our pockets fully loaded, we mounted up on our horses—well, after my brother apologized to his pig for not riding him instead. Considering Thingy had his trotters full with three bouncy new babies, I'm guessing he didn't mind so much. Mal hacked a hole in the wall, and we rode out into the Overworld with Nan in a fancy saddle on her white horse, Hortense. Behind us came Mal's cow Connor and all of Jarro's extra horses and llamas and his cat Meowy. See, that's what Chug and I decided to do while everybody in Cornucopia was in here arguing. We snuck out and took back all of our animals. It wasn't hard to find the only herd of horses and llamas in town, and Jarro's mom didn't even bring Meowy inside. We hid all the animals in Nan's forest until everyone left, and it was a huge relief, knowing no one had to worry about leaving our pets behind.

Sure, Chug and I lost our entire store's inventory, but I can make anything we need. The Overworld is full of raw materials, and Krog's pockets contained both a chest and a shulker box. Turns out he'd stolen most of the good stuff from town already, so really, we left with more than we started with. We couldn't manage to grab all of Jarro's mushrooms, but I'm sure he can find some more. After all, we decided to build our town right by the ocean, near the mushroom island.

We call it Discovery.

See, our old town was called Cornucopia. It was supposed to be a place of plenty, where everything was always available all the time—at a price!—and everyone had what they needed and could be content.

But what we've learned is that contentment is nice and all, but real satisfaction and growth can only come when you get out of your comfort zone and experience life. When we began our journey, I could buy a hoe from Elder Stu. Then I learned that I could craft my own hoe. And now I know that . . . well, I wasn't meant to hoe pumpkins in the first place. I was meant to build, experiment, explore, and create.

See? Full circle. So Discovery it is.

It's already coming along nicely. We're building parks and museums and gardens and a stage in the middle of downtown for music and theater productions. There's plenty of space for fields and forests and lots of room for new folks to join us. We put up signs outside of Cornucopia and also in the old village, pointing the way toward us. And we found another village on the other side of the mountains, too. Beyond that village, things start to get cold, and we encountered our first real snow. Maybe one day we'll go adventuring over there. Nan says there's a thing called a bear that's even bigger than a horse, and I'd like to see that—as long as I can keep Chug from hugging it.

We hear about Cornucopia whenever our folks visit, and it sounds like we got out just in time. The Elders cracked down on their laws, and Elder Stu is reveling in his role as the only crafter in town. A few folks have snuck out to come see me, and I'm always happy to get new crafters started with a lesson or two. At least the Elders had the good sense to put Krog in a jail made of obsidian, and now they check the floor every day. Tini and Livi apparently think he can be rehabilitated, but for now, he's behind bars. And no one has heard of the brigands again, but if they do find a way out of the Nether, we'll be ready for them.

Nan is alive and well and loves to sit in the rocking chair on her front porch and watch the town go by. Then, when things get too busy or too boring—you never know which one you're going to get, because it's still a very new sort of place—she goes to her back porch and sits in her other rocking chair and watches the ocean.

Mal has a small cow farm and a mine. Chug and I have our store. Jarro rents horses and llamas and is trying to figure out what to do with donkeys. And Lenna is our town historian. She spends her days in the library, reading Nan's books to learn about our Founders and adding our own lore to new books. Whenever anyone pops in with a question, she's determined to find the answer, whether in a book that already exists or on another adventure. There's always something new to learn, she says, and always more books that need to be written.

It's like Nan said—we're descended from adventurers, and

each one of us possesses that spirit of discovery, that yearning to see what's over the next hill. For me, it's more of a yearning to see what kind of new potion I can make, but I know that the best way to find ingredients is to saddle up and take my traveling workshop along with my friends, wherever they're going.

Believe me: Life is better beyond the wall.

EPILOGUE 2

DISCOVERY BOOGALOO

CHUG

 Still sticking around for more, huh?

I can see why. We have some entertaining story-tellers in Discovery. Everyone here came from somewhere else, so there's always something new to learn or see. Or eat. Like that new glow berry pie recipe Nan is working on. It really warms the tummy, you know?

But listen—this is where our story ends.

We found what we needed, and we built something great. Our ancestors, I think, would be proud. Me and Mal and Tok go back to Cornucopia sometimes to check in on our parents, and they even visit us out here every now and then. A few people from town who were sick of all the rules have already moved to Discovery permanently, which is why you can buy Inka's melons in the open air market. They taste sweeter out here, somehow. My mom likes the ocean so much she's thinking of selling the farm to one of my uncles and moving out here to retire, if she can just convince my dad. Tok promised to provide him with unlimited hoes pies, and with all the crowding back home,

the pie market here.

t.

e happy.

We all got what we needed.

What else do you need to know?

Or—were you here to buy a pet pig?

We currently have two available, but I hope you're ready for an extensive adoption interview. We need to make sure Thingy's sons will be going to only the best homes. They're used to a bedtime story every night, and you can't ever, ever mention bacon, and . . .

Oh. Jarro?

He's right next door.

Tell him we're having salmon for dinner, would you?

EPILOGUE 3

THE FINAL FRONTIER

JARRO

 I understand completely, and I think I can help.

So, the bigger piglet is actually the quiet one, while the small one is quite the troublemaker. If you get them both, they kind of balance each other out. You know what they say about pigs—if you're going to have one, you might as well have a whole sty. I hope you're ready to write Chug lots of letters detailing their daily habits and growth. For a guy who hates writing, he sure does love reading about his piglets.

But if you really came over here just to make sure I'm okay, don't worry. I'm doing great. Yeah, I'm always going to be worried about the brigands finding us again. And yeah, I know we're pretty close to the place where the worst moment of my life happened. But with the help of my friends, I'm working through it. I'm at peace. I have my horses and my llamas and my donkeys, plus a few mooshrooms and a glow berry greenhouse. Business is booming, and Meowy loves the fresh fish. We're happy by the ocean, really. I don't miss my life back home, and I don't miss who I used to be. Out here, I'm worth something. I have people who believe in me.

I'm beginning to believe in myself.

If I had to sum it up, I would say this.

All you need to know is that I have the four best friends in the world, and together, beyond the wall, we built a future we can be proud of.

ABOUT THE AUTHOR

DELILAH S. DAWSON is the author of the *New York Times* bestseller *Star Wars: Phasma*, as well as *Star Wars: Galaxy's Edge: Black Spire, Mine,* the Hit series, the Blud series, the creator-owned comics *Ladycastle, Sparrowhawk,* and *Star Pig,* and the Shadow series (written as Lila Bowen). With Kevin Hearne, she co-writes the Tales of Pell. She lives in Georgia with her family.

delilahsdawson.com
Twitter: @DelilahSDawson
Instagram: @DelilahSDawson

ABOUT THE TYPE

This book was set in Electra, a typeface designed for Linotype by W. A. Dwiggins, the renowned type designer (1880–1956). Electra is a fluid typeface, avoiding the contrasts of thick and thin strokes that are prevalent in most modern typefaces.

DISCOVER MORE MINECRAFT

HAVE YOU READ THEM ALL?

- [ ] *The Island* by Max Brooks
- [ ] *The Crash* by Tracey Baptiste
- [ ] *The Lost Journals* by Mur Lafferty
- [ ] *The End* by Catherynne M. Valente
- [ ] *The Voyage* by Jason Fry
- [ ] *The Rise of the Arch-Illager* by Matt Forbeck
- [ ] *The Shipwreck* by C. B. Lee
- [ ] *The Mountain* by Max Brooks
- [ ] *The Dragon* by Nicky Drayden
- [ ] *Mob Squad* by Delilah S. Dawson
- [ ] *The Haven Trials* by Suyi Davies
- [ ] *Mob Squad: Never Say Nether* by Delilah S. Dawson
- [ ] *Zombies!* by Nick Eliopulos
- [ ] *Mob Squad: Don't Fear the Creeper* by Delilah S. Dawson
- [ ] *Castle Redstone* by Sarwat Chadda

Penguin
Random
House